D0122273

CRIMSON SUMMER

Also by *New York Times* bestselling author Heather Graham

CRIMSON SUMMER
DANGER IN NUMBERS

New York Confidential

THE FINAL DECEPTION
A LETHAL LEGACY
A DANGEROUS GAME
A PERFECT OBSESSION
FLAWLESS

Krewe of Hunters

THE UNKNOWN
THE FORBIDDEN
THE UNFORGIVEN
DREAMING DEATH
DEADLY TOUCH
SEEING DARKNESS
THE STALKING
THE SEEKERS
THE SUMMONING
ECHOES OF EVIL
PALE AS DEATH
FADE TO BLACK
WICKED DEEDS
DARK RITES
DYING BREATH
DARKEST JOURNEY
DEADLY FATE
HAUNTED DESTINY
THE HIDDEN
THE FORGOTTEN
THE SILENCED
THE BETRAYED
THE HEXED
THE CURSED
THE NIGHT IS FOREVER

THE NIGHT IS ALIVE
THE NIGHT IS WATCHING
THE UNINVITED
THE UNSPOKEN
THE UNHOLY
THE UNSEEN
THE EVIL INSIDE
SACRED EVIL
HEART OF EVIL
PHANTOM EVIL

Cafferty & Quinn

THE DEAD PLAY ON
WAKING THE DEAD
LET THE DEAD SLEEP

Harrison Investigations

NIGHTWALKER
THE SÉANCE
THE PRESENCE
UNHALLOWED GROUND
THE DEATH DEALER
THE DEAD ROOM
THE VISION
GHOST WALK
HAUNTED

Bone Island

GHOST MOON
GHOST NIGHT
GHOST SHADOW

The Flynn Brothers

DEADLY GIFT
DEADLY HARVEST
DEADLY NIGHT

Look for Heather Graham's next novel,
SOUND OF DARKNESS,
available soon from MIRA.

* * * * *

For additional books by Heather Graham,
visit her website, www.theoriginalheathergraham.com.

CRIMSON SUMMER

HEATHER GRAHAM

mira

ISBN-13: 978-0-7783-1182-9

Crimson Summer

For questions and comments about the quality of this book, please contact us at CustomerService@Harlequin.com.

Mira
22 Adelaide St. West, 41st Floor
Toronto, Ontario M5H 4E3, Canada
BookClubbish.com

Printed in U.S.A.

For Sierra Lipa with thanks.
Missing you in South Florida!

CRIMSON SUMMER

PROLOGUE

The sun was out, inching its way up in the sky, casting golden rays and creating a beautiful display of color over the shading mangroves and cypress growing richly in the area. The sunlight touched on the streams running throughout the Everglades, the great "River of Grass" stretching over two hundred acres in southern and central portions of Florida, creating a glittering glow of nature.

The sky was gold and red at the horizon, and brilliantly blue above, with only a few soft puffs of clouds littered about. Diamonds and crystals seemed to float on the water.

Such beauty. Such peace.

Then there was the crime scene.

The bodies lay strewn and drenched with blood. The rich, natural earth hues of the Everglades were caught in a surreal image, greens and browns spattered liberally with the color red as if an angry child had swung a sopping paint-brush around.

Aidan Cypress had never understood why the mocking-bird had been made Florida's state bird—not when it seemed that vultures ruled the skies overhead. Never more so than today.

Now, as he stood overlooking the scene with his crew and special agents from the FDLE, trying to control the crime scene against the circling vultures, Aidan couldn't help but wonder just what had happened and why it had happened this way—and grit his teeth knowing there would be speculation.

Stooping down by the body of a man Aidan believed to be in his midthirties—with dark hair, olive complexion, possibly six feet in height, medium build—he noted the shaft of an arrow protruding from the man's gut.

All the dead had been killed with arrows, hatchets, axes and knives. Because whoever had done this had apparently tried to make it look like a historical Native American rampage.

Except the killers hadn't begun to understand there were differences in the weaponry and customs between the nations and tribes of the indigenous peoples across the country.

In South Florida, the dead man's coloring could mean many things; Aidan himself was a member of the Seminole tribe of Florida, though somewhere in his lineage, some-one had been white—most probably from northern Europe originally. He had a bronze complexion, thick, straight hair that was almost ebony…and green eyes.

South Florida was home to those who had come from Cuba, Central and South America and probably every island out there. The area was truly a giant melting pot. That's how his family had begun. In a way, history had created the Seminole tribe because there had been a time when settlers had called any indigenous person in Florida a Seminole.

But while the killers had tried to make this look like a massacre of old, the dead men were not Seminole. They were, Aidan believed, Latino. He could see tattoos on the lower arms of a few of the dead who had been wearing T-shirts; a single word was visible in the artwork on the man in front of him—*Hermandad.*

Spanish for "Brotherhood."

"What the hell happened here, Aidan?"

Aidan looked up to see that John Schultz—Special Agent John Schultz, Florida Department of Law Enforcement—was standing by his side.

John went on. "It's like a scene out of an old cowboys and Indians movie!"

Aidan stared at John as he rose, bristling—and yet he knew what it looked like at first glance.

"Quaking aspen," Aidan said.

"Quaking aspen?" John repeated blankly.

"It's not native to this area. Look at the arrow. That wasn't made by any Seminole, Miccosukee or other Florida Native American. That is a western wood."

"Yeah, well, things travel these days."

Aidan shook his head. He liked John and respected him. The older agent was experienced, a few years shy of retirement. The tall, gray-haired man had recently suffered a heart attack, had taken the prescribed time off and come back to the field. They'd worked together dozens of times before. He could be abrasive—he had a sometimes-unhappy tendency to say what he thought, before thinking it through.

A few years back John had been partnered with a young woman named Amy Larson. It had taken John a long time to accept her age—and the fact she was female. Once he'd realized her value, though, he'd become her strongest supporter.

But Amy wasn't here today.

And Aidan missed her. She softened John's rough edges.

She was still on holiday somewhere with Hunter Forrest, the FBI agent she'd started dating. They were off on an island enjoying exotic breezes and one another's company minus all the blood and mayhem.

Aidan stopped lamenting the absence of his favorite FDLE agent and waved away a giant vulture trying to hone in on a nearby body.

Half of the corpses were already missing eyes and bits and pieces of skin and soft tissue.

Aidan sighed and looked around. There were twenty bodies, all of them male, between the ages of twenty and forty, he estimated.

Because he'd noted the tattoos on a few of them, and using his own years of experience, he theorized the dead were members of a gang. Florida had many such gangs. Most were recruits from the various drug cartels, resolved to hold dominion over their territories.

He looked at John, trying to be patient, understanding and professional enough to control his temper. "You know, you may be the special agent, but I'm the forensics expert, and this was not something perpetrated by any of the Florida tribes—or any tribe anywhere. I can guarantee you no one sent out a war party to slaughter some gang members. Someone tried—ridiculously—to make this look like some Natives did this."

"Hey, sorry, you're right. Forgive me—just...look

around!" John said quickly and sincerely. "It's just at first sight…well, I mean—wow. You're right. I'm sorry."

The apology was earnest. "Okay. Let's figure out what really happened."

The corpses were in something of a clearing right by a natural stream making its way through hammocks thick with cypress trees and mangroves and all kinds of underbrush.

While the area was customarily filled with many birds—herons, cranes, falcons, hawks and more—it was the vultures who had staked out a claim. The bodies lay with arrows and axes protruding from their heads, guts or chests, as if they'd fought in a bloody battle. And now they succumbed to decay on the damp and redolent earth.

John followed Aidan's gaze and winced. "It's a mess. Okay, well…all right. I'm going to go over and interview the man who found this."

"Jimmy Osceola," Aidan said. "He's been fishing this little area all his life, and he does tours. Two birds with one stone. Members of his family work with him and all of them fish and take tourists out here. He has a great little place right off I-75. It's called Fresh Catch, and his catch is about as fresh as it gets. Catfish. He's a good guy, John."

"I believe you. But we're going to need a break here—you and your team have to find something for me to go on."

Aidan stared at him, gloved hands unclenching at his sides.

John was rough around the edges and said whatever came to mind, but he was a good cop.

He'd be hell-bent on finding out just what had gone on here.

Aidan told him what he'd heard. "Jimmy was out with a boatload of tourists—they're right over there. See—two couples, a kid who just started at FIU and two middle-aged women. The first officers on the scene made sure they all stayed. Go talk to them. They look like they came upon a bloodbath—oh, wait, they did."

John arched a brow to him and said, "Yeah. I got it."

He headed off to talk to Jimmy Osceola and the group with him.

Aidan studied the crime scene again, as a whole.

First, what the hell had all these men been doing out here? A few of them looked to have been wearing suits; most were in T-shirts and jeans.

The few bodies he had noted—not touching any of them, that was the medical examiner's purview—seemed to bear that same tattoo. *Hermandad.*

That meant a gang of enforcers in his mind, and he was sure it was a good guess.

Had a big drug deal been planned?

They were on state land, but it was state land traveled only by the local tribes who knew it. The park service rangers also came through, and the occasional tourist who arranged for a special excursion into the wilds.

Bird-watchers, often enough.

All they'd see today, however, would be the vultures.

"Aidan."

He heard his name spoken by a quiet female voice and he swung around.

Amy Larson was not enjoying an exotic island vacation.

She was standing just feet from him, having carefully avoided stepping on any of the bodies, pools of blood or possible evidence. She was in a navy pantsuit, white cotton shirt and serviceable black sneakers—obviously back to work.

No matter how all-business her wardrobe, Amy had blue-crystal eyes that displayed empathy and caring. She was great at both assuring witnesses *and* staring down suspects.

"What are you doing here, Amy?" Aidan asked her. "You're supposed to be sunbathing somewhere, playing in the surf with Hunter."

"I was."

"So what happened?"

"It was great. Champagne, chocolates, sun, surf, sand..." She sighed.

"And?"

"And a little red horse—like the one from last month's crime scene—delivered right to the room," she said.

When He opened the second seal,
I heard the second living creature saying,
"Come and see."
And another horse, fiery red, went out.
And it was granted to the one who sat on it
to take peace from the earth,
and that people should kill one another;
and there was given to him a great sword.

— Revelation 6:3-4

1

"I'm surprised you've agreed to talk to me," Hunter Forrest told Ethan Morrison.

The man was being held in jail pending trial.

Without bond.

Morrison was rich—he could pay whatever was asked. But sitting across the table from Hunter, he didn't appear to be worth much. He was just a middle-aged man in a prison suit.

He'd waived his right to have his attorney present while speaking with Hunter.

The whole thing seemed to be a game to him. Ethan Morrison believed that the astronomical price he was paying his army of lawyers would get him off.

But it wouldn't. There was a slew of evidence against him and he was facing state and federal charges for murder and conspiracy to commit murder. And the feds were even weighing a charge of treason, since Morrison had used privately run immigrant detention centers to acquire his victims.

The man had created a cult peopled by the desperate and the hungry, ready to do his bidding to reach a nirvana Morrison promised.

He had ordered the murder of two women who were seeking asylum after having his sons kidnap them from a detention center. Both women had been killed in the manner of some obscene rite. And Morrison had been seeking a third sacrifice, a woman who had escaped him, when he'd decided he needed to kill Amy, as well.

But Amy had challenged him, Hunter thought. She was a law enforcement officer—not desperate and afraid, which didn't connect in Morrison's misogynistic mind.

In the end, his attempts at murder had been witnessed by many law enforcement officers. He would go down, along with his sons and those others he had brought with him on his murder spree.

There was no such thing as a good murder, but Morrison's crimes had been especially heinous; the women had suffered horribly.

The judge hadn't given an inch. Morrison was welcome to every high-priced attorney out there, and they could try every defense under the sun. Morrison's attorneys *had* tried everything.

But the judge had the right to hold him until trial, and the man was still being held. And the same high-priced attorneys were still assuring him that once he got to trial he would be deemed innocent.

Still, it appeared that having lost his appeal for bail, Morrison was taking it all in stride. He sat across the table from Hunter in the interrogation room with a casual air and a smile on his face.

"I'm entertained when I speak with you, Special Agent Forrest," Morrison said. "Frankly, I'd rather speak with that Florida girl, Miss Special Agent Larson, but can't say it's all that interesting in here, so…well, you'll do!"

Hunter shrugged. "I doubt Special Agent Larson has any interest in seeing you. You tried to kill her."

"She's so elegant—and kick-ass at the same time. I must admit, I haven't met many women like her. You can break them all, though. But I guess you're enjoying that? Of course, you're both so professional, but…is she kick-ass in bed? I'll bet she is."

"What she is happens to be nowhere near you, Morrison. She's busy. You tried to kill her and you failed. She's on to other matters."

"And I'll bet you were one of those other matters she was on!"

Hunter again ignored him. Morrison wanted a reaction.

"Now, let's see. You killed two women and were attempting to kill a third innocent victim *and* Special Agent Larson at the same time. I'm not an attorney, but I know whatever help you give us just might keep you from a needle in the arm."

"I didn't kill anyone."

"Two women were killed under your order—that means you're as guilty of the murders. I'm sure you know already, conspiracy to commit murder draws the same consequences."

"If someone can prove it. Seriously, how can you prove it?"

"That will all come up in court. But there's more going

on. You could make life a little easier on yourself if you wanted to talk to me about what is happening now."

"What's happening now?" Morrison asked innocently.

Hunter laughed softly. "Mr. Morrison—"

"Pastor Morrison. I was ordained."

"Online?"

"It's real," Morrison said, his tone still pleasant.

"So, you had yourself ordained online for a makeshift religion to suit your purposes," Hunter said.

"Ah, my purpose is to bring forgiveness and goodness to all."

"By murdering people."

Morrison shrugged and smiled. "Again I say, I didn't murder anyone."

"Well, *I'd say* half your congregation is now sitting in jail awaiting trial, as well. You really want this life—" Hunter paused and swept his arms out, indicating Morrison's imprisonment "—for your sons? They did kill people, and the attorneys are still debating on adding more federal and state charges, but this state still has a death penalty, so…"

"We're going to be all right," Morrison said smugly.

Hunter leaned closer. "You really think no one will break? That they're completely loyal? I mean, it might have been something when you were free—and they were free—and you had a goal in front of you, but now… Your boys had everything they could desire all their lives—you think they're going to be happy with prison, facing the death penalty?"

Hunter thought he saw a slight crack in the smiling facade Morrison was giving him.

"We'll be all right," he said.

Hunter nodded thoughtfully and grinned slowly himself. "I see. You really buy the whole 'Four Horsemen of the Apocalypse' thing. Or do you? You think you're going to be saved because you gathered up a few souls, tortured a few sinners to death?" Hunter was no stranger to the logic abused by apocalypse cults, and he could debate this all day. He leaned closer still. "Hallelujah. If you're embracing the Four Horsemen of the Apocalypse, you seem to have a lot of your messages mixed. Bad things will happen—but that sure doesn't mean good things for the people causing the bad things. Think about the rest of the New Testament. The message about kindness to one's fellow man. You're not ignorant. You can't think it won't matter if you—or your sons—face lethal injection *and* the years of prison time it will take to get to that lethal injection because you'll be honored in another life? Please!"

"You have to prove—"

"Oh, trust me. In court, it will be proven your sons killed two women."

Morrison shook his head.

But Hunter continued to smile. The man's face had changed. He definitely doubted he would wind up sitting on golden clouds. He was buying the concept his lawyers would get him off.

For years, his money had bought him anything he desired.

He didn't sound quite so certain when he spoke again.

"I'll give you nothing—I have nothing to give. I didn't kill anyone, and my attorneys will have to see what so-called proof you have against my boys."

"You're a smart man, Morrison," Hunter said. "You know we have a stack of witnesses. Your boys are facing lethal injection. But if you can tell us what else you know that might allow us to save the lives of others, we might be able to keep them from the death penalty."

"My boys will not die. None of us will even be incarcerated after this sham is over," Morrison said.

Hunter decided he should get to the point.

"You heard about the men who were found murdered in the Everglades?" Hunter asked. The massacre was already on the news. The offices of the FDLE and the FBI had put out statements, but details were withheld until next of kin had been notified.

Morrison started to laugh. "A massacre in the Everglades! Cool. They probably deserved to die, but then again, so do their killers."

"And who were their killers? You seem to know," Hunter said.

"Oh, I don't know," Morrison told him. "Just...well, what did they say? The bodies of twenty men? Had to be gang members up to something. They all deserve each other. And they have absolutely nothing to do with me."

"I think they do."

"I'm in here—how could I have done anything?"

"Voices carry, right?"

"What? Are you getting poetic on me, Special Agent Forrest?"

"We all know prisoners communicate with each other, and that in the United States even a man like you has legal rights. Far more than the women who died in your sacrifices."

"Ah, but I'm a prisoner, and everyone you think I'm associated with is also in jail—facing the death penalty, as you say. So...couldn't have anything to do with me."

"But you're involved."

"And what makes you say that?"

"A little red horse," Hunter said. "When we found that

poor woman on a cross out in the Everglades—your doing—
we found a little white horse. Then, in the Bahamas, Amy
and I received a little red horse."

"You—and Amy! Aw, see, what are you bitching about?
You met that sweet little piece investigating me!"

Hunter felt his temper soaring. The man was trying to
get a rise out of him. He wouldn't reward him with any reaction. Turn the tables.

"I know you're involved. But I think someone else is pulling your strings. Someone way bigger than you is in charge
of this. You're just one of his marionettes, dancing at the
will of someone controlling it all. But you could save yourself by helping us."

Morrison's face tightened; Hunter had hit a nerve. The
threat of lethal injection didn't bother the man because he
couldn't believe that he, Ethan Morrison, would ever face
execution.

Being called a puppet…well, he didn't like that.

Morrison started to stand, but he had shackles on his wrists
attached to a metal bar secured to the table.

"I'm done talking to you," he said. "Guard!" he called.

Hunter sat back. There was nothing he could do. Morrison did have rights; it was surprising they had gotten this far.

The door to the room opened; a guard had arrived as
summoned.

But as he was led away, Morrison called back.

"Bring the kick-ass cutie to see me! Maybe I'll talk to her."

Hunter didn't respond. He waited until Morrison had
been taken away, then he rose and left the room. He collected his service weapon on the way out of the facility.

Morrison was taunting them all. He wouldn't tell Amy
anything.

But there were twenty dead already.

Hunter paused while walking toward his car. It was a beautiful day. Soft white clouds traveled across a stunning blue sky. There was a slight breeze. Leaves and branches danced within it.

Twenty dead…on such a beautiful morning.

He needed to drive south. By now, the crime scene investigators would have pored over the site of the murders, and the medical examiners had surely arrived. But twenty dead…

Amy had gone straight to the site.

Hunter thought briefly about the time in the Bahamas he and Amy had shared, weary and elated—celebrating the case they'd solved. They hadn't been together that long, but he could no longer imagine a life without waking up beside her.

They should have known it wasn't over.

When the killings had started, linked to a white horse and a cult…

Maybe, just maybe, none of this was related.

Twenty men dead in the Everglades. Looked like a cartel hit…a gang war.

But they had received the little red horse, and the timing couldn't be a coincidence.

The bodies would be gone by the time he reached the scene. But there would be crime scene photos, and Amy would have sketched everything she saw, as well; sometimes her artistic eye picked up on little details that weren't so vividly caught by a camera.

He still needed to see for himself where the bodies had lain in comparison to the roads and the water. They had to know how the dead had come to be where they were.

He keyed the ignition, then dialed Amy over the car's speakerphone.

"Hey," he said when she picked up.

"Hey," she returned. "Did you get anything from Morrison at all?"

"No."

"Did he lawyer up?"

"No, he was willing to see me. He bristled when I suggested he was a puppet." He paused. "And he wants to talk to you."

"I guess I should see him, then. Better you saw him first, though. I'm here with Aidan, John and local police. At the crime scene."

"I'm on my way to you."

"Should I head to you instead?"

"No. I think we need to find out who the new players are in this game. I'm not sure what Morrison may or may not know. He was the 'white horse.' We've moved on to the 'red horse.' I told Morrison he was just a little part in a bigger plan, but sadly, I believe I'm right. There is someone out there playing with the biblical apocalypse—or rather the Four Horsemen of the Apocalypse. And we've entered the second stage."

"All right. I'm not sure how much longer we can keep the witnesses here. They're all distraught, but then…well, it's hard to blame them. And Aidan is worried someone is trying to blame the Seminole tribe. But here's what's strange, Hunter. They staged the scene but staged it badly. The arrows and hatchets aren't from this area. I don't think they understood that the Seminole and Miccosukee tribes dress differently and live differently than the indigenous tribes in the West. Different climate—different cultures. So, none of the weapons were anything that could be found locally. All the arrows and hatchets are made from wood from trees that only grow in western states. And all the victims have tats—they belonged to the Hermandad, or Brotherhood."

"Interesting. Suspected distributors for Manuel Garcia, who moves from country to country in South America while keeping his business going. I would think this was just a gang warfare situation—if it weren't for the red horse. Anyway, I'm driving there now. If we decide Morrison might talk to you and tell us something useful, we'll get you in to see him tonight or tomorrow. Let's see what else we can discover from Jimmy and the witnesses. I'm assuming there was more than one medical examiner called in?"

"Five of them were called—they're here now," Amy told him.

"Has Aidan found anything?"

"His team is busy. They've found some footprints. They waited for the medical examiners, but I think they'll have to dust the weapons for prints once the bodies are at the morgue. I'm searching the area, too. We haven't found anything else notable yet. I'm going to talk to the witnesses—if we can call them that—in a minute. Talk to the guide, Jimmy Osceola. Aidan told me Jimmy said he noticed the bodies because…there's so much blood. He couldn't understand why the green of the Glades had turned red. He pulled into the hammock and got out and asked his tour group to wait while he investigated—but they followed him. Hunter, it's really…"

"Bad," he said softly.

"It's…a massacre."

"You've done some drawings?"

Amy was a talented artist. And while there might be hundreds—thousands in this case—of crime scene photographs, Amy's sketches sometimes caught what a camera didn't see.

"Of course," she said.

"Good."

Hunter thought back to the case that had brought him to Florida.

For him, it had started when the body of a girl had been found near a tiny town south of Micanopy. The young woman's body had been slashed and bloodied, but the slashes on her face had been made to resemble a devil's horns.

Then there had been a second victim, left out in the wilderness.

After a lot of digging, they'd discovered that Ethan Morrison, an entrepreneur and multimillionaire, had used others as pawns, convincing his followers that the great apocalypse was coming—and they were saving the souls of the women, cleansing them, according to the 'first horseman,' and allowing their souls a chance for the rewards that lay beyond.

But they'd caught Ethan Morrison—in the act of trying to "cleanse" Amy and another young woman.

It had been so damned satisfying to see them all locked up. But now this.

Amy spoke softly. "Hunter...this is truly a horrible scene. I suppose it could be compared to the Saint Valentine's Day Massacre—a rival gang killing since the victims all have tattoos. Is it just coincidence we received that red horse? What is the endgame in this, Hunter?"

"An apocalypse, or someone's version of it, and most likely it has to do with power and money. And right now, someone is out there preaching the ways of the rider upon a red horse."

Red, the color of blood.

Twenty men murdered. Without seeing it, he could imagine the earth seeped with it.

"I'm on my way," he said.

★ ★ ★

Amy Larson smiled weakly at Aidan.

Aidan was right. She shouldn't have been here; she had several days of vacation left. But she and Hunter had both known they needed to come back.

They had begun their vacation with such relief, so happy to spend time together as a couple, knowing a horrible man was in jail. Then the little red horse had shown up along with their room service.

They should have known the cult killing had only been the beginning. There were Four Horsemen of the Apocalypse in the Book of Revelation; they had managed to stop only the first, the "white horseman."

"Yep. A little red horse arrived with room service—along with the champagne," she said to Aidan, picking up the conversation they'd been having before Hunter had called. "We immediately went to the staff, the kitchen…everywhere at the resort. Of course, no one knew anything about it. Their employees' backgrounds are being researched by FBI techs, but it could have been added after the tray was set in front of the door. We tried to pursue it, and we're still pursuing it, but…so far, nothing has led anywhere."

"Oh," Aidan said, staring back at her.

"Hunter is leaving the facility upstate. He interviewed Ethan Morrison."

"Ah, good. I'd have never thought these incidents could be related—cult killings, strange gang-style executions. I admit, I was confused to see you. This was called in just a few hours ago. If he's seen Morrison, I assume Hunter has heard about what happened here?"

"Yes, he's heard. As soon as I found the horse, I called

my supervisor, Director Mickey Hampton, at FDLE. And as soon as he heard about this massacre, Mickey called me."

"This is so crazy," Aidan murmured. "A kid's plastic toy. Delivered to you with the chocolate and champagne."

She shrugged and offered him another dry smile. "Yep. Mickey called the FBI, and Hunter's supervisor called him. He was already on his way to talk to Morrison when the news regarding this bloodbath came in. With the little horse having arrived at our room, we could only assume something was up. Either we were being threatened or some new crime had occurred. Morrison agreed to see Hunter right away, and I imagine he is probably delighting in all this. Amazing how fast news travels, but it does just about travel with the speed of light these days."

She inhaled and exhaled, wondering how such warped human beings could exist, despite the many bad things she had seen in law enforcement.

Morrison was a special kind of sick. A narcissist who really didn't care a thing about other people. A sociopath.

"Yes, I can easily believe his involvement—or lack thereof—would have him enjoying every little tidbit he hears about," Aidan said. "I'm willing to bet you're right, that he is just about licking his lips and laughing his ass off. He's in jail—his case solved. Not!" He shook his head, tightening his lips. "Even if he's not part of this, knowing it happened will amuse him to no end. Then again, we're putting everything on the arrival of that toy. Possibly—just possibly—he's not involved in any way. This could be something else, anything else," Aidan said.

"It could be."

"You don't think so."

"And neither do you."

"Okay," Aidan said, frowning. "But—"

Amy only vaguely heard him. She was looking over the crime scene, taking it all in as a complete unit.

She was grateful Aidan was on this case. He was one of the best forensic experts she'd ever known. Members of his team were very carefully seeking any clue: a cigarette butt, a gum wrapper, a hair, a fiber, a footprint—anything—that could help in the investigation.

But she knew what she was looking for. "There it is," she said softly.

"There what is? You mean there's something in that pool of blood? We didn't start going through on blood work and weapons yet. Medical examiners have jurisdiction over the bodies first."

"I'm not touching the body!" she promised.

She dug in her pocket for gloves and quickly pulled them on. Then she moved gingerly past one corpse to another— one with an ax protruding from its forehead—and hunkered down.

And found what she had been seeking.

And dreading.

"What...? Damn! How did you see that?" Aidan demanded, following her and moving just as carefully as she reached into the blood and collected a small object.

"You weren't looking for it," Amy said. "It's red and covered in blood and dirt. And everything here is red—and covered in dirt. You would have gotten to it when you started on the blood pools."

"Blood, red and dirt," Aidan agreed. "But I should have seen it already."

"Hey, you're human and you would have found it," she

said. "If I wasn't specifically looking for it, I wouldn't have seen it until the entire ground had been combed."

"My people—"

"Are combing the ground in a grid like you taught them, and they haven't gotten here yet!"

She held the small object between her thumb and forefinger to show him. Amy had found a tiny red horse.

They'd seen one just like it before, except that during the previous cult killings it had been white, and it had fallen from the body of a woman stabbed, slashed and tied to a cross.

This was the same kind of little toy, except it was red.

Amy pulled a clear evidence bag from her pocket, and secured the figurine. Then she reached into her pocket again, producing another evidence bag. In it was the same little red horse, the one she had received with champagne and chocolates in the Bahamas.

"That's the one delivered to you with room service," Aidan muttered, indicating the evidence bag she'd brought with her. "This killer, these killers...they're mocking us. Or they're after you. They were before, or they know how deeply you and Hunter are involved in this, and they're taunting you. Bizarre. They couldn't have known before that you and Hunter would be involved. And maybe, at first, it hadn't mattered. But now...this little red horse delivered to you—obviously they're after you. Or challenging you to stop them. Or they believe they can't be stopped this time, and they want to rub your noses in it, and maybe again..."

"Maybe again what?"

"Maybe turn you into one of their sacrifices," Aidan said unhappily.

She shrugged. "Aidan, we cut off one of the snake's heads

and three grow back. The game will change this time. But I think you're right—they're taunting us. Whoever is doing this has a plan we haven't seen yet—a plan that includes all Four Horsemen of the Apocalypse. They didn't care we stopped Ethan Morrison and his cult. It's a Revelation, Aidan. The red horse signifies war. I'm afraid this is just another beginning. We're going to be seeing slaughter everywhere, unless we find this snake's head and chop it off. Someone somewhere has decided we're not just going to see murder, we're going to see battlefields of dead."

She paused for a minute, looking out at the bloody scene again.

"This time they're going to war. And they don't give a damn that we know it. But I wonder. Is this really someone who believes in biblical prophecy—or someone out for personal gain?"

Aidan rose and looked out at the blood-soaked ground, as well.

"I wish I knew. But they are trying to sow as much dissent as they can. First, this was done close to Seminole lands. Though if they'd really wanted it to appear that the tribe is responsible, they might have studied more about our customs. Yes, this looks like a battleground when the fighting is over except it's all wrong. These killers might just be racists, too—the kind who don't know much about history. And it sure appears the victims were members of a gang or cartel."

"Who better to have a gang war than a cartel?" Amy murmured.

"War. They want war."

"Why?" she murmured, but the question was rhetorical. She continued. "If we knew the answer to that…well. Anyway, I'm going to go and talk to Jimmy and his boatload of tourists and see what they know."

"John is with them now. I'll walk you over."

Amy smiled grimly as they approached Jimmy Osceola, John Schultz and the group around him.

John was her partner. He'd been sidelined on medical leave for a few weeks, but he was back. He stared at her with surprise as she walked toward the group. He excused himself to greet her with a quick hug and a question in his eyes. She shrugged and gave him another grim smile; he knew she'd explain her presence when she could.

Amy had known the tour guide, Jimmy Osceola, from the time she was young; she and her family had often eaten at his restaurant. And as soon as she started her work in law enforcement, Jimmy had always been helpful when the state of Florida needed assistance with crimes that took place in the Everglades or infringed on tribal land.

Her first case with the FDLE had involved bodies in oil barrels sunk into the swampy ground. Jimmy had helped her and other law enforcement officials manage the in and out of the geography of the deep Glades area where the barrels had been sunk. He had to be sixty; he looked more like forty. He had a handsome face with high cheekbones, deep-set, large eyes and a headful of hair that showed only a few streaks of gray.

"Amy!" Jimmy said, greeting her as she arrived where he was standing beside one of the local county police cars. She thought he was about to give her a hug, too, but decided against it because of the circumstances.

He quickly introduced her to the group of tourists. "Folks, you've met John Schultz with the Florida Department of Law Enforcement. This is Special Agent Amy Larson, his partner."

"Hello, and thank you for helping," Amy said, waiting for John or Jimmy to introduce the group.

"This is Ben and Ginny Marks," Jimmy continued quickly, indicating an older couple.

"Snowbirds!" Ginny Marks said. She was an attractive woman with steel-gray hair cut in a contemporary bob, petite and offering a quick—if nervous—smile.

"And this young man here is David Ghent," Jimmy continued.

David Ghent stepped forward to shake Amy's hand. He appeared to be in his midtwenties, tall and lean with a headful of wild brown hair.

"I'm a law student, Florida State," he told her, as if he needed to explain why he'd been on the airboat.

She nodded. Jimmy went on to introduce a woman Amy reckoned to be in her midforties. "Audrey Benson," the woman said as she gave Amy a firm handshake. "I'm on vacation, from Chicago. I'm an attorney there."

"And I'm an attorney, too, go figure!" another woman said, stepping forward. She was younger than Audrey Benson, slim and dark-haired and in her mid to late thirties. "I'm Daisy Driver, and I work out of Tallahassee," she said.

"So many lawyers," a middle-aged man with the group said. He had thinning light hair, and a pleasant face, and his arm protectively around the woman at his side. "I'm Geoff Nevins and this is my wife, Celia. Too bad we don't need legal help at this minute—we had no idea we were joining a tour full of lawyers, and an almost lawyer!" he added, smiling at David Ghent. His smile faded. "This is awful. Just awful. But I don't see how we can help. We've been speaking with your partner already. I mean, I'm happy to help, but…" His voice faded.

"It had to have been recent," Jimmy Osceola told her. "I

brought a group through this area yesterday—it's my customary route. And many people use the canals for fishing—you can get some great catfish here, and even snook. I was talking about local birds, pointing out a blue heron—"

"And I saw something in the grass," David Ghent interrupted quietly.

"And it all looked strange. I've seen the sun change the color of the landscape, but not…not like it's changed now. So, I pulled the boat up and walked out and then…kept my distance and called it in," Jimmy said. "I thought you were on vacation."

"I was," Amy said simply. "Did anyone see anyone leaving the area, around the area—"

"I thought I saw a skunk ape!" Ginny Marks said.

"Skunk ape," John muttered.

"There is no such thing as a skunk ape," her husband, Ben, whispered to her.

"You don't know that!" Ginny insisted. "There are all kinds of creatures we haven't recognized that then prove to exist. Like the megalodon shark."

"I didn't see anything," Audrey Benson said.

The others shook their heads, as well.

"Um, Special Agent Larson," Daisy Driver said, "do you think we could go soon? We've been here awhile now, and I don't mean to be heartless or noncaring, but the stench around here is getting bad and I think about a thousand South Florida mosquitoes have found me. We've told all this to Special Agent Schultz, and I'm afraid we arrived after the fact and can't tell you anything else."

"Yes, yes, of course," Amy said. "But we will need your information in case we need to contact you," she added, reaching into her jacket pocket for a notepad to pass around the group and a pack of her cards to hand out.

"They already have my card," John said.

"We'll need you to contact us if you recall anything else. Except," she added, turning to Ginny, "quickly tell me about the skunk ape."

She heard a collective sigh from the group.

But that didn't deter Ginny Marks.

"Oh, right when we pulled off—it was over there. Big— bigger than a man, and that's why I say skunk ape. That thing was moving through the brush right by the road. Highway. Small highway, I guess. John told us years and years ago before they had I-95 and the turnpike that people used to go north by that road. I guess cop cars and fishermen and gator catchers and whoever come that way now," Ginny said. "Anyway, I'm telling you, I saw something. Big and walking upright. Like the skunk ape they've shown on TV. I didn't see where it went. It was moving through the brush by the road, and then... I don't know. It crossed the road or disappeared into the brush on all fours or something."

"Thank you," Amy told her.

"We can go?" Audrey Benson asked. She shivered, as if she were seeing the carnage for the first time. "I... I mean, it's terrible, but I heard the police saying something about the dead men all being part of a gang, a violent gang probably, and—"

"Those who live by the sword die by the sword?" David Ghent whispered.

"Well, something like that," Audrey murmured. "Of course, no man has the right to take another man's life."

"Violent people may die violent deaths," Jimmy Osceola said quietly. "But I guess if we're done... These poor people wound up on a tour that wasn't intended to turn out like this."

"If my partner agrees, you're free to go," John told the group.

Amy nodded, thanked the group again and noted every-one darting looks back at the scene, shuddering, as Jimmy led the way to his tour boat.

When they were gone, John turned to Amy. "What the hell? Young woman, you're supposed to be on vacation!"

"Long story," she said.

She turned to see Aidan was still standing near, apparently listening to what was said and waiting to hear if she or John wanted him doing anything specifically.

His crew of workers, all in their crime scene vests, was in the field now at the area where Amy had found the little red horse.

They were excellent at their forensic work; and while Aidan might be waiting for her and John, nothing was going on that he would miss.

"So," she said. "What do we think?" He arched a brow to her. "Did that tourist see a skunk ape?"

"Skunk ape," John said, shaking his head. "Amy, why are you here? Where's Hunter? Oh, no, you two didn't have a falling-out already, did you?"

She shook her head.

"I'm back because of a little red horse," she said. "Come on, I'll explain. But first...humor me. Hey," she said to Aidan. "Your crew is on this. Want to help me and John? I'm going to go and figure out just where the skunk ape went."

"What? There's no skunk ape," John said, sighing.

She looked at him and shrugged. "'A rose by any other name...'"

"Is not a skunk ape!" John protested.

"Whatever it was, I'm going to find out where it went!"

2

"A skunk ape killed the men?" Hunter asked, skeptical.

He'd arrived at the scene at last. The bodies had already been taken to the morgue.

It was sickening to see—and smell—the amount of blood that drenched the ground where they had lain.

But one of Aidan Cypress's people had directed Hunter to the edge of the road and the heavy growth of brush and trees there. That's where he'd find John Schultz, Aidan and Amy.

They'd been looking for signs of a skunk ape.

Hunter had seen the three of them, spread out along the road, just as he'd been told. He had waved to John and Aidan and come straight over to Amy.

"Maybe," Amy said, apparently choosing to ignore his sarcasm. "Define skunk ape. Someone killed them—or several *someones*—so the evidence suggests. There were a lot of dead men out here, as you know," she told him. She gave him a grimace.

And he gave her a grim look back.

It wasn't easy to be back. Their time to laugh, play on the beach and just be together already seemed brief and far away.

Amy knew he respected her as an FDLE agent. They had met because they had worked together on the cult case, not sure of each other at first, but respect had come before either of them had admitted to attraction. Now he knew he was in love with her, and not just "in love," but committed.

He knew FBI agents who were married to or with other FBI agents, but they weren't in the same units. Being together and working together was not something approved in law enforcement, but she was FDLE and he was FBI.

Their work happened to keep intertwining.

He should have known. He should have known that the case they had met on and just worked together wasn't going to be the end.

Hunter knew how cults worked. He had been a kid whose parents had seen the light; and therefore, he'd survived his first years growing up in a cult. He'd come in on the previous case specifically because he could remember the way that power had been wielded, how promises had become threats, how one man or a group of men—or women—could control others. It was his area of specialty.

The mind was a dangerous playground.

But this was a different kind of deadly game.

"Have we heard anything from the medical examiner's office yet? You said there were five of them out here?"

"Three from the county—the bodies have been taken to the county morgue—one from FDLE and one from the

FBI," she told him. "They have IDs on several of the men—drug runners. But lower echelon drug runners. They all had a tiny scorpion tattooed on them somewhere on their bodies—and the word *Hermandad*. Oh, and apparently each also had *Los Zapatos* tattooed on them near their little scorpions."

"Brotherhood," Hunter murmured. "And 'the Shoes'? That's a new one to me."

"Records show it's an indication they were low-level street warriors—getting the drugs out there and proving themselves to try to move up in the hierarchy. The Brotherhood is a cartel out of Colombia—but you know that, right?"

He nodded. "So, there will be retaliation." He cocked his head to the side. "The street warrior gang is called 'the Shoes.' Something that goes along with walking?"

"I don't know why—that's just what they're called," Amy said. "You're right. If you're pounding the pavement, pushing drugs, shoes are good. But it's tattooed on them! Anyway. Moving onward, because of the arrows and hatchets, the team had a press conference right away."

"And that was good. Morrison had heard about this, just via the news, by the time I got there. And people need to know that besides murdering people, whoever is guilty is trying to stir up all the trouble they can in the state. And maybe beyond."

She shrugged. "Hunter, this state is a mixture of everyone. Tons of people getting along, but you have an incident like this and people start becoming paranoid. My boss has been working with the media, and I think he's made it clear we're looking at something that has to do with gang associations and nothing else."

He nodded somberly, studying her. Amy kept her dark brown hair in a braid when she was working, and she always wore a plain pantsuit and tailored white shirt on the job. She was still striking. Her eyes were green and gold and seemed to radiate like the sun. Her face was stunning—she had high cheekbones, an expressive mouth and a perfect nose. She'd never had to rely on her looks, though. Her dad had been a cop and she'd known she was going to be law enforcement in one way or another since she'd been a girl. She had one brother, who was a cop in Virginia.

Hunter had known he would become FBI because he and his parents had been rescued from their increasingly dangerous cult by an FBI agent. And he understood Amy. Their pasts had been different but with the same outcome—they both wanted to stop bad things from happening to others.

It was never easy.

But after his morning with Morrison, Hunter knew they were facing a case that was going to take every agency—across the country, he imagined—to solve.

Because of the second horse.

"Someone out there has a plan," he said. "I don't think Morrison was the top dog. So who is it?"

"But Morrison wouldn't give you anything?"

He hesitated, looking around the scene.

The cult killing that had first brought him to South Florida had occurred about fifty miles south of where they were now.

The Everglades—the great "River of Grass" that dominated much of the southern peninsula—stretched from Lake Okeechobee to the Atlantic basin. For many, it was a no-man's-land inhabited by alligators, all kinds of snakes, mosquitoes and zillions of other insects.

To some, it was a haven for bird-watchers.

For others—from the original tribes to all those who'd

moved here recently—the Everglades meant a livelihood, peace and a way of life. Big sugar had once dominated a lot of the acreage and it still did. But there were miles and miles of nothing, as well.

Maybe not "nothing." Many tour companies used the canal that had brought Jimmy Osceola and his group here. Some in motorboats, some in airboats and some even came through this way by the roads via bus tours.

By night, the wetlands were empty of people.

There would be few witnesses, if any. Only the brave— or those who knew the area well—would venture here by night.

"So, what do we know about your skunk ape?" he asked her.

She pulled out her phone and drew up her notes, giving him the names of those on Jimmy Osceola's ride along with a brief description of the group. And a woman named Ginny Marks who told them that she'd seen a skunk ape.

"Or," she finished, "something, or someone, else."

"What made her say skunk ape?" he asked.

"The size of whoever or whatever she saw moving around."

"And did you find anything?"

"Yes. I don't know if everyone came by the road, but some people did. I'm trying to figure out how anyone got the dead men out here from the get-go. They were killed here—they bled out here. But what would twenty lower-level drug runners be doing out here? Along with the men who killed them?"

"We need to get vice in on this from the local departments," Hunter said.

"Mickey is working on that angle."

"Good. So—"

"The brush is trampled. Someone came in from the road. We're looking for anything that might have caught on twigs or branches, footprints or anything else we can find. Believe it or not, there's been no rain here for a day or two, but the ground is always damp. We should find something. Aidan will get his crew—once they've finished where they are— and see what they can find. I had to look for the skunk ape, of course. But I'm still trying to figure out how someone was still around—the men were killed late last night or early this morning. The medical examiners are still working. And if the skunk ape wasn't involved, why not call something like this in?"

"The only report came from Jimmy Osceola?"

"Yep."

"Okay. I say we go home."

"What?" she demanded, stunned.

"I need to talk to home base. I promise you these guys are on our radar. I want to know more about the cartel and where to expect retaliation."

"You think this will happen again?" Amy asked.

"Whether they're guilty or not, the rival gangs will be suspected by the Hermandad. So yes, others are going to meet a similar fate somewhere."

"War," Amy muttered.

He nodded. He'd needed to come to the crime scene to study it, but now he was ready to leave.

"You did some sketches, though, right?"

She nodded. "Of course, and photographers captured it all."

"There's nothing else we can do here. I say we go."

"Where?" Amy asked, and she managed something that

resembled a smile. "My home is up in the middle of the state, your home is in the DC area. We both just came from the Caribbean!"

"Good point," he told her. "I saw a decent-looking chain hotel east of here. I say we settle in for the night."

"Hey!" John Schultz approached them and shook Hunter's hand. Hunter liked Schultz, though he'd had to accept the man was rough around the edges. Amy had laughed telling him about how hard it had been for Schultz to accept a young woman as his partner at first. But he was a good cop and a passionate one.

"So, what about Morrison?" John asked him.

"I didn't get a damned thing. I'm just hoping I unnerved him a little."

John shook his head, his teeth gritting. "That…maniac! He thinks money can buy anything. Well, let's hope to hell he's wrong."

"He's wrong," Hunter assured him.

"I'm heading out," John said. He made a face. "Still trying to watch my hours and lay low." He hesitated. "We're not alone on this, you know."

"We do know," Amy assured him.

"And we're out of here, too," Hunter said.

"I guess you're not heading back to the Bahamas," John asked.

"No." Hunter shook his head. "We'll all catch up again first thing in the morning."

"You're staying in the area?"

"Yep."

John nodded. "Yeah, me, too. There's a hotel just east of here—"

Amy interrupted him with a soft tap.

"I guess we'll see you at breakfast," she told him.

John lifted a hand, turning to head back to his car, which he'd parked off the road closer to the water.

"I want to say good night to Aidan," Amy told Hunter.

"Yeah. I'd like to see him, too."

They walked over to Aidan, who was hunkered down by a bush.

He turned around as they approached him.

"Hunter, hey," Aidan said, looking up but not rising. "Sorry to see you back so quickly."

"Sorry to be back so quickly. You found evidence of the skunk ape?"

Aidan rose, dusting his gloved hands together.

"Believe it or not," he said, "I did. Okay, skunk ape? I don't know. Large hulking two-legged creature, yes. I'm sure Amy has filled you in. Twenty men dead. How anyone talked that group into being out here in the middle of nowhere, I don't know. There's evidence of cars, and people coming through toward the water from cars. People—the dead or their killers—might have come by water, too, as there's a lot of trampled ground near the waterway. Whatever happened, it happened fast—even with arrows and hatchets. I haven't learned much from the MEs yet, but from preliminary reports, there weren't many defensive wounds. Some of the men were armed—and I'm assuming they knew how to use their weapons, but they were attacked so swiftly and thoroughly they never drew them. There's splattered blood along the roadway. That would account for someone maybe checking to make sure the dead men were all dead, though they died last night or in the wee hours of this morning." He stood, shaking his head. "There's something I didn't think of—and we let Jimmy go."

"Oh? What?" Amy asked him.

"He was telling me he was accustomed to strange things in the Everglades and on the roads that cut through them. Well, let's face it—we've all seen very strange things here. But Jimmy was telling me just last week he'd seen two men out here who appeared to be fishing without knowing how to fish. And there was a big old gator sitting on the bank, not moving, just minding its business. The men whooped and screamed like little girls. He thought they were tourists who didn't really know what they were doing."

"But they might have been involved in what happened here," Hunter said. "We'll talk to Jimmy. He's a tolerant guy, but he doesn't have a lot patience for people who come out on python challenges and the like without knowing anything about the region. If he noticed they didn't belong here, then they didn't belong here. Yes, they could have been a pair of tourists who just thought they knew what they were doing. But they could have been doing some kind of recon. Thanks, Aidan."

"Call me if you need anything or think I can help. Of course, I'll report any findings to you," Aidan said. He frowned. "Who is taking lead here?"

"We let our bosses sort that kind of thing out," Hunter told him. "As soon as we know, we'll let you know. I'm figuring we're going to be a joint task force."

Aidan nodded. "Well, go home." He paused to frown, likely remembering Amy lived a few hours north and Hunter didn't even live in the state. "Or go wherever you're going and try to pretend it's the Bahamas. Hey, it is Florida. You'll still have sunlight come the morning!"

Hunter saw the sun was fading from the sky.

And he thought the sky was beautiful. Golds, crimsons,

mauves...all shooting across the heavens and seeming to lower like a blanket over the land.

"Yep, it's still Florida," Hunter said. "But somehow I have a feeling we're not going to have time to worry about the hotel pool or amenities. Anyway, talk to you tomorrow."

"Thanks, Aidan," Amy said.

"Hey!" Aidan called as they walked away. They turned back. "You're the good guys. You deserved your vacation. Try not to let this ruin the days you had."

"We have to work it, you know."

"I do. And no matter what happens or where it leads, I'll be here to help."

"Thank you!" Amy said.

Hunter grinned and told him, "You're part of the good guys, too, Aidan. Thanks."

Hunter nodded and he and Amy turned to leave at last.

"Where are your things?" Hunter asked her. "Did you rent a car?"

"I did. I'm next to the forensic van over there. Meet you at the hotel."

"I'll follow you out of here."

She smiled at that. "I'm a big girl. I have a gun and I know how to use it."

"Good. Want to follow me?" he teased.

"I'll protect you," she promised. "You had my back..."

"You do pretty well on your own. And I'm glad you have my back, too," he said.

"You follow me," she said. "I know where I'm going."

"Hey!" he protested.

"I'm local," she reminded him with pretended superiority, before adding seriously, "I don't think these people—these killers—are still around anywhere. But it's a good thing we have one another's backs. It's when someone doesn't have your back that you wind up in trouble."

"You're so right," he said softly.

She nodded and hurried ahead of him. They weren't parked near each other, so he let her start out before falling in behind her.

At the hotel, he put his personal card on the room—they'd give the bill to whichever agency did claim lead when the time came.

Hunter was anxious to pull his computer out, but when they'd entered their room and closed the door, he pulled her into his arms and held her for a minute.

"You know...we're both going to work this."

"It's what we do," she reminded him.

"I know. I just wish..."

"That we'd met at a swinging singles bar and I was a schoolteacher?"

"No," he protested. "No, I wouldn't have cared if you were a CEO or an attorney—or a nurse or a doctor."

"And I wouldn't have cared if you were, either!" she said. She touched his hair and grinned at him as he held her, and then scrambled from his hold. "I have to shower. That crime scene..."

"I have to shower, too. But I want to see what's going on with this gang, who the rivals might be and whatever else they have on record. You go on, I'll get started."

She nodded. "I want to find out about the witnesses."

"You mean the tourists in Jimmy's boat?"

"Yes."

"You think one of them knows something?"

"I think it's always prudent to find out everything you can about anyone you come across while investigating a crime."

"Ah, excellent. Okay, go shower!"

"And don't touch me when I come out—not until you've been in!"

"Yes, ma'am," he said. "I'll do everything in my power to resist."

She wrinkled her nose at him and hurried into the bathroom.

Hunter set up his computer, leaving room at the desk for Amy and her laptop. But before he delved into his research, he made a call to Assistant Director Charles Garza—his superior and the man who had sent him to Florida on the cult case that had finally landed Ethan Morrison in jail.

"So," Garza said, "the murdered men were all part of the Hermandad?"

"We're assuming. They all have the tattoos, though some haven't been identified yet. But they had another tattoo, a scorpion, and lettering that defined them as Los Zapatos, or 'the Shoes.' They were foot soldiers. I hadn't heard of that before."

"They're lower echelon. Vice squads across the country have been notified. It's the way of entry into the cartel."

"All right, then, from what I can surmise, someone managed to kill twenty men—who usually hung out in the worst urban neighborhoods—in the Everglades. What we can't figure is how anyone got them all out to a no-man's-land and killed them there. Even if they were the fringes of a gang, there's going to be gang retaliation. Their attempt to make it look like an old Western movie was ludicrous— which you know and handled well at the press conference."

"Thank you, Hunter. This is all I can tell you—the men killed would be deemed expendable by their cartel. Shoes. Walking the pavement. Just getting into it and hoping to make their mark. This cartel is all over the world. Governments across South America have been trying to cut down on their outpouring of drugs, but... Oh, here's something. There was a real problem about a year ago with one of the men in the gang. He was cutting MDMA with other compounds in a way that was sending dozens of people to local hospitals in Miami. The man arrested wouldn't give up anything and mysteriously managed to hang himself while awaiting trial. Whether it's a common practice among 'the Shoes' or not—trying to make more money for themselves or their overlords—we don't know. Anyway, that's all that I can give you right now."

"Thank you."

"This will be joint, naturally. What happened is Florida jurisdiction, and while we sort it all out, we're on a task force. There will be a meeting tomorrow at the local FDLE offices."

"Right."

"I talked to Mickey Hampton. I know John Schultz and Amy Larson will be on the team."

"Great."

"Amy is with you?"

He glanced over at the bathroom door; Amy was just emerging from her shower. She'd donned a long cotton tee and was industriously drying her hair with a towel. He smiled.

"Amy is with me, yes. So is John Schultz, same hotel. We're just east of the crime scene."

"All right, keep me posted, and of course, I'll get back to you with anything I can."

They ended the call.

"That was Garza?" Amy asked.

He nodded. "If not for the red horses we found, it might have been retaliation, or a message from other drug pushers. Apparently, a 'shoe' was arrested for cutting his drugs a while back, but managed to commit suicide in jail. If it was suicide. Might have been a message."

"I'm sure it was a message," Amy said. She dug in her bag for her computer, drawing up the second chair at the little round table/desk combo in the hotel room. "And the murdered men in the Everglades might have been chosen for being lower echelon—expendable. But even so, to save face, Hermandad is going to have to retaliate. And then others will get into it."

"And we'll have gang and turf wars all over."

"How the hell do we stop that?" Amy wondered.

He leaned back, watching her. She was already searching on her computer.

"You're seeing what you can find on the witnesses who were with Jimmy and found the bodies?"

She nodded.

"Because you think one of them was involved?"

"Intuition," she told him with a grimace and a shrug.

"Doesn't Jimmy take that route all the time?"

"He does."

He pulled out his phone again. He had Jimmy Osceola's number. He'd gotten it from Aidan. He dialed, wanting to know about the strange fishermen he'd told Aidan about.

Jimmy answered right away.

"You know something?" Jimmy asked. "Sorry, I can't shake this!"

"No, and I'm sorry to call you so late. Aidan was telling me you saw some strange people a few days ago in the area where the bodies were found."

"Idiots. You know—we have a problem down here with invasive snakes. Sometimes, people had pets that got too big and they thought the humane thing was to let them go in the wild. Then sometimes storms have wrecked reptile habitats and the like. But we have a challenge down here to try and control the numbers. But you get idiots shooting across neighborhoods that border the Everglades, as well. And idiots out in the canals and waterways. I thought it was a grand pair of idiots. They were in camouflage. And honestly, no one wears camouflage out here. Normal clothes! And they had ridiculous fishing gear—giant rods and gear that would immediately tangle in the mangrove roots. I was going by, pointing out Old Sam—I've seen that big old gator in the same place my whole life—and when the men saw him they freaked out! He was basking. Not hunting, not moving, just basking in the sun. I mean, I'm not making light of an alligator's abilities, it's just that…well, you don't get in on a territorial dispute. You watch out at mating season, and you don't go walking around with your miniature poodle. But anyone who spends time out here knows you leave a basking alligator alone—you're not its natural prey. And they screamed when they saw him. Hey, I mean, alligators scare a lot of people, but…well, they should have been expecting an alligator. You know, in the Everglades."

"Jimmy, did you get a look at any of the dead men today? Would you know if the men you saw before were among them?"

"Hunter, I didn't look at the dead men. I know police procedure. I backed away and dialed 911."

"Right. Thanks. But, Jimmy, would you mind coming down to the morgue tomorrow?"

"Would I mind? Sure. Only an idiot wants to go look at dead men. Will I? Yes."

"Thank you. I'm figuring to get there around nine."

"I'll be there. My son can take out the early tours."

"Thank you."

"These people...they abused land we hold unique. I will happily help in any way."

He ended the call. Amy had been listening while prowling through the computer.

"What if the men Jimmy saw were among the dead?" she asked.

"It will be a step toward finding out how they wound up out there."

"Right," she murmured.

"Anything on the tourists?" he asked her.

She shrugged. "They look like an ordinary tour group. Ginny Marks—who saw the skunk ape—and her husband, Ben, are snowbirds down from Michigan. They are both retired schoolteachers and own a condo on Miami Beach and spend five or six months here every year. We know that David Ghent is in law school at Florida State. And two in the group are attorneys—Audrey Benson, forty-four, from Chicago, criminal law, and Daisy Driver, thirty-three, from Tallahassee, family law. Rounded out by Geoff Nevins and his wife, Celia, in their late forties, from Illinois. They were on vacation. They own a convenience store where they both work with several family members."

"They don't sound like a group of hardened criminals."

"There's a criminal attorney in there," she reminded him.

"Prosecutor, or defense attorney?"

"Defense. I'm trying to find out if she's defended anyone

gang-related, but so far, all I'm seeing are domestic disputes and assault and battery. She's a junior partner."

"Ah," he said, rising. "We can keep investigating that."

"Where are you going?" Amy asked him.

She smelled amazing—maybe just the smell of soap was amazing to him after the day. But if one "wore" soap, Amy wore it well. And the simple T-shirt, lacking the temptations of lace frills or see-through fabric, was ridiculously seductive.

"Shower," he said.

He hurried in, leaving her to work, hoping the morning would bring them closer to the answers they needed.

The hot water felt delicious.

He hoped he wore the scent of soap as well as Amy.

When he emerged, he paused just to make sure he wasn't interrupting her discovery of an information gem, then took the laptop out of her hands and set it down.

"We know we have to live our lives, too," he said softly. "We always have to care but keep a distance. We can't ever be jaded, but we need to forget work sometimes, and think about ourselves and our friends and families." He shook his head. "We both know we have to be involved in this, but…sometimes we have to let it wait, too, and forget the bad for a while."

She slid from her chair and walked over to the bed, stripping the covers away.

"No chocolates on the pillows," she said.

"I don't think this hotel offers turn-down service," he said.

She smiled at him and slid into bed. He wasn't at all sure what she was thinking or feeling. He crawled in next to her and was startled when she rolled onto him, lying halfway up his chest.

"You're right," she whispered huskily, a light in her eyes. "Sometimes I just want to forget about everything."

Her T-shirt had slid up and he felt her bare skin against his. Soft, sleek, smooth and fragrant.

He grinned. "I live to serve," he promised her.

It was a while before they slept.

But the time was well spent.

For a brief spell, they could, and did, forget the bad.

3

The county morgue seldom handled twenty murder cases in a day, but the autopsy area was large enough for the steel beds to be laid out in an orderly fashion.

Hunter met up with Dr. Angela Rodriguez first; they were soon joined by John Schultz, and then Jimmy Osceola.

Amy had gone on to the lab to see what—if anything—Aidan and his team had discovered.

"Obviously, I didn't do the autopsies on all the bodies, but I don't think any of us has any surprises for you. Six of the men were killed with arrows, five with hatchets and the remaining victims were killed with knives. I'm going to suggest that those wielding the weapons were experienced with them, so death was quick in all cases. And I'm assuming that was so no one could retaliate," Dr. Rodriguez told them.

Jimmy was tight-faced and grim, but he waited silently as Hunter explained to Dr. Rodriguez that they were trying to find out if two of the men had been at the crime scene before the event.

Then with Hunter and John Schultz, Jimmy took a walk along the rows of the dead.

The men had been young, Hunter noted. The youngest maybe early twenties, the oldest perhaps thirty-five. They had been in fit physical condition.

It was astounding to Hunter that these men, healthy and most probably adept with knives and guns, had been taken down en masse.

He was studying one of the scorpion tattoos when Jimmy Osceola let out a sound.

Jimmy was one body behind him, and when Hunter turned, Jimmy looked at him.

"This man," he said. "This man was one of the two in the boat screaming at the alligator, wearing camouflage."

Dr. Rodriguez was following them with a clipboard.

"You're sure?" Hunter asked Jimmy.

He nodded solemnly.

Hunter looked at Dr. Rodriguez, arching his brows, as John Schultz came over to see the body in question.

"We do have an ID on this man. Frank Suarez, born in Venezuela, but he's an American citizen, naturalized when he was eighteen. Came here with his parents when he was ten. He did get into trouble when he was in high school for stealing beer from a convenience store. That's why his prints gave us his identity," she said. She shook her head. "They were found with their weapons, but not one of the men had a wallet or identification on them."

"Was their clothing rifled with, or did it appear they

had gone there without their identification papers?" John asked her.

"I don't know. I was one of the doctors at the scene, but the way the men were killed and the way they fell…if their clothing had been rifled by someone searching for something, they did a good job of it." She hesitated. "Even for us, with this—" she extended her arm to indicate the room "—this being what we do, that was one bloody crime scene on a marshy, overgrown spit of ground. I wish I could tell you for sure, but I can't."

"Thank you," John said.

She went on. "Obviously, stomach contents on the men are being analyzed. Nothing fresh that I could identify right away."

Jimmy made a strange sound. He'd seemed fine until he'd heard the words *fresh* and *stomach contents*.

His eyes, Hunter thought, were distant.

"Hunter, John," Jimmy said. He was pointing across a row of the victims on their steel autopsy gurneys.

They both followed his line of vision. He was pointing at the body of another man. In life, the body was that of someone who had also been young, early twenties. The bodies had been covered other than their faces, allowing Jimmy to find the men he had seen, and perhaps more so than with some of the others, the man appeared to be sleeping. He had shaggy blond hair and looked like he belonged at a sixties rock concert.

"That's the other guy," Jimmy said.

Hunter walked around one of the rows of the dead over to the corpse Jimmy had indicated. Dr. Rodriguez and John followed him, with the ME looking first for a number on the toe tag and then referring to her clipboard.

"Charles Gould, graduated from a local junior college, and working as an assistant manager for Valley Fun Foods," she said. "Born in Miramar, Florida, and here most of his life. He was arrested on a charge of assault and battery, but the case was dismissed on a technicality. Unmarried and his parents are deceased and nothing on file tells us anything about next of kin or friendships. I'm sure the different tech facilities in the task force will seek more information on him."

"Jimmy?" Hunter asked, looking back across the room. Jimmy hadn't followed them. "This is the man you saw?"

Jimmy nodded.

"You're sure?" John asked.

"I am sure," Jimmy said.

"We've recorded everything we know about the men we were able to identify," Dr. Rodriguez said. "And our reports are on their way to the FBI and the FDLE," she said, acknowledging John and Hunter.

"Thank you," Hunter said.

"There are several of us working this, naturally," Dr. Rodriguez said. "Here, and in the lab. And we'll be diligent and prompt with all information."

"We know that, and appreciate your help," Hunter told her.

They left the autopsy room, stripping off the paper lab coats and disposable gloves Dr. Rodriguez had provided.

Out on the sidewalk, Hunter and John both thanked Jimmy Osceola.

He nodded gravely. "I am always willing to do what I can. You know that. I must admit, it's given me the creeps. I've spent my life learning the way of the waterways and hammocks, the alligators, moccasins and now the big guys, the boas and other constrictors eating everything in sight.

Now I'm wondering what other idiots might be out there. But here's what I don't get at all! The two scoping the place out are dead! I'd have thought it was the murderers or executioners or whatever who would have been checking on the terrain."

"Unless someone local was in on it who already knew the terrain," Hunter said.

"By local—"

"We're going to have to dig into the families," Hunter said, interrupting Jimmy. "We're looking at a South American cartel, yes. But as we've seen, we have plenty of home-grown terrorist and criminal types, and they can come from any group. The one kid you saw looks like a hippie out of a picture from Woodstock. You get one man like Ethan Morrison, and he corrupts an entire group of people, usually those lost or depressed or desperately seeking something from life. In this case, we're not looking at a cult—we're looking at a major criminal enterprise. A drug-running cartel. That will include murder, extortion, prostitution and more. Anyone growing up around here might have come out to the Everglades with a school group—a tour group. Lots of people love airboats, and even the fact that you can find areas where no cell phone will work. You have helped us incredibly today, Jimmy. We know an invitation of some kind must have gone out to the deceased before the event. And maybe to be sure it was as remote as they'd been told, the two you saw came to check it out. Now we have to hope we can find out something about them. And since you saw them and know they were out there, we know there is something to find."

"Just what he said," John told Jimmy.

Jimmy nodded. "It's my home. It's my land. You let me

know if you need anything else I can possibly give you." He frowned suddenly. "Where's Amy?"

"Meeting with Aidan. They're going to see a few attorneys, among others," Hunter told him.

"Oh?" Jimmy asked. Then he said, "Oh! They've gone back to interview the witnesses. But they weren't witnesses—not to the actual crime."

"But they were with you when you came upon the scene," Hunter said. "Amy is going to meet with everyone who was on the trip. She talked to Aidan this morning about possible evidence his crew might have collected, but they're not coming up with hair, fibers, litter…they have one cigarette butt and they're working on DNA from that. Anyway, there might be something someone saw. Amy and Aidan will talk to them. Then later, maybe John and I will interview them again."

"I don't get it," Jimmy said, shaking his head.

"Ginny Marks saw what she thought was a skunk ape," John said.

"Hey, in all my years out here, I've yet to see a skunk ape," Jimmy informed them, sighing for patience.

"And in all my years—not as close to the land as you, but I know the area—I've yet to see a Florida panther. They're rare, but they're out there," John said.

"So, you think there really is a skunk ape?" Jimmy asked, looking at John, confused and skeptical.

Hunter laughed softly, shaking his head. "We know someone was out there. Maybe, now that time has gone by, someone will remember something else."

Jimmy shook his head, letting out a long sigh again.

"I wish I'd seen something. But you know, come upon a scene like that and you find you're just staring—not looking around. Anyway, I'm out of here. I think I may drive out to the beach. I may go stay in a hotel at the beach! I love my area of this state, but I could use some sun and sand!"

"Enjoy," Hunter said.

Jimmy waved and nodded and headed toward his car.

John turned to Hunter. "I think it was a good idea for Amy and Aidan to do individual interviews—and good that neither of us is with them in case we want to go back for any reason. What now?"

"Now I say we head to the closest FDLE office and look at the information we have on the identified dead men. And get going on their families," Hunter said.

"Yes. Those young kids—they must have parents who are going to grieve. Sibling or cousins or friends who are going to miss them."

"And who might know something about what they were doing out in the wilderness where they were killed," Hunter said. "We'd best get on it."

John nodded. "There's an office just east. I'll text you the address."

Hunter nodded and walked to his own car. After he buckled into the driver's seat, he checked the email on his phone.

True to her word, Dr. Rodriguez had sent him the files she had.

He wondered how much carnage they had a chance of stopping. One thing was sure: the Hermandad was a fierce and far-reaching crime machine.

And they were going to want revenge.

Where and when that revenge would come was the question.

Because once this war started, death would come like

a field of dominos knocking one another over in a wave that might be impossible to stop.

"Everyone is making fun of me. Even my husband," Ginny Marks said, shooting her husband a warning glare. "But...hard to recall it all exactly. I mean, I'd always wanted to take that tour. I'd see the signs for Jimmy's restaurant and tours dozens of times. And every time I'd see a sign, I'd say, hey, I want to do that! Friends had gone out with him and they said no one in the world could explain the terrain and the birds and wildlife like Jimmy Osceola. He was showing us a bird...a beautiful heron. And then...then he was moving the boat next to the ground and getting out and warning us to stay in and...wow. Everything was slow—we were moving along slowly, and then time seemed to jumble. I was looking at the heron and then we were all looking out on the land beyond the canal and the world...the whole world around us seemed red. And I saw it—or him—or whatever I saw. Big and hulking by the brush and the tree line right by the road."

"I really didn't see anything," Ben Marks said.

They were sitting on the patio of the condo the Markses owned in Boca Raton—one that faced the intracoastal waterway, a world away from the Everglades.

Ginny had insisted on brewing coffee for them.

Aidan had agreed they needed it.

"We believe you did see someone, Ginny," Amy told her. "Maybe not a skunk ape," she acknowledged, "but possibly a big man."

"In a big black outfit, yeah, maybe," she wondered.

"Why not a gorilla costume?" her husband asked.

"Ben! I saw something. I am retired—I don't have dementia! Someone else saw what I saw!" she claimed.

"What makes you say that?" Amy asked.

"I heard someone!" Ginny told her.

"You heard someone," Aidan said. "Out by the road, or—"

"On the boat!" Ginny said. "I don't know who it was, but right when I saw whoever or whatever it was, I heard someone say, 'Ass!'"

"Someone...who?" Amy asked.

She shook her head. "I don't know. Jimmy Osceola was at the back of the boat with the motor or whatever, moving us along as he talked. There are five benches on the boat. Ben and I were in the middle. That other couple—the folks from Michigan... Geoff and Celia—were in the row in front of us. The attorney girls—sorry, I'm sixty-three, they're both girls to me—had a row each, as did the kid, David. He was right behind us, and Audrey Benson was behind him and Daisy... I forget her last name, but anyway, she was in the front seat—it's a little seat on account of the way the nose of the boat was made."

"But you have no idea who spoke?" Aidan asked.

"Or if you imagined it, along with a skunk ape," Ben said, shaking his head.

"I am not imagining!" Ginny said.

"I'm sorry," her husband said, giving her an apologetic grimace that turned into a weak smile. "Ginny, honey, it was traumatic! All those bodies, all that blood...even from a distance. It was horrible. But you two know that," he added softly, turning back to look at Amy and Aidan.

"Yes, of course it was traumatic, but I am completely of sound mind and reason. You know someone or something was out there. If they were supposed to be out there, why hadn't they called the police? And I heard what I heard. Someone on that boat whispered, 'Ass!'"

Ginny had drawn up straight in her chair. She appeared almost regal—and certainly of sound mind and reason.

"I believe you," Amy assured her. "Of course, the word could have referred to anyone."

"It could have. But after sleeping on it, I think someone on our boat knew the skunk ape—or whatever or whoever," Ginny said.

"Oh, honey! That's like a conspiracy theory!" Ben told her sorrowfully.

"Anything is possible," Amy said.

Because, in truth, she believed it *was* a conspiracy. She just wished Ginny knew who had spoken.

"Anything," Aidan agreed.

"Did you get any useful clues from the crime scene?" Ben asked him.

"A lot of bodies," Aidan said dryly, adding quickly, "In truth, we didn't get much from the area, but we will trace the hatchets and arrows that were used and left behind. I can almost guarantee they will have come from the American West, possibly Nevada. But we'll see." He looked at Amy.

She nodded. It seemed he thought they had everything they could get, but she had one more question.

"Mrs. Marks, why didn't you mention this yesterday?"

"You didn't even tell *me*," Ben muttered.

"Yesterday, everyone was making fun of me for saying I'd seen a skunk ape. I wasn't going to give anyone more fuel with which to deride me," she said.

"I see," Aidan murmured.

"And more," Ginny said. "I was scared with the others

around. I mean—and I'm not a crazy conspiracy-theorist—but what if whoever said the word *ass* was part of it? If they knew I heard them…well, it wouldn't be safe for me, would it?"

"Smart," Amy said. "But you should have called me."

"I would have." She gave her husband a dry glance. "*Everyone* on that boat was making fun of me. I would have called later."

"When I was bowling, right?" her husband asked.

"You shouldn't make fun of your wife," Ginny told him.

Ben Marks shook his head. "Ginny, I'm not making fun of you, I swear it! I just—"

"You don't believe in a skunk ape. And worse!" she told Amy and Aidan. "He won't accept the fact that my hearing is better than his!"

"Hey!" Ben protested.

"He needs a hearing aid," Ginny said. "But that would mean that he was old."

"We're the same age!" Ben protested.

"Right. Old. Anyway, I did hear what I heard," Ginny said.

"We believe you," Aidan assured her. "And as Amy said, you were smart. As Ben says, it's unlikely an odd assortment of tourists was involved, but careful is always best, right, Amy?"

"Right. By the way, did you know any of the others before the trip?"

Ginny and Ben both shook their heads.

"Okay, thank you again. And if anything comes up—"

"We'll call you," Ginny promised. "I won't hold anything back anymore—to you," she told her husband.

"And I won't make fun of you, I promise. Except I really don't believe in a skunk ape."

"Okay, I don't even believe in a skunk ape!" Ginny said. "But…it gave me a way to tell you that someone had been out there!"

"Smart," Amy told her.

She and Aidan thanked the couple and headed out of their condo.

"So, someone else saw the mystery person in the bush," Aidan said, sliding into the passenger seat of Amy's rental car. "But Ginny didn't know if it was a man or woman, much less which man or woman."

"But you believe her?" Amy said.

"I do."

"And whoever it was," Amy said, "they were calling whoever it was that was leaving the scene an ass."

"We sure have a lot of whoever people out there," Aidan said. "So…hmm. My money is on the kid."

"David Ghent? The law student?" Amy asked.

"What say you?"

She shrugged. "Possibly. I'd say maybe a little cog in a giant machine. I don't know if he's old enough to have orchestrated something like this."

"We've both seen what young people are capable of," Aidan reminded her.

"I want to talk to him, yes. But I say we head to the attorneys next. Audrey Benson out of Chicago and Daisy Driver out of Tallahassee, Florida. I'm afraid one or both might be planning on leaving the area soon."

"Tallahassee is in the state."

"So, we start with Audrey Benson."

"You're FDLE. I'm forensics along for the ride."

"You don't like my logic?"

"I love your logic," he told her. "Let's do it!"

Frank Suarez might have just been a kid who had gotten into a little bit of trouble. But his background hadn't boded well for him.

His mother had died of cancer about three years after they'd come to the States. His father had kicked him out of the house the minute he'd turned eighteen.

Juan Suarez had not been a nice man—judging by his son's social media. The man had raised pit bulls for fighting—until the state had shut him down. He'd done a stint in prison himself. He'd run a repair shop until last autumn when he'd had a heart attack while yelling at a customer over the price of new ball bearings.

"There's no one to even call on the kid," Hunter said, sitting at the conference table they'd been allotted at the office.

"The other kid...not so good, either. No father's name recorded on his birth certificate. Mother was a prostitute. She died of complications due to a botched abortion." John shook his head, leaning back. "I don't even know who to talk to for these kids...young men, I guess. No siblings, parents dead or unknown."

Hunter had hacked into Frank Suarez's social media easily enough. Frank hadn't been stupid—he'd posted absolutely nothing about criminal activity, being with a gang. He had pictures from a local bar—with his arm around an attractive young woman. She had dark hair that waved around her shoulders but was held back from her face with a band and was wearing short white shorts and a midriff halter top. The outfit looked as if it might be a uniform for the cocktail waitresses at the venue.

"Carlos O'Malley's," Hunter said.

"What?"

"Place looks cool and truly South Florida," Hunter said. "Carlos O'Malley's." He'd seen the name of the place on a sign across the bar behind Frank and the young woman. "They advertise a corned beef and cabbage night *and* a salsa night each week that offers the 'best churrasco in town!'"

"And we're going to Carlos O'Malley's—why?"

"We're going to meet a girl."

He turned his computer around for John to see the screen.

"He probably just took a picture with her because she's pretty."

"You got anything else?"

"No," John admitted.

"Then let's go."

They left their setup in the conference room; they had a board going with pictures of the crime scene and all the information they had.

They were just starting out when Amy called him.

"You've got something?" he asked her, his phone on speaker.

"Don't know if it will pan out, but Ginny Marks—"

"The skunk ape lady?" John said.

"We know she saw something, John," Amy said. "And she told us today she heard someone else in the boat say the word *ass* when she was seeing her skunk ape—or whatever."

"Ass?" John said.

"John, I think someone on Jimmy's tour boat had something to do with the massacre. I think they purposely took that tour, wanting to make sure it got called in and the bodies didn't rot for days before someone got to them. And that

69

person muttered 'ass' when they could see someone else at the scene or leaving the scene," Amy said.

"Possible, not probable," John said.

"I'm going with possible," Amy said.

"We're heading over to see the lawyers," Aidan's voice came through. Amy apparently had her phone on speaker, too. "Still with Amy. Hanging in. My folks are working it at the lab, not to worry."

"We're going to go hang out at a bar," John said, flashing a grin at Hunter.

Hunter just shook his head.

"We're going to a place called Carlos O'Malley's," he said.

"Hunter's looking for a girl," John teased.

Hunter just shook his head again.

"The victims who Jimmy Osceola saw pretending to fish have no family. They were ripe for being picked up by a gang and the cartel. But I found one picture on a social media page belonging to Frank Suarez. We're checking it out. I think he was standing with a bartender there."

"Okay. We'll keep in touch. We're heading to a posh hotel. Audrey Benson is staying on the water. Nice. Oh, we did have coffee on a lovely balcony this morning," Amy told them. "We'll keep in touch."

She ended the call.

Hunter glanced over at John. "You do know Amy and I are not the kind of people who get jealous over perceived wrongs, right?"

"Of course I know! That's why I can tease," John said. "Oh, come on, we've got to be light and easy sometimes. Spent the morning in the morgue—I still need to wash that off! I mean, long shower tonight, but hey, we need mental showers, too, right?"

"Yes," Hunter said. "True. I like that. A mental shower. So, onward to the bar."

"Onward to the bar. I mean, why not? It's not like we have a pack of solid clues to follow. Who knows, maybe we'll find a skunk ape at the bar."

"Maybe we will," Hunter said lightly. "A skunk ape in human clothing. No, with what's going on here, that's an insult to skunk apes everywhere. Let's just hope we can find that girl. And that she knows something about what her dead friend was up to."

Amy and Aidan arrived at the hotel where Audrey Benson was staying just in time to meet her down in the lobby; she was checking out.

"I'm heading home, yes," she said, surprised to turn from the counter to see the two of them standing there, waiting for her. "I'm afraid seeing twenty dead men in a field is all the excitement I care to have in Florida."

"We're sorry your trip turned out to be so brutal," Aidan said. "It is an amazing state—our sunshine, our geography and the incredible differences you can find from top to bottom."

"Oh, I haven't turned against Florida," Audrey said. "I just think this little time out for sun and fun has come to an end. I'll be back."

"Chicago is a great city, too," Amy offered. "Second City, museums, jazz... It's a great place to live."

"I'm glad you like it," Audrey said. "But—"

"We just had a few more questions for you," Amy told her.

"Oh? Okay. You know, we didn't witness what happened. We just witnessed the aftermath."

"Right. But Ginny Marks—"

"Forgive me, but that woman has a screw loose."

"Well, someone had been in the exact place where she claimed to have seen a skunk ape."

Audrey sighed. "You never know. I guess someone could have been out there—saw the bodies and ran!"

"Or maybe someone having something to do with the murders was checking out the results of the massacre," Aidan suggested.

"I suppose that's possible."

"You are an attorney. Practicing criminal law," Aidan said. "I'm sure you've heard all sorts of things in your career. I mean, you are a defense attorney."

"And I'm evil because of that?" Audrey asked.

"Not at all!" Amy assured her. "Every American deserves the best defense—we're innocent until proven guilty in this country. But you probably have heard just about every story possible. We were wondering if you had any perspective on what happened."

Audrey was thoughtful, and then shook her head, her lips solemnly pursed.

"And you didn't see anything?" Amy asked her.

"No. If Ginny saw something, I don't know what it was, and I didn't see it," Audrey said.

"Did you hear anything?" Aidan asked.

She frowned. "Hear anything? I heard birds…there was a light breeze. Leaves and all were rustling…and Jimmy was telling us about the terrain, the history…then, it seems to me, I just remember silence. And Jimmy telling us to stay in the boat. But not even the grass or any of the foliage—even the distance—couldn't hide what we saw."

"But no one else on the boat said anything?" Aidan asked.

"We all began talking, I think. I don't remember anything specific because we were all scared and horrified," Audrey said. She glanced at her watch. "I'm so sorry, but I don't want to miss my plane. I'm a junior partner, and you can reach me easily at my firm, but I must get to the airport. Again, I don't know what more I could say or do that could help, but please don't hesitate. I guess it's a Florida matter now, though."

"I'm afraid something like this brings in the federal government, too," Amy said pleasantly. "So, thank you. We have plenty of reach and if anything comes up we'll find you in Chicago."

Audrey gave them what appeared to be a forced smile, picked up her bag and hurried to exit the hotel.

Aidan looked at Amy. "I'm going to check with the lab. Where next? The second attorney or the kid I find to be a little suspicious and you find to be...a kid."

"I never said he wasn't suspicious."

"You're the detective."

"Aidan, your instincts are always good," Amy said. "So, let's go see the kid."

"All right! Let's find the kid," Aidan said. He laughed softly. "Maybe he's at a bar, too."

Amy sighed. "I'll call him."

She pulled out her phone, but before she could dial, it rang.

She didn't recognize the number; there was no caller ID.

She didn't answer with her name or identify herself as FDLE. She just said hello.

For a minute, there was nothing.

Then a soft chuckle sounded.

"Hello? No, 'Larson, here,' or 'Amy Larson, FDLE,' or perhaps 'Special Agent Larson'?"

"Who is this? And what do you want?" she said. Something about their tone rubbed her the wrong way.

The soft chuckle sounded again. "I just wanted to hear the sweet and melodic sound of your voice, Special Agent Larson. Do you like to ride? Do you ever go horseback riding, Amy? Horses are such amazing animals, carrying even greater amazement on their backs, such as those with power. Oh! Yes, I called for more than a quiz on horseback riding."

"Who is this? Why did you call?" Amy asked, shaking her head at Aidan, who was looking at her worriedly. She lifted a finger for him to wait before speaking.

"To hear your voice," the caller said.

"Okay. You heard my voice."

"Such an intriguing woman," the caller said.

"You've heard my voice, now why did you call?"

"Oh, well. I thought I should let you know that red horses have a great time in New York City. A really, really great time!"

The line went dead in her hands.

4

Carlos O'Malley's was an attractive venue. It was decorated with shamrocks and pictured little leprechauns here and there on soft-lime-green walls.

There were flags from many nations lining the bar.

A large area with eight high-top tables stretched out in front of the bar, with a dining room that might easily seat about two hundred people to the right side after entry.

Hunter and John looked around for a minute after entering. It was almost two o'clock, which meant the lunch crowd was thinning out, but servers were hurrying around, clearing checks and then tables.

The serving staff was all female, young and attractive. And they were all wearing the shorts and halter tops worn by the girl in the picture with Frank Suarez.

"So…" John said. "Hmm."

One of the young women walked up to them.

"Hi, can I help you? Bar, high-top or do you prefer the dining room?" she asked.

"High-top, I guess," Hunter said. "Thanks."

She was not the girl in the picture. He was hoping to find the young woman without asking someone else about her.

"Take your pick!" she said cheerfully. "Special today is fish and chips! And Sonja will be right with you."

"You know what?" John said as they chose a high-top with a clear view of the restaurant. "Fish and chips sound good. Feds eat lunch, too, right?"

"Yep. Feds eat lunch."

"Look!" John said, lightly kicking Hunter beneath the table. "Sonja—it's her."

He saw the young woman speaking briefly with the hostess who had greeted them; it was the girl from Frank Suarez's social media post.

She walked over to them with a pad and pen in hand.

"Good afternoon, gentlemen. What can I get you? Oh, I'm sorry—I see you don't have menus yet. I'll get those for you, but can I get you something to drink?"

"I know it's a bar, but you got any good coffee?" John asked.

"Of course! And you, sir?" she said to Hunter.

"Coffee, too, please, and some water. And we don't need menus—we'll both take the fish and chips, thank you," he said.

She nodded. "Sure! That will be quick. I'll be right back with your coffee."

She left them.

"Do we get to eat before we grill her?" John asked.

"During. I'm going to ask her if we can speak with her privately when her shift is over. I don't think she's going to break down with tons of information while working."

"I like the plan," John said.

Hunter thanked her when she brought their coffee and water. And then he asked, "Sonja, right?"

She frowned, and then smiled. "I'm Sonja."

"I want to be honest. We're here specifically to see you."

"Oh?"

She was very pretty, with dark eyes, dark hair and a sweet smile. Of course, appearance didn't make a person capable or incapable of evil. But there was something about her smile, about her open friendliness. But then, she was a server. Tips would not be so great if she weren't friendly and outgoing, cheerful with patrons.

"Why?" she asked, her smile fading to a frown.

"We found a picture of you on social media with a young man," Hunter said.

"Okay," she said carefully.

"I'm Special Agent Hunter Forrest, with the FBI. Special Agent Schultz here is Florida Department of Law Enforcement."

She looked truly puzzled.

"And you're looking for me? I'm the kid who never even downloaded a movie illegally!" she told them.

Hunter nodded. "I believe that." He reached into his pocket to produce a printed copy of the picture. "But do you know this young man?"

"Of course I do. That's Frank."

"He's a regular customer?" John asked.

She nodded. "A really sweet guy. Always tips well. A little sad. He grew up horribly." She hesitated, lowering her head. She was evidently shaky. She stopped speaking, look-ing at the two of them. "Hey, he's kind of a sad case, you know. Sucky time growing up! He's polite to everyone here. When he speaks on the phone, he goes outside so he doesn't bother other people. Never comes in without being polite and tipping well."

"Do you know him well?" John questioned.

"So, we've never gone out, but he has asked me, and… I've said we could do a movie sometime when I have time off and he's available. Sometimes I work the late shift. This is a good and cool place to work—nice people, we cover for each other—but Frank waits for me if I'm working late, closing up. Sometimes we talk. He never drinks too much—a beer, at tops two. We have been planning a date. It just hasn't happened yet."

"He comes in alone?" Hunter asked.

"Yeah, always." She nodded, then frowned. "Except…"

"Except?" Hunter said gently.

"So there was one day when someone came in to meet him. Carlos—this place is really owned by a man named Carlos O'Malley—was helping the bartender. It was busy, around five, cocktail hour, two-for-one beers. And this man walked in. Frank was at that table over there—" she paused to indicate one of the high-top tables a few feet from where they were seated "—when this man walked in and went up to Frank. Carlos started swearing behind the bar. I never got to the table because Carlos went over. He's a big, tough-looking guy himself. And I heard him say something about calling the police, and the other man said he had a right to be there, and Carlos said it was his establishment and he had a right to serve and not serve who he chose. And Frank… Frank was mortified! He smiled at Carlos and said not to worry, that they would get out—and he made the other guy leave with him. The next time Frank came in he apologized to Carlos right away. I don't know what the conversation was, but... Carlos was okay with Frank. Just not the other guy."

"Thank you," Hunter said quietly.

"There's no reason that Frank can't keep coming in, right?" Sonja asked.

"I'm afraid we have bad news," Hunter said gently. "Frank won't be in anymore. He was killed."

The tray she had been holding crashed to the floor. Hunter slid out of his stool to help her pick it up.

"I'm so sorry," he said.

"Please sit, we'll get this!" John said, joining Hunter. Together they collected pieces of broken glass.

Sonja took Hunter's chair and looked as if she'd been blindsided.

John took the tray with the broken glass to the bar; Hunter knew he'd be asking to speak with Carlos O'Malley.

"I... I... I never knew a friend who...died," Sonja said. She stared at Hunter. "You said you're FBI? That means something terrible happened."

"I'm afraid so. You must have heard about the massacre in the Everglades," he said.

"Frank was...he was killed there? Among those men?"

"You didn't know he was in a gang?"

She shook her head. "He was just...a sweet kid. I knew about his background. He could have been so mean and so horrible with what life had thrown at him, but he was sweet and kind and...oh, my gosh!"

A big man with a headful of dark graying hair and blue

eyes came walking around to the table. He was wearing an apron and Hunter figured he had to be Carlos O'Malley.

He offered a handshake to Hunter, introducing himself. He looked sorrowfully at Sonja.

"I'm sorry to hear about that boy. You want some time, Sonja? I know all of you thought of Frank as a great customer, and he always said you were the best. Would you like to go home? We're not busy at all. I'll have Milton take you home."

"I'd rather be with people, except..."

"Go take some time in the office," O'Malley said.

She nodded and looked at Hunter and John. "I... I'm so sorry. I don't think that... I can only tell you that he was a good guy."

"Thank you," Hunter told her gently.

He looked at O'Malley, already liking the man for being so decent to Sonja. There were bosses who would have told her to get back to work.

"Mr. O'Malley—" Hunter began.

"Yes, it's really my name. Mom is Cuban, Dad is from County Cork. And Frank Suarez was one of the dead men at that massacre?"

"Yes," John said gravely.

"Well, he was a good regular. He usually came alone. He really liked Sonja, but he was happy with any of the waitresses. He'd watch sporting events on the large screen and cheer and boo along with everyone. I suspected he might have some unsavory connections, but he never brought that here. Then one day Octavius Ripley comes in and sits down with him. And I will not have that kind of person in my place."

"Octavius Ripley?" Hunter asked, glancing at John. A local criminal?

"Yeah, I know of him," John said. "Palm Beach County had a solid attempted murder case against him—until the victim succumbed in the hospital. There were no other witnesses, and the physical evidence wound up being 'tainted.' Law enforcement was furious and frustrated and left wondering just what the hell else we have unsolved that might have involved his handiwork. We believe he is part of one of the cartels."

"Hermandad," Hunter muttered.

"Possibly. Or possibly a rival," John said. "That's the problem. Nothing is on paper. We've tried bugs at various places, and they've all been found. This has been an uphill battle. We've tried putting people on a hot seat—nothing. O'Malley, you were right to throw him out—he is a dangerous man."

"Oh, I'm aware. I keep a shotgun," Carlos O'Malley said. "And I promise you, I know how to use it. I have a permit, and a permit for the Smith and Wesson I carry, too." He shook his head. "I don't know… I'm sure Frank must have been involved with Octavius…somehow. He swore to me I'd never see the man in here again, which makes me wonder… Octavius doesn't like people who go against him. I'm surprised the kid managed to get him out of here that day."

Hunter nodded. "Thank you," he told O'Malley. "We'll have to speak with him."

"Good luck. The guy will tell you he doesn't have to speak to you. He'll call his lawyer. He'll tell you to arrest him or leave him the hell alone."

"We'll do our best."

"I hope you do find out what happened," O'Malley told

them. "I mean, I guess gang members know they might...be murdered. Or die violently. But that Frank... I'm so sorry he got into it all. Because he was sweet at heart. He just needed something to cling to so badly! Too bad he didn't meet Sonja first. She's a great girl with a great heart. She might have steered him straight."

The hostess brought them their fish and chips—nervously placing them on the table, giving everyone an equally nervous smile and hurrying away.

"Enjoy, please," O'Malley said. "On me."

"No, please, let me have a bill," Hunter said. He made a face. "We need to tip our waitress."

"Okay, sure," O'Malley said. "If you think I can help you with anything else, please don't hesitate."

"We won't," Hunter promised.

As O'Malley left them, Hunter's phone rang. It was Assistant Director Garza.

His voice came tensely through "They're at it again, Hunter. This time, twelve dead in an alley in New York City."

Amy saw Hunter was just ending a call as she and Aidan headed into Carlos O'Malley's Pub. She had decided they needed to discuss the call she'd received before they kept moving.

As they walked in and were greeted by a friendly hostess, Amy smiled and pointed out the table they'd be joining.

Hunter and John rose as she approached the table with Aidan, both frowning in curiosity.

"We were going to call you and head into the office," John said.

"I got a call from an unknown male voice about red horses in New York City," Amy said quickly.

Hunter's face went still. "And I just got a call from Garza about twelve men shot and killed in a New York alley," he said.

Amy sank into a chair at the table. "So we're too late to stop anything."

John slammed his hand on the table. "It's damned hard when we don't know what to stop. You two think the second horse—the red horse—of the apocalypse is in play? And the red horse is about war. So, someone is inciting a gang war. I just don't get it. Why?"

"We don't know," Hunter said. He looked at Amy. "If we knew why, I'd like to think we could stop what's going on. I know many people will think that gang members deserve whatever's coming to them, but we don't know how many are barely more than kids who have been steered in the wrong direction but might have straightened up. I don't have the right to choose who lives and who dies, and that's why we have a justice system. We have to do everything we can to keep this from escalating."

Amy nodded, lowering her head for a minute. She loved how Hunter thought.

"We just heard one of the dead men might have been decent—given the chance," John said.

"Ah," Amy muttered. "We were headed to the next witness when I got the call and we figured we should meet up."

"Garza wants me to go to New York," Hunter said.

"Are you leaving soon?" Amy asked.

"Tomorrow morning. Today I'm on the prowl for a man named Octavius Ripley."

"Familiar name. He's suspected of…many things. In many places," Amy said.

"I believe he might be a major player in Hermandad," Hunter told her.

"And he might be," she agreed.

Aidan interjected. "I'm taking Amy's phone back to the lab—if she's with you now, Hunter, I'll see it gets back to the hotel by tonight."

John rose. "All right. I'll go see the young woman attorney from Tallahassee. That's where you were headed, right, Amy?"

"Attorney Daisy Driver, then the college student David Ghent, and last, the middle-aged tourists, Celia and Geoff Nivens," Amy said.

"What? You get two people and I get the rest?" John said.

"Hey, every one of us is going to talk to every one of them," Amy protested.

"Just teasing you—I like the idea of a bunch of interrogations," John assured her.

"Ask nice questions, John," Amy said. "They're not in the hot seat. We're hoping they can give us something. Ginny said she heard someone in the boat saying the word *ass* right when she saw the skunk ape. I think one of the passengers might have been there to make sure the deed was done—and also discovered."

"I'll be so nice you'd pass out if you saw me," John promised her.

"That will be interesting," Aidan said. "Hey, so you two have had lunch, huh? Was it good?"

"Delicious," John assured him. "Fish and chips, today's special."

Aidan looked at Amy. "I'm hanging out with Hunter from now on," he told her.

"You're allowed to stop for lunch," Amy assured him.

He shook his head. "Nah, I want to see what we can find out about the number that called you. My bet is it's a burner phone purchased with cash. But we can never know, and if we can trace the call, it might help." He rose. "I'm out of here. Oh, wait. Amy, you were driving."

"I can drop you at the lab on my way," John told him.

"No, take the rental," Amy said to Aidan.

"We'll all head out," Hunter said. "Except I'm waiting on some calls. This Octavius Ripley is on a few watch lists. I'm getting reports on where I might find him."

"I'll give Mickey a call, too," Amy added. "If a local is on the FBI lists, Mickey will have something on him."

"You'll use Hunter's phone because I'm taking yours," Aidan reminded her.

She nodded. "Sure."

Aidan grinned, reached for her phone, then he and John headed out.

Hunter handed Amy his phone. "Want the fish and chips? It's a good meal."

She nodded. "Sounds great."

The hostess sent another young waitress over to them. Hunter ordered for her while she called Mickey.

"Garza already called me," Mickey told her. "He wants Hunter in New York, after the fact, but he also said they have local agents working up there. Anyway, we have an address for Octavius Ripley. Convoluted story, but one of our undercover agents found it. He keeps it under the name of an aunt. The aunt happens to be dead, but somehow, the property is still in her name. I'll text the address. You're about forty-five minutes away. The man may or may not be there, or he may refuse to see you, but since his people were murdered, he might be happy to do so."

Amy let her supervisor know to contact her on Hunter's phone—the number she was calling from—since hers was on the way to the lab.

She ended the call, and relayed the information to Hunter.

He nodded. "We'll head out. I'll get your fish and chips to go. I think they offer salsa with it—want some?"

She laughed. "Dry and neat as I'll be eating in a car."

"You got it."

Amy watched him head toward the bar and speak with their young waitress. She let out a long breath. Another massacre in New York—and Garza was sending Hunter. He was federal—she was state. But while the events were most certainly orchestrated by the same power, she was responsible only for finding out what had gone down in Florida.

"She'll be right here," Hunter told her when he got back to the table. "Got you an iced tea to go, too," he added, studying his phone. "Mickey sent me the address. I've got directions set up in Maps. We're good to go. This is going to be interesting."

"Or a total dud. He won't be there—or despite the murders, he may refuse to talk to us."

"Well, it's a scenic drive. Florida horse country is a beautiful area."

Their waitress brought Amy's food and a paper cup of tea. They thanked her and left to go out on the road.

"So, Garza is sending you to New York—even though New York has first-class FBI offices there, and surely dozens of exceptional agents."

"Because it's connected," Hunter said.

"Of course. But they'll have taken the bodies. Forensics will be done with their sweep of the alley, I imagine."

"Yes."

"But you'll think it out in your mind's eye."

He glanced at her and smiled. "You do it all the time."

She grimaced and took a bite of her fish. "Well, we got nice food, anyway!" she said cheerfully.

He nodded.

"What's wrong?" she asked when he was silent.

"I just wish..." His voice trailed.

"You don't want to go to New York."

"Nothing wrong with New York. I love the Big Apple."

"But?"

"I don't like this. The red horse at our resort. The red horse at the crime scene. And the fact *you* got a call about red horses in New York."

"You're afraid to leave me. Hunter, I've been doing law enforcement a long time. I am good at my job."

"I know."

"And John will have my back."

"I know."

"I see. You just don't think John will have my back as well as you would have my back."

He glanced at her with a quick smirk. "Maybe I feel I *need* to have you at my back."

She grinned at that.

"Hunter, like it or not, we're deeply involved in this. Along with teams in both areas. And whoever is doing this is having too much fun taunting me to want to take me out right now."

"You're probably right there," he acknowledged.

She laughed softly. "I know."

She finished her food and crumpled up the paper and put the trash together.

A minute later, Hunter suddenly pulled into a parking lot—it was a phone store. "I think you need your own phone on you," he said. "Get one of those things where you pay for data and get the phone free."

Luckily, the store was almost empty. It took Amy only a few minutes to get a temporary phone. The clerk was very helpful and set it up so that calls to her number would be diverted to the temporary one until she deactivated it.

Back in the car, she leaned back against the seat and closed her eyes.

They reached the impressive estate where Octavius Ripley was reportedly living. There was a guard at the gate of the development, but Hunter's credentials allowed them an easy entrance. At the house, they parked on the street and took the winding pathway up to the house. It was surrounded by paddocks and there was a large barn in the back.

The door was opened by a cheerful housekeeper who was slightly plump and wearing an apron, but didn't seem to expect anyone who might be after her boss at the door. Whatever his criminal enterprises might be, the man apparently kept them away from his home.

She invited them in and led them to a parlor at the side of the house.

"Mr. Ripley went down to the barn a while ago. We had a foal about a month ago, and he does dote on that little filly! He should be back soon. Would you like coffee or anything while you wait?" she asked.

"Not a thing, thank you. We're fine," Hunter told her.

"As soon as he's back, I'll let him know that you're here," she promised. "Oh, I'm Milly if you need anything! And you said that you're Hunter Forrest and Amy Larson?"

"Right, thank you!" Amy said.

"And you're with the FBI?" Milly asked.

"Hunter is FBI. I'm Florida Department of Law Enforcement," Amy said.

"Thank you. And not to worry—Octavius is always happy to be helpful!"

She left them seated in two plush armchairs that faced a large window and the garden.

"That was easy enough," Amy said.

"I'm always curious. How does a dead woman still own a piece of property?"

Amy shook her head. "Legalities in changing title? Which he's probably stretching out."

"But he's apparently been questioned before."

"And he knows no one has any solid evidence against him. Why not appear to be nice and helpful?"

Amy looked out over the garden. It was beautiful, filled with foliage and flowers native to the area. Two arched hibiscus bushes curled around a tiled path to a bench that was shaded by palm trees.

She stood up and walked around the room, studying the shelves. They were filled with books and dozens of board games.

Many of the books were law books. Several of those were on Florida law.

She was reading titles when she heard Hunter grunt with impatience and rise, as well.

"This is taking too long. Let's head out to the barn. I'm worried sweet and friendly grandma-looking Milly might have been warning him to get out."

"Possibly," Amy said. "That would change my opinion of her."

"Hey, be nice. We got lucky. She invited us in here."

"I'll be nice!" Amy promised. She turned and headed out of the room, calling for the housekeeper. The woman emerged through the grand foyer, presumably from the kitchen, wiping her hands on her apron.

"Yes?"

"We're just going to run out to the barn," Amy said cheerfully.

"Oh, but there's the baby out there—" Milly said.

"I love horses!" Amy told her. "We'll be quiet and discreet, no worries. Because Mr. Ripley has been gone a long while now, right?"

The housekeeper frowned, looking a bit puzzled. "Yes, yes, he has. It's been well over an hour. Maybe even two hours. But he does stay out there, makes phone calls, just sits in the barn…loves his horses, he does!"

Amy started out, making sure to smile, and Hunter—smiling at Milly, too—quickly followed behind her.

The lawns and paddocks that stretched out around the property were beautifully tended. Rows of hedges defined areas, lines of trees surrounded others. Rich grassland seemed to stretch forever or at least to the next line of trees, probably indicating another owner's property line.

There was a dirt and stone trail from the back of the house to the barn. It was a large red structure reminiscent of those found in the northeast or American West, both long ago and today.

Two large doors leading into the structure were wide open.

Looking in even in the afternoon daylight, the back of the barn was in darkness and shadow like a stygian pit.

Amy set her hand toward her back, ready to draw her Glock if necessary, intuition warning her that something was wrong.

Hunter was behind her.

He had her back.

"Mr. Ripley!" she called, veering toward the left side of the structure; the wooden panels would help her if there was someone inside ready to shoot rather than chat.

There was no answer. She looked at Hunter.

He indicated silently that they both take a side. She continued to the left while he took the right side.

"Mr. Ripley!" she called again.

Horses snorted and kicked at their stalls. She heard what sounded like a distressed whinny, but while she did love horses, she wasn't an expert in horse language.

She glanced over at Hunter. He signaled her again, sliding against the wall. She did the same, her Glock now ready in her hands.

"Ripley! Are you in here?" Hunter called.

The pounding against the stalls continued; the horses were highly agitated.

There was suddenly light; Hunter had hit the switch.

"Ah, hell!" he muttered.

She silently echoed his sentiment. They had found Octavius Ripley, but he wasn't going to be giving them any information.

The man sat in an old wooden chair with a TV-tray table at his side. His phone lay on the table along with a little book.

He sat with his arms and hands resting on the arms of the chair and his head was back, almost as if he had fallen asleep there.

But he hadn't.

A hatchet was stuck into the middle of the bald spot on top of his head.

And blood flowed over his open eyes and his face.

5

It was dark by the time the medical examiner came out and a forensic team arrived to go through any possible clue.

Hunter talked with Milly while Amy worked with the local forensic crew. Aidan and John were on their way out. Aidan was just waiting on more results regarding Amy's phone call.

There had been some confusion at first. Local authorities hadn't understood bringing Aidan in or why an FBI agent was taking charge of the investigation. But the lead county detective on the case—Jenson Estrella—was smart, reasonable and a team player. He knew about the massacre in the Everglades, and if it was related, he was glad to let the FBI and FDLE take charge.

"You guys have the best resources and funding," Jenson told him. "And you know what the hell is going on."

Hunter told him they only wished they knew what was going on, but they were following all the leads that they could, no matter how weak. They'd come here because of Ripley's known association with one of the dead men from the massacre.

"I'll work with your partner, then, and let you talk to the housekeeper." Jenson Estrella was probably in his midthirties, medium in height and build, with a slightly worn face and sharp eyes. "Obviously, my lieutenant will want us kept in the loop."

"Right, and we need everyone involved in what's happening."

Hunter didn't believe the housekeeper—whose full name was Mildred Marie Grissom—could have been involved in any way. The news of what had happened—while she had been in the house—had sent her into hysterical tears.

Dr. Rodriguez—who had been called in since she had handled the massacre in the Everglades and she had been able to come directly—had given Milly a mild sedative. Not enough to knock her out cold, but enough so she could cope and respond to questions.

Hunter sat with her in the kitchen. She'd wanted to make coffee; it was the kind of thing people needed to do sometimes when faced with a shocking tragedy. He wasn't sure many of the people caught in Octavius Ripley's criminal empire would consider it a tragedy, but again Hunter thought he had kept that kind of business out of his home.

"Someone did that to Octavius. While I was right here," she said, for at least the twentieth time.

Hunter just let her talk.

She shook her head. "It's a gated community. A big one, yes, because of the way it's zoned. There are prize horses in the barns and stalls around here," she said. "Show horses... and pets, too, of course. But the community...the houses are big and nice. And there are usually gardeners and trainers and all kinds of people around. And the gatehouse...well, I guess there are ways in. And there isn't a wall around the whole community because it's acres and acres and...there just isn't a wall. But I can't see how someone just came in and... The back door. I mean, there's a back door to the barn. But Octavius was usually smart! There's a camera that records everyone coming in. There are cameras that record the back door, and even cameras that cover all the windows. Octavius had a room upstairs and there are screens that show anyone coming near the house, but...there's only one that shows the barn and it's at the front of the barn. The back door is always kept locked. And it's small. People around here feel protected most of the time. They won't anymore. But the fear is that a prized horse will be stolen, not that a vicious murderer would take an ax to a man's head!"

"Did any service people call here today?" Hunter asked.

She shook her head. "No one," she said.

"Do you know anyone who would do this to him?" he asked her.

Again, she shook her head. "I'm not stupid, Special Agent Forrest. I know there are rumors about Octavius being in-volved with one of the cartels, and that he helps people laun-der money, and I don't know what else. The FBI has come to talk to him before—they have nothing on him. But you know that, don't you?"

"Milly, I'm going to be honest with you. We know Oc-tavius knew a young man named Frank Suarez. And Frank was with the group of men who were killed in the Everglades in the massacre. I'm sure you've heard about it. The news was everywhere."

"Of course I knew about it," she said. She seemed to be looking past him, at something far away, not in the kitchen.

She was remembering something.

And she wasn't sure whether she should say it or not.

"Octavius is dead, Milly. I can see you cared about him, and I'm sorry. But you don't need to hide anything. He can't be hurt by anything you have to say."

She blinked and she looked at him again. "What about me?" she whispered. "Can I be hurt?"

He hesitated.

You could never guarantee anyone's safety, not unless you had them in protective custody; and even then, though rarely, killers got through.

"Is there a reason you should be afraid?" he asked. "This person killed Octavius when you were nearby. And whoever it was didn't come for you."

"I don't think there's a reason, but I don't want an ax in my head. I know you probably think Octavius was a horrible man. But he was a good boss, a kind boss. I'm a widow. I have children living in Saint Augustine. He never minds when I need to take a trip up to see them. He never minded, that is. And he paid me well. I stayed because…this was easy for me. I have one of those orderly minds and I love cleanliness. And as you can see, it's a big house. I could hire people to come to do the windows and scrub the floors. All I had to do was manage the house." She hesitated, wincing. "When the FBI came before—a few years ago now—he told me not to worry, to always welcome a law enforcement officer. So, when you came today…"

"You welcomed us in."

She didn't sob or make a sound, but a few tears slid down her cheeks.

"I don't know anything about his business. I just answered an ad one day about a decade ago. We hit it off, and he never once complained about anything I did. And as I said, I could ask for time off." She winced with a sad smile. "He told me I kept the place in such order he was fine when I needed to leave for a few days. He knew I'd get it all back in shipshape as soon as I returned. Then, too, he did a lot of traveling. When he was gone, I was free to take all the time I wanted. In fact, I had my daughter and son-in-law and their kids down a few times when he was out of town. With his permission, naturally."

"I'm sure," Hunter said. "Milly, if Mr. Ripley is gone and you're gone, who tends to the horses?"

"Oh, Jake takes care of the horses. Whether I'm here or not."

"Jake?"

"Jake Barry. He's a great guy. He works for a lot of the families here. Everyone wants him. He's like a horse whisperer."

"But he wasn't here today?"

"No. But he liked Octavius, too. Said Octavius knew that he—Jake—knew what he was doing with horses and he didn't try to leave him pages of instructions. He respected him."

"We'll talk to Jake."

"Jake would never do anything like this! Oh, my God! He's the kindest and most gentle human being I've ever met. Dogs love him, horses love him—cats even cozy up to him right away."

"We aren't going after Jake, Milly. We'll just talk to him. Maybe he's seen someone lurking around."

She nodded. "I... I don't believe this has happened!"

The sedative had helped. She seemed less distraught, but tears did still trickle down her cheeks.

"Milly, I don't think you should stay here tonight—"

"Oh, no! I'd never stay here knowing...knowing what happened! I—I can go to Saint Augustine. Stay with my son or daughter." She frowned. "I just don't know...my driving... I mean, my driving is fine. I'm a good driver. But I feel so..."

"Milly, Dr. Rodriguez gave you a sedative, you know that. And no, you should never drive if you've had a sedative. But my partner, Amy—or Special Agent Larson—is with the Florida Department of Law Enforcement. She'll get one of their people to drive you. It's a few hours up the coast, and no, you shouldn't be driving that—or any—distance. And if they're knotted up, we have local FBI offices, too. We'll get you up there. We can even get someone to help you pack some belongings if you'd like."

She shook her head. "I would just need a few things I can grab myself. I keep a little stock of clothing at my daughter's house." She tried to smile again. "My grands do love me."

He nodded, setting his hand on hers. "I'm sorry, Milly."

She nodded. His phone was buzzing. He glanced at it.

Amy was calling him from the barn. He was glad they'd stopped to get her a temporary phone.

"Hey, do you need me?" he asked, answering quickly.

"Yes and no. I don't need you out here. But I am worried about Milly."

"Oh?" He looked at Milly, wondering if his instincts were off—if the woman had managed to split a man's skull with a hatchet and then walk back in, calmly clean up and not raise the least protest when they headed out to the barn.

"Dr. Rodriguez doesn't think Octavius Ripley had been dead for more than an hour or two when she arrived. Hunter, I believe the killer might have just done the deed right around the time we arrived. He might have known we were there. And if we hadn't come, he might have walked right in the back door and—"

"Understood," Hunter told her.

Would Milly be safe in Saint Augustine? Would her daughter, son-in-law and children be safe if she were with them?

The killer had come for Octavius. He had known the man's habits.

Hunter thought the killer probably even knew there were cameras, where they faced and what they recorded.

Milly had told him workmen were often in the complex. Gardeners, painters...all manner of trades were practiced on properties like this.

"I need to get someone on the guards at the gate. We need information on everyone who comes in here for work, and we'll need a list of all residents, too."

"I already called Mickey," Amy told him. "He's on his way here, but he's set all the necessary links into motion. We'll have all of it in our phones soon. Hunter, do you have any idea how many people come into a massive complex of estates like this?"

"That's why we need a task force."

Milly was watching him. He wanted to explain to her why she needed to be in protective custody before she heard him saying it.

"I'll be out in a few minutes," he told Amy.

They ended the call.

Milly was turning pale as she stared at him. "What?" she whispered.

"Milly, I'd like you to go into protective custody."

She looked chagrined and sat back in her chair.

"You're going to arrest me?" she asked.

"No, nothing like that." He hesitated just briefly. "Milly, the killer might have been on the property when Amy and I arrived."

"Oh," she murmured. "Oh, how horrible! He must have slipped away then, while you were waiting to talk to Octavius! Oh, if I'd just gone out to the barn to tell him when you arrived…"

"You might be dead yourself," Hunter said gently.

"I should have sent you right out! Your gun would beat a hatchet!"

"Milly, the killer might have disappeared right before we got here, or right when we got here. But we don't know if he might have come into the house looking for something, perhaps. And if he had come in, if he believes you know something, that there is something in here that you might know about—"

"Octavius never spoke to me about business!" she said.

"I believe you. But a killer might suspect something," Hunter said.

"What exactly is protective custody?" she asked him. "Do you want me to go and stay in a cell?"

"No, Milly. A hotel room—with an agent watching over you at all times."

He thought she might protest; she didn't. She let out a long sigh.

"So, a hotel room. And someone will bring me meals?"

"Yes, Milly, someone will bring you meals."

"Whatever I want?"

"Within reason," he told her, smiling.

"Okay. I will need things. Right?"

He nodded and told her, "We have several places down here—safe houses. I'll see you're given the best care we can possibly give."

She was quiet a minute.

"The horses!" she said. "There are four of them. The mare is Nellie, the stallion is Bolt, the new little filly is Shenandoah and the old gelding is Fred."

"Don't worry, we'll see to the horses."

"I know that the family down the street is wonderful. And they could take them in."

"We will see to all that," he assured her.

Again, she was quiet. Then she looked at him, shook her head and wiped tears from her face.

"I think protective custody is going to be just fine."

"So, how was the Bahamas?"

Amy had expected the call from her older brother, Linc. She should have called him. Instead, she'd now be trying to explain calmly and rationally that she was fine, and she and Hunter were back, and the Bahamas had been great, but they were both working the case.

She had been observing the work of the crime scene techs and sketching the scene when the call had come. Horses remained in a few of the stalls, anxious still, snorting and kicking at the wood of their quarters. She had talked to the horses at first, heedless of a few of the crime scene techs watching her, and she liked to believe she had calmed them down. She'd also looked at all the stalls that held horses; only a few were empty. She didn't believe the killer had come near any of the animals. But the horses had seen the killer.

Too bad they couldn't talk.

And now her brother was on the line, and she needed to explain why it had been important for Hunter and her to return.

"The Bahamas were beautiful, Linc," she started, planning to rush through an explanation.

But he cut her off. "The Bahamas were beautiful, Linc," he said, imitating her voice.

"But we're back. You see, there was a massacre in the Everglades. And naturally, despite the many agents in the country both local and federal, Hunter and I just had to work it."

Her brother was a cop—a detective in Virginia. He'd gone there for Laura, the woman who became his wife, and had fallen in love with the state.

He had always been a good big brother—other than the teasing, of course, which went along with the fact he was older.

Their dad had been a cop. They'd grown up knowing all the trials and difficulties—and the danger. It just always seemed hard for men to accept the fact that while they might be biologically stronger, women could often be better shots, trained in different self-defense arts—and sometimes capable of dealing better with situations that demanded patience, cunning and/or the ability to negotiate.

Amy knew her brother and her parents were proud of her. And of course they did worry. But with their children raised and on their own, her folks were seeing the world. They'd been in the Bahamas—now they were heading on to see the pyramids at Giza, something they hadn't done yet.

"Yes, I'm back," she said plainly. "Lincoln, there was a red horse delivered to us with room service. And there was an-other at the crime scene. And now a man we came to ques-tion because of his probable place in the hierarchy of the Hermandad has been found murdered in his stable with an ax to the back of the skull."

"I'm just calling because you're my sister, and though I may have painted mustaches on you when you slept as a kid, I love you," Lincoln said. "And guess what, we get news in Virginia! And I'm still from Florida and I can only imag-ine… Anyway, I just want you to know I'm here if you need me. And if you don't want to be haunted by sorrowful, hurt stares for the rest of your life when you see Mom and Dad, I'm suggesting you give them a call and tell them you're on the case, business as usual, and you're okay."

Amy smiled as she listened, imagining Linc. He was a few years older, a respectable six-two, with dark brown hair like her own and magnetic hazel eyes. She'd heard he was excel-lent in an interrogation room, able to convey a knowledge of a crime a suspect hadn't admitted to—even when he didn't know. Without raising his voice or a hand, he could draw out confessions by tripping people up.

She kept working as she answered his call, for the sketches she used for her personal work on a case, and for those who were interested in what the mind's eye saw that the camera did not. She did her sketches with a number 2 pencil, simple and easy, and she always had one in her purse; she could hold the phone between her head and shoulder while she worked.

She wasn't putting the phone on speaker here.

She was at a crime scene. Everyone didn't need to know the intricacies of her family.

"You know about the men killed in New York, right?" Linc asked her.

"We heard."

"I figured Hunter's bosses would be on it. But you're in Florida."

"Yeah. Garza is pulling Hunter up there."

"They think the murders in New York are connected to your case?"

"The red horse, Linc. War."

"And gang war can take down a lot of people. Don't worry, every law enforcement agency in the country is watching this."

"And we might need every one of them. Linc, we have no idea where this will happen next. Yet."

"But a red horse, hmm. Keep studying the Book of Revelation," Linc said. "And go beyond the obvious meaning as you did last time."

"Of course. Thanks."

"Okay, well, keep me posted as to what part of the world you're in. And you may be over twenty-one—wait, you're almost thirty now—but call Mom and Dad."

"Will do. I'm just at the scene right now. Love you. Talk later," she said, ending the call with her brother.

She glanced at the sketch, surprised at what she had done and how good it was considering the twisted way she'd been standing. And she saw something she really hadn't noticed until she'd drawn it.

Her sketch was of one of the few empty stalls.

The structure on this open stall was slightly different than what appeared around it; the wood grain was running differently.

She glanced at one of the women from the forensic team.

"May I?"

"Walk around the position of the chair, Detective, if you will," the woman told her.

Amy nodded, walking carefully into the stall and then hunkering down at the odd pattern in the wood.

It was a door—almost like a doggy door. A secret, hidden entrance...for a dog? She guessed it was about the right size for a German shepherd.

In front of it, the hay on the floor was scattered and dusty.

And she saw a pattern there, too. As though someone's knees had been dragging in their effort to crawl in, and then stand. A heel print was visible. Just how much good it might prove to be, she didn't know. But she did guess now that Octavius Ripley's killer had come through the property— most likely on foot—and slipped into the barn through the strange little dog-size entry. She backed carefully away and headed back to the forensic woman.

"I think the killer entered the room from that stall. There's a hidden door, and there's a heel print. I don't know how much good it can do—"

"You never know! Thank you. We'll do our best and be especially vigilant there—and beyond."

"Thanks," Amy said. The technician had her phone out and was immediately calling someone to come and take a cast of the print and to start on the area in the stall.

Amy saw Hunter was heading her way, walking slowly as he surveyed everything around him.

"Hey," she called to him. "Did you get Milly to stay in protective custody?"

"I did. And did you—"

"I believe I know how the killer got in. He was already on the grounds—past the guards. I think he walked through different properties to get here. Carrying his ax, but if he appeared to be a gardener, no one would have noticed."

"We start checking people who came through to work on the estates," Hunter said. "I've been called into our local office."

"Of course. You have to go to New York."

He cast his head slightly to the side. "I hope you're not going to mind. *We* have to go to New York."

She frowned. "Hunter, I can't just call in sick and go with you."

"You've been assigned to come with me."

"But I'm a state employee—"

"Temporarily assigned to the bureau. The powers that be—in very high ranks—have determined we worked the cult case so well together that it's important we stay on this. Of course, we'll have a task force meeting in the office before we leave in the morning—local, state and federal law enforcement is to be on top of everything."

"They're expecting more," Amy said.

"Aren't you?" he asked her.

"So, the feds are in charge," Amy said.

"Technically, but come on, when do I work like that?"

"I did think you were a bit arrogant when we met," Amy said.

"It was hitting close to home," he reminded her.

"Okay, I'll give you that." She shook her head. "Hunter, I just think one of us should be here. Now we have the murder of Octavius Ripley on top of the massacre. And we know he was most probably involved in one way or another with what happened. We have a chance…"

"I know."

She sighed. "But we're going to New York."

"We'll keep in close contact with John. And Aidan."

"Aidan is in forensics. He isn't a detective."

"He could be, and that's half the point—but his ability to

see a crime scene and analyze what he sees quickly is his talent. Hey, none of this came from me. It is what it is."

"All right. So, a task force meeting in the morning—"

"They're sending a jet for us."

"So that we can work."

"Which we'd be doing, anyway."

"Well, then, I guess we're going to New York. But for now—"

"Every piece of information they have on Octavius Ripley is being sent to us," he assured her, "along with what they have on the Hermandad and Los Zapatos, plus everything they have on these properties, and whatever they find here, including the names of everyone who was working and even everyone who was on a visitors' list." Hunter looked around the barn, slowly and carefully, and then looked at Amy. "I don't think we can learn anything else here."

"What do you want to bet the killer came in under a fake name?" Amy asked.

"Quite possibly. And he would have had good fake ID for it, too. This is a major operation if someone is trying to start gang wars across the country. But we'll find out which ID was fake, and we'll get sketches going—"

"See. I should be here. There's so much still to do. I should be doing sketches."

"You're just on loan to do a follow-up investigation on the killings there, and to help make a determination if these killings are related and what they mean—and what will happen next."

"On loan—I feel like a library book!"

"It's not that bad."

"Hmm. And the FBI has lead."

"This is crossing state lines."

"Yeah, I know."

"We could just…quit," Hunter suggested.

She smiled. "You can't quit and you know it!" she told him. "Your fate was sealed the minute you were rescued by an FBI agent!"

"And your whole family are cops."

"Okay, we're not quitting."

"But we can quit for tonight," he told her. "And we have that nice cheap taxpayer room to go back to."

She nodded slowly and then asked him, "Milly is really going to be okay?"

"She has agreed. She doesn't want to go to her children and endanger them. She wants to be able to see them in the future. She's fine. And since the killer was still here when we arrived, I agree it's safest."

"So…" Amy said the word softly and let out a long sigh.

"So?"

"I think I'm ready to head back to the cheap hotel room."

"Let's go, then," Hunter said.

But he went first to the woman heading the forensic team, introducing himself, and thanking her and the others.

Hunter was a good-looking man. He also had a natural courtesy about him that could draw out the best in others.

At last, they left the barn with its bloodstained floor and restless horses.

They were headed to New York.

In truth, Amy loved New York City.

It was just…in her mind, it was not the right time to be leaving Florida.

There were still answers to be discovered here.

6

There was a knock at the door.

Hunter snapped to a sitting position, reaching instantly for his gun, set on the nightstand at the side of the bed.

Amy, too, had snapped to the same position, and reached for her weapon, as well. They hadn't been expecting anyone. And their conversation on the way to the hotel had been about the fact they weren't going to solve anything instantly. They were in it for the long haul, and they needed a decent dinner and a good night's sleep.

They'd found a chain steakhouse on their way to the "cheap chain hotel," and it had offered fish, vegetarian and chicken dishes, as well. He'd opted for the chicken, Amy had gotten the steak, and they'd shared both.

It was late when they reached their room. Late when they

still found themselves in the shower together, teasing and washing and the "washing" became teasing, stroking and caressing, and so far, they hadn't slept at all. They had been curled together, drifting off, in fact, when the knock had sounded at the door.

"It's just me!" John Schultz called out.

"And me, Aidan!" came a second voice through the door.

"Come on, put your clothes on! Get out here," John called. "Every day can't be the Bahamas!"

"You know, he was better behaved when he was sick," Amy muttered, shaking her head. Of course, Hunter knew she cared about her partner, even if he had given her a bit of grief when he had first been partnered with a young female agent at FDLE.

They were both already half-dressed by the time he finished speaking. Another minute and Amy nodded, so Hunter threw the door open.

"What the hell, John, it's late. People are sleeping," he said.

"Right, like you were sleeping," John said.

"We were about to be sleeping!" Amy said.

"Hey, sorry!" Aidan told her, grimacing, and shaking his head at John behind John's back.

"What is it?" Hunter said. "Well, come in."

"We will. Hey, looks like some of us knocked off early today. Some of us didn't."

"Not that bad," Aidan told them. "John found a steakhouse."

Amy glanced at Hunter, a half smile on her lips.

"You're not supposed to be eating a lot of red meat," she reminded John.

"He ordered the chicken, honestly," Aidan told her.

"Yeah," John said, pointing at Aidan, "*He* kept staring at me and making noises in his throat when the menu came."

"Because he cares about you," Amy said.

"Yeah. So, yeah. Chicken was fine. Anyway…before tomorrow's task force meeting, and you guys taking off…"

John and Aidan walked in; John took the seat at the desk. Amy straightened the covers and plopped on the bed.

Aidan took the second chair from the little table, and Hunter sat next to Amy on the bed.

Aidan pulled out a cell phone and slid it over to Amy. "Brought this back for you. We pulled the data from it at the lab, but didn't get anything useful."

John leaned forward. "Okay, so, we went through the rest of the witness list. We talked to the attorney from Tallahassee, Daisy Driver, and Celia and Geoff Nivens, and the kid, David Ghent."

"And?" Hunter asked.

"I asked them all if they'd heard anyone say anything," John said. "And the kid—David Ghent—started laughing. He said it was hard to tell, he'd been listening to the 'old folks' make noises all day. But then he asked *me* if someone had heard something, and something about him seemed off."

"Interesting," Hunter said. "Did you feel the same?" he asked Aidan.

"I'm not sure I like him, so I might be putting personal feeling into this. But he did seem to be…squirrelly, if that makes any sense."

"Gotcha," Hunter said. "So, we need to keep an eye on him. Do we know if he's planning on heading back to school?"

"It doesn't seem he's planning on going back, but I guess he was taking some special course down here for the current session and that he plans on returning in the fall. He was raving about a guest lecturer in the 'defense of law,' or something like that. He said it was fun being on the boat with two attorneys. Watching their different styles even in a public situation was a learning experience. But his reaction to the question about hearing something...it disturbed me."

"You didn't tell him who told us, did you?" Amy asked.

"No! Of course not," John said, frowning in protest.

"All right, we need to see to it that someone is discreetly watching David Ghent. Ryan is being assigned to us—"

"Great!" Aidan said. "John, you didn't get to work with him much, but he's a young agent, and very much on it. I'm seeing a great future for him."

"Aidan, I met Ryan," John said impatiently. "And yeah, he's good. He's going to watch David Ghent?"

"I'll see to it," Hunter assured him.

"Then—"

"We know Octavius Ripley and Frank Suarez knew each other, and there had to be an important association because Frank Suarez got Ripley out of a bar he liked before there was trouble. So, I'm wondering if there was supposed to be a deal between the Hermandad and another gang, group or arm of a different cartel. Maybe Ripley assigned Frank Suarez and someone else to check out the area, and that was why Jimmy saw them when they were pretending to be fishermen," Hunter said. "While it's still a strand of hay in a haystack, I think we need to sift through every human being who got into the estates where Ripley was living. It's not going to be someone who was officially heading to Ripley's place. Start on the lists tomorrow of service people and visitors who were there. It will be tedious, but hunt them all down—"

"And check them all out online?" John asked.

Hunter shook his head. "See people."

"Yeah, yeah, watch their reactions," John said.

"John, you know you need to see everyone in person, and you need to find out if anyone you see behaves suspiciously or thinks they've seen something suspicious."

John sighed. "Yeah, I know that. And yeah, it's got to be done. Ryan will be watching the kid, so Aidan...you still with me? Can you leave the lab that long?"

"Yes. I'm an excellent lab technician, but I also have some of the best people working for me, and they'll be reporting to me throughout the day," Aidan assured him. He looked at Hunter and Amy. "I'd like to stay on this."

"That's great," Amy assured him. "As John was saying, as long as it's okay with your supervisor."

"I have permission from the powers that be," Aidan assured her.

"In the morning there will be a task force meeting at 8:00 a.m.," Hunter reminded them. "Then, get on the interviews if you will. Find the man who killed Octavius Ripley, and we'll start to untangle this knot."

"Right. Well, then, we'll let you get some sleep," John said, rising.

"Good night," Aidan said.

"Think they're really going to sleep?" John asked Aidan as they left.

"John!" Aidan chastised.

Hunter closed the door on him.

Amy looked at Hunter and smirked. "Good thing John will never know the truth."

"I think John knows the truth," Hunter said.

Amy laughed. "No, that we're really going to sleep, that we already had a great night."

"Well, you never know…"

"I do. I'm going to crash and sleep the minute I hit the pillow again."

But they did sleep, knowing the alarm would ring early. And that it would be another long day.

The room was filled with officers and agents.

Some were federal agents, some were state agents and some were local police.

Amy spoke, using the large screen with police photographs, her own sketches and her words to describe the scene Jimmy Osceola had first discovered in the Everglades. She went on to explain their discovery that Frank Suarez and Octavius Ripley had known one another and, with that connection, they'd then found Octavius Ripley, murdered.

She described each of the people who had been with Jimmy on his tour boat: the retired couple, Ginny and Ben Marks; the two attorneys, Audrey Benson of Chicago and Daisy Driver of Tallahassee; the law student, David Ghent; and the middle-aged tourists, Celia and Geoff Nevins, from the Chicago area.

"Please understand we have nothing concrete on any of these people, but David Ghent has aroused suspicion by his manner. To that end, Special Agent Ryan Anders will be discreetly following him and watching his actions. We'll be comparing the situation in New York with what happened here as it's highly likely the Hermandad went after these men in a revenge play. We are still trying to determine how the members of Hermandad were lured to the Everglades, but one of the dead men was seen at the site on a previous occasion, suggesting he was surveying the area before the group went out there. Nothing in the reports from the medical examiners suggests they were forced to their point of execution." She went on to say they would be questioning Ethan Morrison again, and possibly interviewing his sons while they awaited trial also.

One of the county deputies raised a hand to speak. "Why are you so certain Ethan Morrison has something to do with this? He's in prison."

"The cult killings had to do with the Four Horsemen of the Apocalypse," Amy explained. "We found a little white horse at the first crime scene. This time, a red horse was sent to us in the Bahamas. And another red horse was found at the crime scene in the Everglades."

"Perhaps that's someone trying to deflect guilt on a simple gang-style killing," another officer said.

"Anything is possible—it's just not probable," Amy said. "We're afraid there is someone at the top of all this, directing different factions to murder and create confusion. What the endgame is, we have no idea. But we do need to find out what's going on."

"Gang members killing gang members," someone muttered.

"We are part of the legal system," Amy reminded him. "We catch killers, no matter who they're targeting. We're asking everyone to be diligent, to follow through. Special Agent John Schultz will be leading here in Florida while we investigate in New York City, and all information needs to be passed on to him. Any discovery you make anywhere. We need to know who ordered the hit, though we believe someone has been sent in to agitate, to cause a killing that brings about retaliation, again and again."

Hunter stepped up after her, reminding them anything heard on the street, any drug bust, anything suspicious, mattered. Certain members of the task force would be following through on researching all those who had come into the gated estates where Octavius had lived and died.

While Hunter was speaking, Amy's phone buzzed in her pocket. She saw she had the number in her phone ID as Ginny Marks.

She quickly answered the phone.

"Amy?" Ginny's voice whispered, filled with fear and dread.

"Yes, it's me. Ginny, what's wrong?"

"I... I'm scared!"

"Why? Did something happen?"

"I saw a man walking around in the parking garage. I'd never seen him before. Then he was in the elevator. He kept smiling at me. He'd pressed a different floor, but when I started to get off, he was going to follow me. Then Sheila from my mah-jongg group hopped on and said I needed to come up to her place because a friend was visiting. I was glad to stay on the elevator! Amy, I know he was following me! And Ben...well, you know Ben. I'm not sure he believes me. I know there is no such thing as a skunk ape. But there are very bad people big enough to look like skunk apes!"

"Ginny, are you saying you think it's the same man?"

"I... No. This man is different. He's tall but not too tall. Not skinny, but not built up. Very average. He was wearing a baseball cap low over his eyes, and he had a brown beard. Amy, please, I think he's still in the building. And I'm so scared. Oh, God, I think I hear someone around the door."

"Did you call the office? Your building has an office, right?"

"They have an office... Amy, I'm terrified!"

"All right, I'm going to get someone local there right away. And I'm coming. Are you still at your friend's place?"

"No, I needed to come back home to warn Ben."

"Don't open your door—make it as hard as possible."

"He's shouting out that it's a delivery and I must sign for it!"

"Do not open your door under any circumstance. Is there any other way out of your condo?"

"No!"

"You don't own a gun, right?"

"Lord, no, we might have shot each other!"

"Okay, I'll have the closest officers there immediately. Stay on the line with me."

Hunter had finished speaking; he was turning the mic over to John as the Florida head of the task force.

Amy grabbed him by the arm and motioned for him to give her his phone. She dialed 911 and identified herself, asking for the closest police to rush to Ginny's condo.

Hunter watched her, frowning. She handed him his phone back and spoke into hers. "Ginny, police are on the way. We're on our way, too. You and Ben put every door you can between you and whoever is trying to get in. Lock them. Pile stuff against them. Go ahead and hang up now so that no one hears you or anything coming over the phone. We'll be there soon."

"What happened?" he demanded. "Do you think she just panicked over a stranger in the elevator?"

"No, I don't."

He started leading her out of the room. "Neither do I. Let's go—and let's hope officers are there quickly. I doubt if there are many gun-toting retirees at their condo, and I believe their 'security' is a sign-in sheet and cameras in the lobby."

They jogged down the hall and out to the parking lot. "What about New York? I thought we were heading straight to the regional airport to hop a bureau jet?"

"I know you—you want to make sure Ginny is safe."

"But will it be…all right?"

He stopped a second to look at her. "That's the great thing about a bureau jet—it will wait. I'll let Garza know we're running late."

As they drove, Amy said, "Hunter, if something has happened to that poor woman…it's going to be because she tried to help. Because she saw something and spoke up. And I wonder if, when they were questioned, others on the tour boat know that she'd heard something."

"We can still hope it was just a delivery."

"It's not a delivery, and we both know it."

They arrived at the scene to discover four county cop cars were pulled up to the condo. A woman tried to stop them as they entered, but Hunter had his ID out and they swept by her, heading for the officer standing guard by the elevator doors.

"We stopped him, sir! Ma'am. We stopped him," the officer said.

"Do you have a man in custody?" Hunter asked.

"No," the officer said with a heavy sigh. "But we have officers searching the building now."

"You're sure someone was trying to break in?" Amy asked.

"Oh, yes. The Marks couple has a bolt and a chain on the door. The chain had been slipped and he was using a cutting tool on the bolt. We're not sure what, but something that wouldn't make the noise of a boring tool or a shot. He was almost in. I think he heard the police arriving and he took off. We're seriously going door by door now to find him. He didn't leave by the front—we've checked the security tape in the lobby. We think he's still in the building."

"We'll join the search," Hunter said. He looked at Amy. "Do you remember the layout of the building from when you visited them?"

"I do—two staircases, east and west," she told him.

"I'll take east," he said.

"West," she replied.

They parted ways, heading in opposite directions on the condo's main floor.

The office was central on the ground floor. As she headed to the stairway on the westward end of the building, she saw the ground floor held much more.

She looked in the gym; a lone woman was working with five-pound weights.

"The officers know I'm here!" she said defensively. She was an older woman, silver-haired, slim and fit.

She probably used the gym often. Amy wasn't sure if she was angry at being disturbed, or if the years gone by had made her grouchy.

"And you're alone?"

"Look around," the woman said. "Yes, obviously, I'm alone. You can see."

Amy could clearly see all the machines in the room and no one else was at any of them, nor was there anyone working with the free weights.

She nodded and went out, stopping next at the laundry room.

Unless the would-be assailant had crawled into a washer or dryer, he wasn't there.

Not enough possible room, though she'd heard of teens daring one another to get into a dryer and then having to have the dryer taken apart to get them out of their knotted mess.

Not in these dryers.

There was also a "social room" with shelves of books and board games. One of the county police officers was in that room, looking around and appearing perplexed.

"Thought I heard something," he said, and shrugged. "But as you can see…"

"Right. Thanks," Amy said. She turned to leave and then hesitated, thinking about the building.

The officer thought he'd heard something.

If he had, it could have come from any room in the area. And she found herself thinking more about the woman in the gym.

Had she been grouchy—or scared?

She stepped back into the gym.

The woman wasn't where she had been. And as Amy stepped in, she heard a soft, gasping cry.

"Idiot bitch!" someone whispered. "Now she's heard you."

Amy had her Glock out and was moving carefully, alert, seeking clear vision in every direction. She couldn't see the woman or the man who had spoken.

She realized the split section in the wall indicated restrooms, his and hers.

She carefully approached the wall.

She didn't speak.

"I know you're there!" the speaker called out. "Do you want this woman to die?"

The woman sobbed. Amy didn't reply. She held dead still by the wall. Barely daring to breathe, she waited.

The woman was suddenly prodded out before her but a man held her in his grip with his left arm.

With his right hand, he held a gun tight against the woman's forehead.

She'd hoped to take him by surprise from behind. But the woman gasped and gave her away.

"I will shoot her!"

The speaker was in his late twenties or early thirties; Amy couldn't tell if he had a gang tattoo because while he wore a T-shirt and his arms were exposed, she could see his arms were almost completely covered in ink.

"I will shoot her."

"Why?" Amy said, trying to draw him out. "You haven't killed anyone yet. You could be arrested for breaking and entering, but…why die over that?"

He stared at her blankly, frowning. Then he briefly lowered his head, and when he looked up, she saw pain in his eyes.

"I haven't killed anyone—yet. Enough to die for!"

"Last chance!" she told him. "Let her go!"

He wasn't dropping the gun. He smiled slowly. "You don't understand," he said. "Someone always has to die."

He pushed the woman away. He was moving the gun, but not taking aim at anything.

"Dead, dead—dead," he said sadly.

"Drop your weapon."

"I can't," he whispered. "It could be worse!"

He held the gun oddly, twisting it.

"Drop it now or I have to fire!"

Amy had no choice.

But it didn't matter, she didn't have a chance.

He twisted the gun around.

"No!" she cried.

He fired—and shot himself in the face.

The morning became afternoon. There were reports to be made.

The sound of the gunshot had brought officers—and Hunter, of course—rushing to the gym.

He quickly saw Amy was fine, a sobbing older woman was being comforted by an officer and there was a dead man on the floor. And he reminded himself Amy was a talented and experienced officer. He knew it.

He would worry, anyway.

They'd been partnered, and it wasn't easy. But all partners cared about the welfare of one another; partners watched out for each other. He knew there was still a part of him that he had to push to the back of his mind—and heart. She could stand on her own.

But he wanted to have her back. Acknowledging that she also had his.

The sound of a gunshot immediately triggered alarm; but in law enforcement, alarm had to be tempered with caution, wisdom and care.

"He shot himself!" Amy explained immediately, assuring Hunter and the police officers who also ran to the sound of the shot she was all right.

It was the man they were seeking who was down.

And down horribly.

His face was gone.

The police officers seemed surprised anyone would shoot themselves in the face.

Hunter wasn't.

"He feared something worse," he said.

"But...what could be worse?" she asked him.

"He probably has a family. Someone he loves. He saved their life or lives by taking his own," Hunter said.

"We won't get facial recognition, that's for sure," one of the officers said.

"No, but we may get prints or other identification," Hunter said.

The medical examiner arrived. For a while, there was a little chaos. Hunter was trying to get even the young police officers who'd been on the search to realize it was now a crime scene—even if the criminal had taken his own life—and had to be treated as such.

Finally, Amy's explanation of what had happened, corroborated by the silver-haired woman—a Mrs. Nancy Regina, a widow who lived in condo 4C—had been taken down by the rep for the local police for the record. The paperwork would be shared by all.

It was somewhat difficult for Amy to get a concise picture of the events. Mrs. Regina—who had always felt safe and surrounded by friends in her condo—was hysterical, saying things in such a jumble Amy had to start over.

She was finally escorted out of the gym by one of the officers, who promised to stay with her until they could find friends for her to be with.

But when Hunter and Amy were ready to leave, they discovered that Mrs. Regina was waiting still to talk to Amy.

Hunter looked at Amy and arched a brow.

"Well, of course I'm going to speak with her," she said. "What about Ginny and Ben?"

"They're already gone, taken to a safe house."

"Great. I hope we have a lot of safe houses," Amy said.

Hunter was beginning to feel the same way. The tour

group might be in danger. But it seemed Ginny had been the one who had worried the killers.

When they entered the room, Nancy Regina leaped to her feet and came rushing over to Amy, hugging her tightly.

Amy allowed the hug, patting the woman on the back.

"It's all over now," Amy assured her.

"Oh, you just don't know how terrified I was. I mean, I was afraid I was going to have a heart attack," Nancy Regina told her.

"I hope you're okay now. We can have you taken to the hospital—"

"No, no. I'm okay. I just wanted you to know how grateful I am you came back...you seemed to know... I was so terrified. I have been trying to see you to apologize—"

"Mrs. Regina, you have nothing to apologize for," Amy told her. Amy glanced at Hunter. He set his hands on the woman's shoulders.

"Mrs. Regina, you were victimized. Amy and I—and all of us—are just grateful you're okay."

But Nancy started to talk again, needing to go over and over it all, Hunter imagined.

She'd been in the gym when the man had run in. She'd tried to explain to him the association mandated gym clothes in the gym, and his T-shirt and denim jeans weren't appropriate. Then she had thought to ask who he was related to in the building, since she'd never seen him before.

His gun had come out—aimed at her—and he'd hidden behind the wall that cleverly concealed the restrooms when Amy had entered. He'd warned the woman if she said a word or gave him away by any means, he wouldn't hesitate to shoot her.

"But he would have killed me, anyway!" she said. "He meant to use me to get out of the building and then...he would have killed me. He was talking to someone on the phone who kept saying no one could identify him, he could leave no witnesses. He kept telling me if I got him out, he'd let me go. All I had to do was make sure no one saw him, and I could get him out of the building as my nephew. But I could hear the man on the phone. If you hadn't come back, Special Agent Larson, he would have killed me."

"But you are fine now," Hunter assured her.

"Am I?" she asked.

"I told you, Mrs. Regina, we can take you to the hospital—"

"No! My health is fine, but what about my future? I'm scared for what might come next!"

"I'm sorry?" Amy said.

Nancy Regina sat up very straight, as if she had rediscovered her dignity. "I'm old—not stupid. He came here to kill Ginny Marks!"

Hunter and Amy looked at one another.

"Why do you say that?"

"Oh, please! Never mind internet or cell phones—there's still nothing faster than people telling people! We all know Ginny and Ben Marks were in that boat that stumbled upon the dead men in the Everglades. Somebody thinks she saw something, and they want to kill her because of it!"

"Yes, I believe you're right," Hunter said. "But, Mrs. Regina—"

"I know what you're going to say. No one was with me in the gym. Only police officers know what happened. The news will report that a suspect in an attempted assault and/or murder died from a self-inflicted wound. But word will get out! People will know I was in here—people who live in the condo. Gossip happens, and it's how everyone knows everything, and someone could just say the wrong thing in a coffee shop! Please, I'm terrified! I heard the man on the phone."

Hunter listened and nodded, glancing at Amy. "All right."

"All right?" the woman murmured worriedly.

"If you want protective custody, we'll see it happens," he told her.

"Oh, thank you! You're wonderful. I mean, not as wonderful as she is. I mean, well, she saved my life. Now I'm babbling again. I'm sorry. I'm just—yeah, I'm old, but I like living, okay?"

"We all like living, and we should all get to live out our natural lives," Amy assured her.

The woman trembled, shaking the chair she sat on.

"That man…he was young. What he did to himself…it was so awful!" She seemed to cringe. "His face…his face… exploded. Why? How could he do that to himself?" she whispered.

Hunter felt for the woman. She had experienced and seen a horrible thing. But now they needed to find the dead man's family. Just in case his bosses were feeling vengeful after he failed in his attempt to kill Ginny Marks.

"Mrs. Regina, I know you've gone over this several times. But you heard him talking to someone on the phone."

"You can trace phone records, right?" she asked.

"We can, but they use burner phones. They're bought with cash and discarded when they're used, so it's very hard to trace," he explained briefly. "Of course, we'll be looking into the phone, but I need you to remember what you heard."

"The man on the phone was loud, but I don't think the man who held me at gunpoint realized it. He said the couple had locked themselves in. The only way he could have reached them was to break down a wall—and he'd be heard.

He was angry, telling whoever it was on the phone they'd told him it was an easy in and out. That's when the guy on the other end of the phone started getting even louder and more forceful, telling him there could be no witnesses, and there could be no failure. And if there was failure, he knew the consequences. But... I heard that. He should have been afraid for his life, he should have given up and surrendered to the police or the FBI or someone. He'd have had a trial. He could have been out in his old age."

Amy looked at Hunter. "We need his identity as quickly as possible."

"No ID on him," Hunter said. "The medical examiner went through his clothing."

"I'm willing to bet his prints will be in the system. And he had to believe that in killing himself, he'd be keeping someone he cared about safe. I can't think of another reason to shoot yourself in the face," Amy said.

Hunter shook his head. "Swearing loyalty to some of these gangs... I'm betting suicide before becoming a snitch has something to do with a code of loyalty. And maybe it's respected, but you're talking about people well versed in violence, so..."

"We need the prints checked as quickly as possible," Amy said.

"What about me?" Nancy asked.

Hunter didn't believe a killer would be after her. The only man she could identify was dead. But then she had heard another man's voice.

And it was true, word about exactly what had happened would get out.

"We'll get you in protective custody. I'll make some calls. For the moment, I'll get an officer to escort you to your condo and stand guard over you," Hunter said.

He walked to the door, saw several police officers holding vigil in the hall and asked one over.

"Officer Browne, sir. How may I help?" the man asked.

"Will you escort Mrs. Regina to her condo and watch over her until other arrangements are made?"

The man nodded. "Lieutenant Anderson has said we're to assist the FDLE and FBI in any way we can. I'm happy to oblige. I'll call in my position."

Hunter thanked him, waited for him to call his lieutenant and then introduced him to Nancy Regina.

Maybe he reminded her of a grandson. Maybe she reminded him of a grandmother. They seemed to hit it off immediately.

When they were gone, Hunter looked at Amy.

"We still have to get to New York."

"I know. But so much needs to be done here."

"We don't work alone."

"Precisely. So, why do we have to be in New York?"

"Amy, come on. We're going to need to see the crime scene, and someone in New York could give us answers to some of the questions we have here."

She nodded unhappily. "One thing."

"Yes?"

"Please. You could go on ahead of me, if necessary. I'm worried, Hunter. That man shot himself in the face. Who does that? We need to find the dead man's family."

"What if they're organized crime, too?"

She shook her head. "We can't assume that. Again, you don't do that to yourself if not for a good reason. I'm willing to bet he has a wife or girlfriend and a child somewhere. That type of thing, Hunter…it's what you do to protect a child. I'm willing to bet anyone involved in this has taken some kind of blood oath."

"That's a little dramatic."

"But possibly true."

He smiled at her. "Okay, the body is already with the ME. The lab will be working on prints. We'll get an identification on him and find out. Ginny and Ben will be protected, and Nancy Regina, too. And we'll find the dead man's family."

There was no one in the room but the two of them then.

He reached out and pulled her close. "The sound of that shot..."

"I worry about you just as much, Hunter," she said softly.

"I know, and honestly, I was worried as much about what was going on. I know you're a crack shot. I figured you got someone."

"You did not."

"I did, and I knew you'd only fire if you had to."

"I never had to. I would have caught him in the forehead, quick and easy, if he hadn't let go of Mrs. Regina. But he turned the gun on himself after letting her go. He could have killed her—and let his suicide be by cop—but he didn't."

"Let's see if we can hurry things along," Hunter said.

He put through another call to Garza, who promised to set things in motion as quickly as possible.

"So, this man went to the condo specifically to kill Ginny Marks, but she was so locked in he couldn't reach her," Garza said. "And then he was holding a hostage, but when Amy got into the picture, he shot himself instead of the woman he was holding."

"Yeah, and Amy is worried because if she had shot him, it would have been a cleaner, easier death."

"So, he might have been worried she wouldn't shoot him, even if he killed the woman. Or she would disable him before he could kill them both."

"We need to know who he is, this young man."

"Crime scene photographs aren't going to do us any good on an identification."

"Right," Hunter acknowledged, turning to look at Amy. "Hey, you can sketch him from memory, right?" he asked her.

"I— Yes, of course. I should have thought of it. I should have started immediately."

She drew out a notepad, shaking her head impatiently as she went to work.

"We'll get an ID on him through prints or Amy's sketch— and get his family to safety," Hunter said. He hesitated. "I know you want us in New York, but we want to interview the rest of the people who were on Jimmy Osceola's tour boat while we're waiting on the ID."

"Go to it," Garza told him. "But you are going to want to get to New York. They've started identifying the dead there."

"And?"

"The dead were members of something called the Saints of the City."

"Saints?" Hunter said skeptically.

"Just people who liked alliteration, I'm assuming."

"Any witnesses call in on a hotline yet?"

"No, and there is something else very odd."

"What's that?"

"No one has come asking about any of the bodies yet. Not a single mother, sister, brother or wife. People are terrified. Your man there just shot himself in the face. There's something massive going on—and it seems there's a top executioner who lets it be known that anyone who fails won't just die themselves, but they'll take everyone they love along with them."

7

Amy had no problem creating a sketch of the dead man.

She had stared straight at him.

When he'd still had a face.

They were quick to snap pictures of the drawing and get them out to law enforcement agencies across the area and beyond, though they were convinced certain events were particular to certain areas. Anything that happened in South Florida was out of South Florida—just as the killers in New York City were out of New York.

They left the condo with Ginny, Ben and Nancy Regina all taken care of. They would be in temporary custody of the FBI, and it was unlikely anyone would get to them.

As they drove—heading out to find and interview the other witnesses—Amy reflected that Ginny had been right.

"Ginny saw someone that day. Someone who disappeared quickly but was also spotted by another passenger in Jimmy's boat. That person thinks Ginny might know who they were."

"But if we knew who it was, we would have hauled them in by now," Hunter argued.

"Not if we didn't have proof of anything."

He shrugged. "I'm not sure. I don't think whoever this is may be sure at all of what Ginny might have said. I think they're determined to tie up all loose ends."

"And they'll keep tying them up," Amy said worriedly. "What about the other people who were with Jimmy Osceola? Or Jimmy himself? Are they in danger?"

He shook his head. "I really don't think so. From what I understand, they were all clueless and making fun of Ginny. And while it's serious business—if suicide is demanded and if there is a chance of getting caught—whoever is orchestrating this is probably not taking a chance on going after specific people if it's unnecessary. Especially those who were on that tour boat." He was quiet a minute. "Then again..."

"One of them is involved. I know it," Amy said.

"But which one? The squirrelly kid, as Aidan suggested? Or maybe an attorney? Some people automatically distrust attorneys."

Amy was thoughtful. "We can offer protective custody to all of them and see who accepts."

"That wouldn't stand up in a court of law, you know. Refusing protective custody is not against the law. And we can't put the entire state into protective custody."

Amy grimaced. "Well, at least there are several law enforcement agencies involved."

"But everyone is going into federal custody. Garza and Hampton decided on that together to make paperwork, housing, everything easier." He was quiet for a minute. "Garza said this is going to go all the way up the chain. He's already working with the director. Field offices and even satellite offices across the country are on alert. Especially in high-population cities like Chicago, Houston, Los Angeles—places where you can find drug and gang activity."

"I still don't understand where this is leading," Amy said. "Gangland war."

"A return to larger instances of organized crime with the heads getting their 'armies' together."

"But how are they tricking each other into showing up to be slaughtered? That still makes no sense."

"And maybe it never will. Maybe the idea is just pure chaos."

Amy leaned back, frustrated. "Can there really be someone out there who has the resources to create this kind of havoc, playing on the Book of Revelation? It's crazy."

"The world has a lot of crazy. And right now, this is our crazy. I think we've reached it. Here are the apartments... David Ghent is supposed to be living in 105."

"That's where John and Aidan found him, yes."

"Okay, so...let's go see the young man. You take the lead. I haven't met him yet."

They parked the car and started along the path. It was an old building, a horseshoe-shaped place with a communal pool and the apartments surrounding it. The rent was probably reasonable and affordable for a college student.

"Wonder if it's for show," Hunter said.

"For show?"

"If this kid has been hired or is under the sway of someone up the chain, this is the perfect place for a struggling college student to live."

"Right." Amy tapped on the door to 105.

After a minute, she tried the doorbell. She knocked again, harder. No answer.

"Well, this is anticlimactic," Hunter muttered.

"Maybe we should have called," Amy said.

"And give people warning?"

"Well, not giving them warning isn't working at the moment."

Hunter grinned at her. "I saw an office down at the end of the pool. Let's go speak with the super or whoever might be in."

There was a young woman behind a desk in the office, leaning back in a swivel chair, studying her phone. She was wearing jeans and a T-shirt and appeared to be college-age herself, and not particularly busy—other than with her social media.

But seeing them, she straightened in her chair, feet on the floor, hands folded over her phone on the desk. She smiled but looked a little nervous. They were both in their business suits; and Amy always thought Hunter had a striking and formidable appearance. People tended to pay attention to him—even if it were to eye him warily.

"Hi! How can I help you?" she asked, sweeping back a strand of long blond hair.

"We were looking for David Ghent, in apartment 105. We were hoping maybe you'd know where he liked to hang out."

She frowned suspiciously and tried to keep smiling. "Is something wrong? Is David in some kind of trouble?"

"No, no, nothing like that," Amy said, hopefully in an assuring manner. "We just wanted to chat for a minute. David isn't in trouble at all."

"Oh, well, that's a relief," the girl said.

"Is he in trouble often?" Amy laughed, grinning as if his being in trouble would just be his age and the fact he was a student.

"Oh, you know, nothing major. He's not a druggie or anything. Just likes mischief and...well, no major trouble. We have rules here. It's an apartment complex, not a dorm or anything like that, but the management has rules about behavior. I'd hate to see he was asked to leave because he's really a good guy. Anyway, I'm willing to bet he's down at the Wing House. It's a block down—a hangout for a lot of us around here. We don't all have cars and it's easy walking."

"Thanks! We'll check it out."

The girl grinned.

"You'll definitely give the place a different look!" she said.

"Should have worn our jeans," Hunter told Amy.

Amy made a face, looking at the girl. "Work. They make you dress up."

"Of course! Let me show you." She stood and walked back to the door with them and pointed down the street. "Right there!"

"Thank you!" Amy told her. "And you are...?"

"Oh, Suzie Marshall! Nice to meet you."

"Amy Larson and Hunter Forrest," Amy told her. "And thank you again."

They waved to her as they started off. Hunter was grinning. "Suck-up," he said.

"Hey, it works!"

"So, it does."

They walked the block to the restaurant.

It was a casual place with bar and high-top tables taking up half of the space. A family consisting of a mom and dad, two kids and probably a grandparent were seated in a booth in the restaurant area. A group of young people was at one of the high-tops.

There were three men at the bar spaced apart, each with a beer or drink, just sitting, speaking with the bartender now and then, or one another, and looking at their cell phones. Strangers, probably, just being polite or friendly at a bar.

But Amy noted one man in particular.

He was in his mid to late twenties, had a scruffy beard, light brown hair down over his ears and wore a baseball cap.

She realized it was Special Agent Ryan Anders, and he was already on the job.

Hunter glanced at the bar and then away, and she knew he had noted Ryan, too. He suppressed a smile.

Anders looked entirely different from the way he had that morning in the task force meeting.

David Ghent was among the young people at the high-top table. He was one of two who were seated at the table while another three young people were just leaning on it, talking and laughing. Beer seemed to be the drink of choice.

They appeared to be any group of college kids, relaxing when they were out of class.

David Ghent saw them standing just inside the entry, apparently letting their eyes adjust to the subdued lighting. His face grew somber and he looked around at his friends, excusing himself and coming to them before they could join him.

"Special Agent Larson," he said. "Super to see you again. Your partner and that forensic guy were out to see me. I'm not sure what else I can tell you, but like I said, I'd love to help."

"Actually, David, we're here to see if we can help you,"

Amy said. "This is Special Agent Hunter Forrest, by the way."

"FDLE?" David asked.

"FBI," Hunter told him.

"Wow—the big guns!" David said. "I mean, I see the news, of course. I knew the FBI was working the case, but… I didn't think you'd bother with me."

"We like to bother with people. That's what we do," Hunter said easily, smiling, and then adding seriously, "As Amy said, we're here to see if you want to go into protective custody."

"What?" he asked. "Why?"

"Ginny Marks was threatened by a man who killed himself rather than be arrested," Hunter explained.

"No! That's horrible!" David exclaimed.

For a moment, Amy thought he was going to immediately say he wanted protection fast.

But he didn't.

"I guess someone thinks the old bat knows something. But trust me, the lady doesn't know anything. I think she wants attention. Oh, man, I'm sorry. She seemed nice enough. Just a little off the deep end, you know?"

"She did see something—someone moving in the bushes just off the highway," Amy said. "We found evidence."

He laughed. "Evidence of a skunk ape?"

Amy smiled sweetly. "Murderer, skunk ape—someone or something."

"But you all stopped her from being hurt, right?" David said.

"Yes, fortunately. But we can't guarantee the rest of you are safe," Amy told him.

He shook his head. "I don't know a damned thing, and

I didn't spout off about a skunk ape. So if there was a bad guy around when we were talking, he knows I didn't see anything by the road. Hey, guys, come on. I've got school. I've got a life."

"David, you should think about it," Hunter said. "And while we're here, we did want to know if there was anything else you could tell us. Did you hear anything in the brush? Or even anything from the people in the boat. Did you see or hear anything at all?"

"Yeah, Jimmy Osceola pointing out birds and talking about them." He shook his head. "Look, it was cool, though odd. I wanted to get a real feel of being in the Everglades. Jimmy has a great reputation—tons of stars on all the travel sites. He's a cool dude, relaxed and easy, and we were all talking before we took off for the tour. Ginny and her husband were nice—the other couple was really nice, too. The ones from Ohio or Wisconsin or...uh, Illinois. Celia and, um, Geoff. They were bright and fun, and it was super to have two lawyers on the tour! They were really cool. They didn't mind talking to me at all, which was nice because they were..." His voice trailed and he paused, shrugged and grinned and finished with, "More experienced!"

"But nothing else at all?" Hunter asked.

David shook his head. "Hey, it felt like *Gilligan's Island*. It was supposed to be a three-hour tour. Instead, it was a massacre and hours and hours, and images in my mind—even though Jimmy kept us at a distance—that will never leave."

"And you're sure you don't want protective custody?" Amy asked him.

He glanced toward his group of friends, all who were talking and laughing. An attractive redhead had taken his seat at the table.

"I'll think about it. And if I decide… I can call you?" he asked.

"Of course," Amy said. "John Schultz will come and escort you, but you have my card, too. Call any of us if you decide you want our assistance."

He gave them a grimace. "The thing is…for how long? You may never find out who did this."

Hunter gave him a smile. "We're pretty persistent."

"But it's true, not every murderer is caught. I mean, they have tons of TV shows on crimes that were never solved, so…right now, I want a life! And you can't keep people in protective custody forever. And I sure as hell don't want to be in one of those programs where you have to change your name and all. So, thank you. I'll still think on it. For now, thank you, but no."

"Fine," Hunter told him. "Your choice. And thanks for talking to us."

"I'd help if I could. I've just got nothing," he said.

They gave him a wave and left. Amy glanced back to see him slide back around his chair, his arm around the attractive redhead.

"Average kid or disciple of a psychopath?" Hunter said lowly.

"Well, his group of friends suggests average kid, though we're referring to a twenty-two-year-old as a kid. I remember being his age, my years in college and those times when you did just enjoy being with friends and…being that young. No responsibilities."

He laughed softly. "I'm a few years older than you. I remember, but vaguely. My life was normal by then, but…"

"Never really normal," Amy said softly.

Hunter shrugged, looking away.

He'd had a very different childhood; his mom, repudiating her family's money and their lack of concern for the poor and downtrodden, had embraced a cult.

His parents hadn't realized just what it meant. They hadn't imagined the brainwashing—or the punishment that would come for those who didn't adhere to all the "teachings," and just what might happen when someone thought differently and wanted out. But they had been lucky: an FBI agent had entered their lives and they had escaped the violence that had befallen other members, ones who hadn't perfectly towed the line.

Since he was a kid, Hunter had been driven to become an agent, and help others out of bad situations.

It wasn't that he had forgotten how to have fun, how to relax or even how to take others into his life.

But it was hard to imagine him as a carefree college student.

"So, what do you think?" she asked him.

"I think it's a good thing Ryan is watching him," Hunter said.

"Me, too," Amy said. "Ryan does an amazing job of changing his appearance."

"The scruffy beard is excellent."

"I doubt if the kid will make him. Ryan will be different again tomorrow. If there is something 'squirrelly' about him, hopefully Ryan will find out what."

"He's good. I think he has a great future ahead of him. And now...the attorney...well, if they are involved in any way..."

"They'll know the law?" Amy suggested dryly.

"Let's start with Daisy Driver. Family law."

"Sounds good. But, Hunter, the protective custody thing

needs to be real if any of them choose it, and I think Celia and Geoff might."

"But they're just on vacation, right? They have jobs to get back to."

"Attorneys have work to get back to also."

Hunter's phone was buzzing. He looked at Amy as he listened and responded. "Get the closest officers out there immediately—" He broke off. "Of course. All right. Amy and I are on the way."

"What is it?" she demanded.

"Your sketch paid off. An anonymous call came in. The name of the man who was supposed to kill Ginny and Ben Marks was Nick Klein. And he left behind a young wife, Melissa, an RN, and a baby, fourteen months old, Cassandra. The closest squad car is on the way."

"Where?"

"North Broward. We'll head straight there."

"Let's go! Hunter, I wonder if… I don't know. I feel badly—even though he was supposed to kill Ginny and Ben and them locking themselves in a room saved them from him… I don't know. I guess I'm wondering if he would have gone through with it. He let Nancy Regina go. I would have fired—you're right—if he hadn't let her go. I'd have killed him. But he let her go and killed himself."

"Amy, he still took on murder for hire. He agreed to kill people."

"I know. I'm just wondering if he could have really done it. When it fell apart, all he wanted to do was make sure he was dead so his family wouldn't be punished."

"We'll get to them. I have the flashers on. We'll be there quickly, I promise."

Hunter used the siren. Still, the journey seemed endless, even when she knew only minutes had passed.

When they reached the small house where Nick Klein had lived, two police cars were pulled up at the front and four officers were out in the yard. Hunter and Amy hurried out of his SUV and over to the man who appeared to be in charge, their credentials out.

"FBI and FDLE," the officer exclaimed. "I'm Peterson, as you can see on my shirt. I'm taking it your agencies called this in. We've got a hostage situation, I believe. We can hear the baby crying now and then, but when my men approached the door, shots were fired through it. Thank God it's all your call now!"

"Anyone hurt?" Hunter asked.

Peterson shook his head. "Grigsby moved in time. Thanks for asking."

"Do you have a line of communication?" Amy asked.

"No, all we got was a shout to get the hell away or 'the bitch' was dead."

Amy looked at Hunter. "We may not have much time," she said. "Back or front?" she asked.

Hunter nodded. "Front—I'll try to distract, talk. Be careful."

"I think I saw the edge of a toddler playset in the yard... the back door may be open if they use it often. You be careful. Hunter, when you approach—"

"I will lay low!"

She smiled weakly.

"Keep an eye on the front," Hunter warned Peterson. "If we fail, he may want to take everyone with him."

"Gotcha!" Peterson assured Hunter.

Amy crouched low, keeping below sight from any of the

windows, and crept quickly around the side of the house. In the back, as she had thought, there was a little plastic play area with a small swing and slide, just the right size for a toddler. There was a small screen-enclosed patio. She hurried to the patio door, slipped inside easily and saw another door.

She could hear Hunter talking; his voice was deep, rich and very loud. He was telling whoever was in there he could give him a life again, save him and his loved ones, if he just threw out his weapon and came out.

She couldn't hear the replies from inside.

She could hear the baby crying and muffled sobs from the woman.

She tried the door and listened to Hunter again.

"This is insanity! I mean, look at what you're trying to do. You've been ordered here to kill Melissa and Cassandra Klein because Nick Klein was assigned to kill another woman—and he failed. But Nick shot himself in the face—killed himself to save them. So, if you kill them and sacrifice yourself, there's no guarantee anyone you love won't be shot, too. Whatever this agreement is, the people pulling the chains aren't following through. Dead. Nick is dead. He had no face. No face left. He did that to himself to save his wife and child. No life is sacred to these guys. They do not keep their deals!"

The back door was unlocked. Amy opened it as silently as she could. She entered the kitchen and quickly moved across it, her weapon drawn and ready.

An archway at the right edge of the kitchen looked out over the living area. She could see a man with shaggy brown hair near the door.

A terrified young woman was seated against the wall by

the front door, arms clutched tightly around her distressed child.

The man was pointing the gun at her—but loosely. He stared at the front door, looking through the small peephole.

Amy knew he could hear Hunter, but not see him.

He had no idea she was in the house.

The terrified young mother looked up and saw Amy. For a moment Amy feared she would scream or give her away. But Amy shook her head and brought her fingers to her lips.

Amy knew she could move quickly and silently.

That she could reach the man.

It was still taking a chance. But she didn't know how long it would be before something went wrong.

"I can't!" he shouted to Hunter. "Nick was a screwup. That was his last chance. I have the house. I will do what I was commanded to do!"

"I can protect you and yours!" Hunter shouted.

Amy took the moment when the man stood still—his gun only loosely aimed at Melissa Klein.

She shot across the room, hitting his hand, and the gun fell to the floor.

He whirled on her, ready to flatten her. She leaped back, steadying her Glock on him.

"I don't want to shoot you!" she told him.

He stared at her, indecisive, and in those seconds the door slammed open—the strength of Hunter and two of the officers crashing through the lock.

The would-be killer spun around, ready to fight, only to be caught by the shoulders, and forced to his knees by Hunter as Officer Peterson hurried around him, securing him with cuffs.

"You don't understand!" the man raged. "Nick was a screwup. But you gotta shoot me, you have to shoot me!"

"You want him?" Peterson asked. "Obviously, this is an FBI matter."

"We'll have him taken to an FDLE holding. We'll meet up there and decide what to do about custody. This man won't get help from the outside, and they'll keep him on suicide watch," Amy said. "Officer Peterson, if your men will take custody of him, Special Agent Forrest and I will take Mrs. Klein and Cassandra."

Amy glanced at Hunter, curious he didn't want to interrogate the man immediately.

But she did know Hunter believed it was sometimes good to let men such as this stew awhile, waiting in a small room with nothing to do, and no one coming.

"Right," Peterson said. "We'll call off the negotiator and SWAT and get to the reports." He let out a sigh. "And we'll let the coroner's office know they won't be needed."

"Yet," the man said morosely.

"What's your name?"

"It doesn't matter."

"Get his ID," Patterson said to one of the officers.

But the officers came up empty-handed.

"Nothing in his pockets," one of them said.

Officers led him out.

Amy had knelt by the sobbing woman and screaming child. "Let me help you to your feet," she told Melissa Klein. "We're taking you with us where you'll be safe. Tell me what you need for the baby right away. Diapers, a change of clothes…"

Holding her daughter tightly to her chest, the woman managed to rise. Amy tried to calm the baby.

"Cassandra! Hey!" She gently touched the child's hair. "It's okay now. Mommy is okay, you're okay."

The baby stared at her with wary eyes, but she was no longer sobbing hysterically. She looked at her mother.

"Why?" Melissa murmured. "He—he said Nick was dead. That's true, isn't it?" she asked Amy with wide, teary eyes.

"Yes, I'm sorry."

Melissa shook her head. She didn't let out any sound as wet tears streamed down her cheeks.

"I told him we'd get by somehow! I told him, but he was so desperate...he lost his job. They had cutbacks and...he was the newest man on their roster. Cassie needs to have treatments and they took his insurance and...he was so upset. He said a real man takes care of his family." She paused, and for a minute, her tears stopped. "That man—he said Nick was supposed to kill someone and screwed it all up. Nick wasn't a killer! I told him to stay away from strange friends offering strange deals. I said we'd get by, that...he wasn't a bad man! That's why he couldn't...oh, God!"

She started sobbing again, clutching the baby.

"I'll find her things," Amy told Hunter.

He nodded, placing an arm around Melissa Klein, and speaking in a gentle tone. "You have Cassie here, Mrs. Klein. You're going to have to be strong. I know you're in pain, but the baby is alive and you're alive, and we're going to need your help to stop the people who tried to manipulate your husband and tried to kill you and your daughter. Lean on me, it's okay. Let's try to get Cassie calmed down, okay?"

Amy looked around the house and found the baby's room. Nothing there was expensive; the wall had been painted by Melissa and Nick, she imagined. They had created artwork that was fun though amateurish, and it was evident the cover on the crib had been hand crocheted with love.

She found a little bag already packed with diapers and a bottle and a pacifier. She picked up the bag and went back to the living room and found Hunter and another officer were ready to take Melissa and the baby out to the car.

"Milk!" Melissa called. "Milk!"

"I'll get it," Amy promised her.

There was a gallon of milk in the refrigerator and a row of clean bottles on the counter. She stuffed a few into the bag and filled one with milk and hurried out to join Hunter, Melissa and little Cassandra.

"We'll be escorting you," Peterson told her. "Two-car escort—nothing unexpected is going to happen to that lady and little girl after this!"

She wasn't sure if it was necessary or not, but it was possible someone could try to ram the car. Stupid, but possible. "This guy is being taken to our offices, right? I don't want Melissa and him in the same place."

Peterson nodded gravely. "And don't worry. He'll have FDLE and the police on his tail—he won't be going anywhere. Strange thing is, I don't think he's much of a threat now. Big man when he can threaten a woman and a baby. Without his gun, he's a strange, sniveling little coward certain he's going to die and oddly accepting of it."

"Don't let him die."

"Suicide watch, not to worry."

She nodded. "Thank you."

"Pleasure to serve the FDLE and the FBI!"

Hunter was in the driver's seat already; Melissa had evidently taken a car seat for Cassandra from her own car. She was still shaky, and another officer was making sure it was tightly set in Hunter's SUV. She looked at Amy anxiously. Amy gave her an assuring smile.

"It's going to be okay," she told Melissa.

Melissa winced and nodded. "Thank you. My baby is alive. I'm alive...but... Nick. I know you can't believe this, but he wasn't a bad man and... I... I loved him."

"I believe you. And I'm sorry," Amy said. "And I know you'll grieve, but maybe you can help us now, and stop the people who tried to use him."

She nodded. Tears trickled down her face again. "That man...he was going to kill my baby, too. Who kills a baby?"

"Very bad people," Amy told her. "Very bad people we need to stop."

"I wish I knew who!" Melissa whispered. "I wish..."

"You may be able to help us with information you don't even know you have," Amy told her.

"I'll try. I promise, I'll try."

Melissa walked around and got into the rear passenger's seat and Amy slid into the front. She saw Hunter nod to Peterson. Two police cars sprang to life; one started out in front of Hunter and another followed once they were back out on the street.

When they were on the road, Amy twisted in her seat and looked back at Melissa. The baby—probably exhausted from the tension and crying—had fallen asleep. Melissa had her head back and her eyes closed.

"I'm awake," she whispered.

"What do you know about Nick's friends?" Amy asked her.

"His old friends? Good friends, friendly guys who like to watch football and barbecue." Her eyes opened and she looked at Amy. "He met some new people I never met.

He said they could help us get out of the horrible hole we crashed into when he lost his job. I asked him if it was anything illegal. He said he didn't think so, but they'd be telling him what to do, and if there was something slightly illegal, they were all sworn to a code of silence and they'd alibi each other and...oh, I don't know why he even tried! Nick just wasn't a violent man."

"He was probably threatened. He stepped into the water a little too deep, and they might have threatened him," Amy said. "But, Amy, do you have any idea of where he met these new friends of his?"

"A bar, I think. Like a friendly college kind of place."

"Do you know the name of it?" Hunter asked, glancing into the rearview mirror at Melissa.

"The Chicken Hut...something like that. That's not right...something to do with chickens."

"The Wing House?" Hunter asked.

"That's it!" Melissa said. "Yes, that's it! The Wing House."

The Wing House. The casual bar where college kids had hung around a high-top table just laughing and chatting.

The bar and eatery where they had so recently talked with David Ghent.

8

Ginny and Ben Marks, Nancy Regina and now Melissa and her baby would be held in protective custody by the FDLE, it had been decided. None of them wanted to give up their lives, but they were all aware they were involved in a situation that might take time.

It was possible at some point they might have to decide sooner rather than later about going into the WITSEC program.

For the time being, they were safe.

With Melissa and the baby safely delivered, Hunter thought they should first warn Ryan Anders about the bar, and then speak with both Garza and Hampton about a way to watch the comings and goings at the bar.

Ryan Anders couldn't watch both the bar and David Ghent.

"And how interesting that we spoke with David Ghent there," Hunter said. He and Amy were on their way back to the FDLE offices.

"And I still think we need to speak with the other witnesses again," Amy said.

"Garza and Hampton sent another team to contact them—in light of what happened with Ginny and Ben Marks. They're being offered protection."

"Do we know what happened? Did either accept?" she asked him.

"I don't know yet."

"Okay, let me check with Mickey…see if we know the name yet of the man who attacked Melissa and the baby." She shook her head. "I know Klein was trying to break in on Ginny and Ben. He failed. He panicked when he heard sirens, I imagine. But the way Melissa sounded…was he just a good guy caught in something he couldn't get out of?"

"I imagine that's possible," Hunter said. "Criminal groups can be like cults—no religious overtones, maybe, but absolute loyalty demanded. Protection, but only when that loyalty is given."

"But Nick Klein blew his own face off, and they still went after Melissa."

"Maybe they think he told her more than he did about what he was up to—and why. Something that could give us a connection."

"She did give us a connection. The bar."

He nodded. "Yes, and we'll see where that will lead. And I admit, I agree with Aidan and John—David Ghent is squirrelly. Except I don't want to give a bad name to squirrels."

Amy smiled at that, but quickly grew serious. "Hunter, this is…seriously, we can't keep everyone in protection forever. The killing is…ridiculous! Killers trying to kill themselves if they fail! I understand the hold is the threat to the families, but…how do they get that far, so completely—and quickly and so often?"

When they arrived at the FDLE facility, they were escorted back to where they could watch the man and speak with the agent in charge, Richard Gonzalez. Through the two-way mirror, they saw the attacker sitting at a tiny table in a small room. He appeared to be in only his boxer shorts.

"We've tried prints, but nothing. He doesn't have a record," Gonzalez told them. "We took his clothes."

"Good idea," Hunter told him.

"He could have had pills sewn into them," Amy said.

"Hey!" the man suddenly shouted. "Hey, you can't do this to me! Leave me in an eight-by-eight room with nothing for hours! I know my rights!"

Gonzalez shrugged. "He went on like that every two minutes at first. Now, he lets ten minutes or so go by before he gets aggressive and starts screaming."

"You want to go first or second?" Hunter asked Amy.

She grinned. "He could be a misogynist. I'll either get something from him, or I'll give up and give him a real man!"

She slipped into the interrogation room, a folder with nothing in it in her hands.

Hunter watched as she entered, at the way the man watched her.

She slid into the chair facing him at the small table.

"So, they sent *you*."

She shrugged. "I'm the one who got the gun out of your hand."

"Yeah? But you couldn't break down the door."

"That's why we work with teams."

"So, what do you want?"

"Your name, for one."

"I'm not telling you."

"Okay, I'll go with 'hey, you,'" Amy said.

"And I'll just go with 'hey, you, asshole'!" he told her.

"Charming. You must be a real hit with the ladies," she said.

"Don't kid yourself. I do all right."

"Sure. They don't have much choice when you put a gun in their faces. Is that how you get yourself taken care of? Or do you just, you know, play with a gun and yourself?"

He would have leaped to his feet. But his handcuffs were chained to the table.

"Bitch."

"I sure can be," Amy said pleasantly. "So, who hired you? And why do you want to die?"

"I don't want to die. No one wants to die. It's just better."

"Better than what?"

"Better to die with a bullet through the brain than...well, there are worse ways to die."

"Why do you have to die at all?"

He started to laugh. "Lady, you are dealing with stuff far beyond anything you think you know!"

"That's why I'm here. Enlighten me."

"It's war!" he said softly. "War—and you're going to lose."

"Who is at war?"

He shook his head and looked down. When he looked at Amy again, there was a hopelessness about him.

"Great gods, I guess."

"I see. The real power is above your pay grade?" Amy said.

"I have nothing to tell you."

"Do you like the chicken wings at the Wing House?"

He frowned, startled. "What?"

"The wings, I hear they are really good. I haven't tried them yet."

He wagged a finger at her. "You're dumb, you know that?"

"I hear perfectly," Amy assured him.

He let out a sound of exasperation. "Stupid! An idiot! Why aren't you home cooking dinner for someone, raising some brats? 'Cause you think you're tough. You carry a gun. Big deal. You shouldn't be doing what you are. You should be—"

"Barefoot and pregnant?" Amy suggested.

"It might mean you could live."

"Strange. You were trying to kill a young woman who was home with a baby."

"She worked. It wasn't enough."

"Ah. So, Nick Klein—"

"Nick Klein didn't get it."

"Get what?"

"That you don't disobey, and you don't fail."

"Who don't you fail?"

"The great gods!"

"I'm sorry. I don't think you believe in great gods, so you're talking about men."

"They may as well be gods."

"How do they get to be gods?" she asked.

He leaned back and looked at her, almost smiling, shaking his head. "Money is the greatest god. Those who wield it are the great gods. You can buy just about anything with money."

"I see. I know Nick was worried about money. Is that what happened to you, too?"

"You know about human instinct, lady?"

"Enlighten me," Amy said.

"Survival!"

"So, why do you want to die?"

"Dammit! I don't want to die. But I'd rather die…easy."

"Like Nick. Blow your own face off?" Amy leaned toward him. "Who hired you or ordered you to kill Melissa and the baby?"

He leaned back. "Gods."

"Save yourself. Tell us who," Amy said quietly.

For a moment, the man looked desperate. "They can reach me. Don't you get it when I say gods? They can reach people!"

"Not here," Amy said.

"You never know where or when," he said. He took a deep breath. "Will."

"Will?"

"It's my name. William."

"William—what? Do you have a surname?"

"No. William is better than 'hey, you,' right?"

"It's a start." She stood. "Do you want anything? Coffee, water, a soda?"

"A thick steak and lobster tails."

"We're all out."

"A shot of Jack Daniel's?"

"All out, too."

"Coffee would be nice. No cream or sugar."

Amy left the room, joining Hunter and Gonzalez behind the glass. William—if that really was his name—waved.

He knew they were there, watching him.

"He really believes someone can get to him in here and kill him in a horrible way," Amy said. "I'm not sure how we convince him otherwise."

"Gods—but money creates gods," Hunter said.

"I've been listening to him. Not just his words, but the cadence in his speech. He said his name is William. And he does a good job of sounding like he came from rural Florida. But I don't think English is his first language," Amy said.

"Sounds like a country boy to me," Gonzalez said.

"She may have something there," Hunter said. "There is a different cadence."

"Ah, hell!" Gonzalez said. "Spanish! It was my first language, and I should have recognized the accent was in there now and then. May I?" he asked.

Hunter nodded. "Go for it!" he told the agent.

Special Agent Richard Gonzalez walked into the room.

"Where's my coffee?" Will asked. "And where's the pretty one? Ah, come on—I don't want you in here!"

"*¿Quieres café?*"

"*Sí*—come on!"

"Your name is Guillermo?" Gonzalez asked.

"In Spanish."

"And your first language was Spanish."

"So?"

"What country?"

"What country are *you* from?"

"This one. My parents were born in Chile," Gonzalez said.

"Well, I'm from this one, too."

"And your background?"

The man, Guillermo, leaned back in his chair. "My folks were Colombian. So what?"

"Are you part of a Colombian cartel?"

Guillermo started to laugh. "What? Is anything that has to do with crime part of a Colombian cartel?"

"Not at all. But you're part of something."

Hunter decided it was time to step in. Amy had silently disappeared and returned with coffee. Hunter nodded, took the cup and stepped into the room.

"Black coffee," he said, placing it on the table. "In other words, you're part of something. It doesn't have to do with any particular nationality, but it does have to do with money. That's how they bring you in. You're desperate, and they offer money. But to get the money, you become part of what may not even look criminal at first. Then they want little things. Steal a few vehicle tags. Maybe filch a purse, or watch someone, take pictures. Then you're dragged into it and warned if you don't follow every rule, something very bad will happen to you. And to everyone you love. And if you fail, they know who you care about, and they'll go after them. The promise is that if you die and don't give anything away, your loved ones will be left alone. Except now you know they don't keep that promise. They had you go after Nick Klein's wife and child. So, dying for them won't do you a damned bit of good."

"No, no, you don't get it at all! Nick screwed up. He talked about the bar!" Guillermo protested. "If I die, there was no association! I don't talk."

"Then what are you so afraid of?" Hunter demanded.

The man shook his head. "I don't know, that's just it.

There are different people. Finders, I'd guess you call them. Different people find people."

"And when you're desperate, they have what you need?"

Guillermo looked at his feet, and then he looked up. "Go to the bar."

"The Wing House. And all this is not associated with one cartel?"

Guillermo shook his head. "This is...different. There's a chain. I'm on the bottom of the chain. I never saw the man who 'found' me before. Everything is on burner phones. Replaced constantly. We're told where to pick them up. The gods are at the top. They give the word when something is to be done. They're going to know that I failed. They'll come for me. They..."

His voice trailed.

"Guillermo, please," Hunter said, leaning closer to him, his hands on the table. "We're going to try to keep you alive. You attempted murder, but we can keep you alive."

The man took a shaky breath. He shook his head. "I was a doubter. A text to one of my burner phones sent me to a location on Route 27. A bunch of nothing in the swamp. I stopped at the GPS location. They told me to beat the brush. I did. And..."

"And?" Hunter asked.

"It was barely a corpse," Guillermo said. "The eyes had been cut out, the face slashed and the head wasn't attached to the remains of the body. The innards had been stripped out of the stomach and half-eaten when I got there. That was what happened to those who weren't loyal. The eyes, the slashes, the ripping out of the guts...they were done when he was alive."

"They sent you to see the body, so you'd know what you had to do," Hunter said. "What *did* you do?"

"Got back into my car and got as far away as I could. And swore I'd be loyal, no matter what the hell was asked of me."

Hunter glanced at the mirror, knowing Amy was watching. She already had her phone out and he knew she was waiting for him to give her the coordinates of the body.

"Do you remember where it was?" Hunter asked.

Guillermo nodded and told him.

It was a stretch off Route 27 that cut through sugar land, Seminole land and the Everglades, and combinations of the three.

Near where they had found a young sacrifice strung up on a cross during the cult killings.

Hunter knew Amy would be on her phone.

FDLE would be heading out, looking for the remains.

"Did you ever find out who it was?" Hunter asked Guillermo.

"Some poor schmuck who screwed up. I was told loyalty was everything. And disloyalty was like treason. And treason was dealt with as in days of old. Decapitation, drawing and quartering...except his limbs were still attached. Just his head had been lopped off. But the eyes..." Guillermo shuddered.

"You're hardly a sweet innocent," Richard Gonzales told the man. "But you're in our custody. Nothing is going to happen to you in our custody. These people have a fear train in motion. They go after weak individuals. I have a team of professional law enforcement here, and I can tell you, these animals will not get in here."

He looked at Hunter, an angry—but solemn—vow in his eyes.

Hunter nodded.

"All right. We're going to find your corpse," he told Guillermo. "And you can be grateful we stopped you before you killed Melissa and Cassandra. Have you killed anyone? We will find out the truth."

"This was to be my first," he said. "And I'm afraid you'll never stop it."

"We have the bar—from two sources," Hunter reminded him.

"Right." He gave them a bitter smile, shaking his head. "But you never know who it might be in there! And it might not be the only, er, recruiting station. You never know who the recruiter might be."

"Who recruited you?"

Guillermo started to laugh. "John Smith!" he said.

"Someone introduced themselves to you as John Smith, and you didn't question the name?"

"Hey, I know a dozen guys really named Juan Garcia, so no, I didn't think anything of anyone saying that their name was John Smith. We were at a bar—it was just 'John' at first. And from him I received my first burner phone. And my first job was just to filch a wallet off one of those sugar barons destroying the Everglades! Then…then came all the stuff about the loyalty oath, and a jewelry store robbery, the corpse along Route 27 and…and then a call about Nick Klein having betrayed the oath and screwed up one time too many and…and the order to kill or be killed." He was quiet a minute. "I didn't even argue about killing a baby. I'd seen the corpse on the side of the road, you see?"

Hunter looked up as Amy came into the room. She had her sketchbook out and she nodded to Richard Gonzalez, who rose to give her his chair so she could set the pad on the table.

"Well, the pretty one is back. That's good, even if…well, even if you're technically the one who made it so that I have to die badly," Guillermo said, grimacing at Amy.

"You're not going to die—not by their hand. And you didn't kill anyone—that we know of," Amy said. "You are going to describe John Smith to me."

"Describe him?" Guillermo said, looking at Amy.

"Yes, describe him. Tall, short, blond, dark? Big nose, dark eyes, light eyes?" Amy asked.

She glanced at Hunter. They were both wondering if her sketch was going to prove to resemble David Ghent.

But the man Guillermo described was tall, over six feet, had short-clipped dark hair and light blue eyes. He had narrow cheekbones, a skinny face and odd flyaway dark brows. Amy listened intently to everything that Guillermo had to say. She showed him her sketch. He looked at her with surprise, then said that his forehead was a little narrower, one little lock of hair fell over it and his mouth was broader.

Amy shaded and adjusted and showed the sketch to Guillermo again.

The man sat back.

"That's him. That's John Smith. Or a damned good likeness of him."

Amy handed the sketch to Richard Gonzalez, who was quickly out of the room, seeing to it that the likeness was sent to agencies across the state and beyond.

"Thank you," she told him.

"What's going to happen to me—if you stop these guys and they don't get me?"

"A lot of solitude, I'm afraid. You did attempt to murder a woman and a baby, and you admitted you were a thief."

"But I helped you. And I didn't kill anyone. Not even

myself—yet," he said dryly. "And if you put me in prison, you know they'll get to me! I… Shoot me. Just shoot me." He took a deep breath. "I don't have a wife. I don't even have a girlfriend. My parents are long gone. But I don't want to die like that poor sucker on the highway."

"You're not going to," Amy assured him.

"We'll see what the courts say. If the information you give us is good enough, we'll see about time served—and witness protection," Hunter told him.

"But for now…?" Guillermo began as Gonzalez came back into the room.

"Have faith in the FDLE," Amy told him. "Tonight, you're going to be safe right here. Tomorrow, you'll be arraigned, and our reports will show you were cooperative. You'll do time and I'm willing to bet you'll enjoy solitary confinement."

"But people are corrupt—"

"Not in my office!" Gonzalez said firmly.

Guillermo looked at Amy. "I helped you, right? I really helped you."

"The sketch is important. Oh, and by the way, Guillermo, the people doing all this aren't gods. They sure as hell aren't magic. There are people who don't sell out their principles for money. There are people out there with integrity. And eventually, even a big money god will fall to them." She rose but addressed him one last time. "If you do go into WIT-SEC, if you choose to live, make sure you tell law enforcement about any little detail that comes back to you—and don't sell out again."

"I just gave you an identity. We're all about never letting anyone know anyone's identity. If they do get ahold of me now, well, anything I want to do in the future is…" He broke off and frowned. "Maybe that doesn't matter. I was afraid. I was going to shoot a baby. Maybe I deserve whatever happens to me."

They had been about to leave, but then Hunter looked at him curiously. "That's the main thing. Loyalty—never give away another's identity?"

"We take an oath," Guillermo said almost in a whisper. "You see one person, the person who recruits you, so to say. You get your phone. You do a couple of small jobs. Then I guess if they believe they've recruited the right person and you're capable of murder, they send you out to see one of the bodies of someone who betrayed them. That way, you know what will happen to you—and/or your loved ones if you fail them or betray them. And while there are gang members and members of cartels involved, this doesn't have anything to do with any nationality, any gang, anything other than…"

"Than?" Hunter asked.

"The gods, I guess, and the main god over all the gods. I don't know how far up the chain you'd have to go to know them."

"What happened to the men in the Everglades?" Hunter asked. "They were all members of a gang."

"I don't know about that. Best I can figure is someone's got a beef with them."

Hunter nodded. "We will note your cooperation when you go before the judge. And you will be guarded in solitary confinement."

"Whatever good that'll do," Guillermo said wearily.

"You think these people have infiltrated the police, the FDLE, prison guards and the FBI?" Amy asked, an edge to her voice.

"You don't understand the kind of money and power they're throwing around," Guillermo said.

"And maybe you don't understand some people have integrity," Amy said.

"I guess that wasn't me."

"Let's hope we prove Amy right," Hunter said. He headed to the door and Amy followed him out with Richard Gonzalez right behind her.

"We'll see what we come up with using Amy's sketch," Hunter told Gonzalez.

"And we'll get whoever he is. Once every agency has that picture, we'll pick him up," Gonzalez said, looking at Amy. "Did you go to art school?"

She nodded. "I took a lot of classes, but I always knew I was going to be a cop."

"Well, whatever—not that we don't have phenomenal artists in the FDLE and in our police forces around the state, but it's a nice talent to bring to the table. And I'm hoping we get to this guy before it's discovered that..."

"His identity is known, and some other 'recruit' is threatened into killing him?" Amy asked.

"It's a hell of a system they have going. Threaten people into killing, and more people into killing the killers," Richard Gonzalez said. He shook his head. "How the hell do you stop it?"

"We have to get to the top of the pyramid," Hunter said flatly.

"Man, but it's so tangled," Gonzalez told him.

"So, we go step by step," Amy said. "Thank you for all your help here."

"We're going to head on out," Hunter told him.

"Yeah, I can imagine. It's been a hell of a long day for you."

"Oh, I don't think we're heading home," Hunter said.

"No?"

Hunter looked at Amy. "I believe we're ready to go bar hopping."

Amy woke with a start. She had dozed off.

She saw Hunter smile, amused she had woken up the way she had.

"Hey, it's all right!" he told her. "You know, we could go home. There are agents from the FBI and the FDLE watching the place."

"I know. And we'll let them watch. But I was thinking…"

"Yes?"

"Well, our up-and-coming young FBI agent, Ryan Anders, can change his appearance in the wink of an eye—he is good. What if our 'recruiter' has the same talents?"

"Yeah, you know, we can't take this thing on alone. We really do need a task force on it."

"I know. But it's so daunting, Hunter. How far up does this pyramid go?"

Hunter was silent for a minute. "To big money—to the gods," he said. "And the thing is, this kind of pyramid scheme is like a cult. You bring people in, and they believe their leaders are like the gods—and money can be a god. The thing is, as we both know, once you get into something like that, it's almost impossible to get out. And either their absolute control just makes this situation look massive, or it is." He glanced at her. "And we have to depend on our fellow officers and agents. Amy, we can't stand in front of everyone who might be in danger and deflect bullets from them."

She sighed softly. "I know. So, should we go home—or to our hotel home? Sleep, and trust in others?"

"We can stop into the bar. Find out if Ryan has changed into someone else and if our young friend David Ghent is there, and maybe just munch on a snack—bar food will be fine right now—and then go home."

"Do you think the owner is involved?"

He shrugged. "The best researchers in both our cyber departments are on it. If he's guilty of anything, they'll find something. And that's the best we can have with no evidence, other than a would-be killer telling us that's where he was recruited. Unless you wanted to ask the owner point-blank if he's aware killers are recruiting among his customers."

"No, then we'd have to stand in front of him to deflect bullets coming his way, I imagine. I'm sure someone would somehow know he'd been questioned by the FBI and FDLE. Cyber sleuths may find something," Amy said. "Okay, let's get some nachos or wings and then get some sleep. Oh!" she said, sitting up straight. "We're still supposed to go to New York, right?"

"Briefly. See the crime scene, discover what we can about the dead and anyone who might be in danger there." He hesitated. "I honestly think our real answers are here, but we do have good people working to get those answers. I don't want to go to New York, but you never know what we might discover there. I can't help it. I'm still thinking Ethan Morrison is involved."

"But involved how? Morrison pulled it all off during the cult killings by pretending he had a secret hotline with God, and his church was everything, and his people were making sacrifices for the greater good. This is...cold-blooded. Money."

"But it's like a cult. And Morrison was a multimillionaire. We're here!"

"Wow. I did sleep awhile, I guess. I'm sorry."

"Don't be sorry. When you're driving and I sleep, I'm not going to be sorry," he teased her. "I'm just going to be glad that I slept."

Amy smiled, then sobered. "Hunter, I can understand this kind of thing better if you convince someone God seeks to cleanse people, or whatever, so they can go to heaven. How...how do you do this just over money?"

He was quiet a minute. "That's why this all reeks of a cult. Loyalty. A common goal like a god with a promise of something better for those who succeed and adhere to the rules, and horror—death like a form of hell—for those who don't. And again, I can't help but believe while Morrison may not know who is at the top, he is involved with what's going on."

"From prison?"

Hunter winced. "There are ways. We know that. Even when mail is censored, there are ways. But he's not calling the shots. Maybe he's an adviser, speaking to those in his 'flock' who still adhere to him as an elevated and holy leader. I don't know."

"So, I should go see Ethan Morrison."

Hunter shrugged. "Maybe. When we're back from New York City, we'll both go. We'll work on his sons—make sure they realize Florida has the death penalty, and they may go up on federal charges. And yeah, they risk the death penalty there also considering the size of their conspiracy. But for now—food!"

They walked into the restaurant where they had found David Ghent earlier along with a barely recognizable Ryan Anders.

Neither was in the place then.

A few young people were seated about at the high-tops and at the bar, but if anyone was involved in plotting a crime or suckering someone into doing so, they were doing a good job of hiding all evil intent. One table was chatting about a calculus exam and another was talking sports teams across the country.

"I'm not seeing anything suspicious," Hunter said.

"So…nachos or wings?" she asked.

"Both."

They didn't see a waitress and so walked up to the bar. The bartender that night was an attractive young brunette. She smiled pleasantly and told them, "This time of night our crew does everything. J.C. cooks, Pete runs liquor and me or the owner cleans. You just ask me for whatever you want and then sit wherever you want. I'll call you or come over when the food is ready. So, what would you like?"

She seemed disappointed they only wanted iced tea for drinks, telling them she mixed one of the meanest cosmopolitans in the south.

"Long day, tea will do," Hunter said.

"Long day—that's why a cosmopolitan would be good!"

Hunter and Amy laughed along with her and stuck with tea. It *had* been a long day. Both tacitly seemed to agree they didn't want a bit of a buzz even before sleep.

With the teas in their hands, they chose a booth. As always, Hunter found a seat that allowed him to watch the front door and the comings and goings in the bar. Amy thought it was more than his FBI training that made him so determined to be vigilant no matter where he was. He'd grown past it, but the things that had happened when he'd been a boy had stayed with him and would always be a part of him.

He'd found a booth, so she slid in next to him, though she could have been to the side.

"Sorry. I should ask where—"

"Hunter, it's okay. It's warm and cuddly this way. It's fine. You're always going to watch the door. Just like the guys in the Mafia."

He groaned softly and slipped an arm around her.

He was just smiling when his warm expression faded.

"We might have some company," he said softly.

9

Hunter had to admit, at that point, he hadn't expected David Ghent to come walking in.

But there he was.

He stood at the door for a second looking at the bar and then at the high-top tables, and apparently dismissing those he saw there.

He looked as if he was about to turn and leave. The pretty bartender waved at him.

"Hey, David!" she called.

He waved back.

"Aren't you coming in?"

"Ah, maybe not. I just remembered some stuff tomorrow. I'm rethinking!" he said lightly. But then as he turned again, he saw Hunter and Amy at the booth.

"Uh, hey!" he called.

Hunter thought the young man was surprised.

And not pleased. But he plastered a smile on his face and came walking over to their booth.

"Were you looking for me again?" he asked.

"No," Amy said, giving him one of her best smiles. "Not at all. This place just looked cool when we were here earlier."

"And we are hungry," Hunter said.

"You get so tired of chain places," Amy said. "The same old stuff over and over again. We're not far from where we're staying, so we figured we'd be different tonight!"

"Oh, well, cool. What did you order? The nachos are great."

"We did order nachos," Amy said.

"And it is called the Wing House. So nachos and wings," Hunter said. "You're welcome to join us."

"No, but thank you..." he began. He paused in his speaking because the young bartender had come over with their orders and plates for them.

"I could have come to the bar," Hunter told her.

"That's okay. I'm not busy. Are you joining them, David?"

"I—"

"There are tons of wings here," Amy said.

"No, no, thank you, I ate earlier. I... I'm going to get some sleep."

"You sure?" the bartender asked him. "I've seen you stay out way later!"

"Yeah, I know, I'm just kind of worn out. But thanks," David said. He pushed back a lock of his hair and managed a better smile. "I thought I might get a second wind if I walked in the door. I just realized I'm exhausted."

Hunter saw the bar door open again. A man with a clean-shaven face with a short dark haircut walked in, dressed in a US Navy uniform.

Hunter realized it was Ryan Anders and completely different in appearance than when they had last seen him.

He could barely recognize the man.

David Ghent would never know he was being followed.

"Sit. Just a second, please?" Amy asked sweetly.

He let out a long sigh but slid into the other side of the booth.

"I've told you everything I can, I swear it!" he said.

"Oh, I believe that," Amy told him. "I'm worried. Have you thought any more about going into protective custody?"

He shrugged. "I just don't think I need to upend my entire life because I went on a tour through the Everglades. I wasn't there when it happened. I had the ill luck to be on that boat." He shook his head. "I don't know why anybody would attack Mrs. Marks. But maybe because she's kind of a crazy lady and might invent something that...well, that turned out to be real." He offered them a rueful grimace. "I've got people to meet, places to go...but I can still call you, right?"

"Anytime," Amy assured him. "You have our numbers. And you can hit 911 or call John Schultz or Aidan Cypress or...anyone. They'll get you to the right place, safe and sound."

"Great. If I ever so much as suspect I'm in trouble, I'll call right away! For now, though, I'll say thank you for the invite, and no thank you, and I'll be on my way."

"Oh, just one more thing," Hunter said.

"What's that?"

"Do you know someone named Bill?"

"Bill?" David said, starting to frown warily.

"Oh, Hunter," Amy said, placing her hand lightly on his arm. "He uses Bill or William to make it easy for people. Guillermo. Do you know a Guillermo?" she asked David.

From the look on his face, he did, whether he denied it or not.

David Ghent appeared to be acutely uncomfortable even though he shrugged. "Hey, it's South Florida. I could know a William or Guillermo. I probably know several Bill/William/Guillermos! Why do you ask?"

"Oh, we came across him," Hunter said lightly.

"Why would I know him?"

"He mentioned this place, too," Amy said. "That's why we're here! When we see a place and someone mentions it again in the same day, well, it makes it worth a stop-in."

"Oh, yeah, right. Ha, ha," David said. He kept a firm smile in place. "Is this guy in trouble? A friend of a friend?"

"We just needed to ask him a few questions, too," Amy said. "Do you think you know him? Are you worried about him?"

"No, no, nothing like that... I guess I assume you only talk to people who are in trouble."

"Well, we try to help people who are in trouble," Amy assured him. "Some people...fall into trouble. They don't mean to be in trouble. They just fall into it, and trouble has a way of going deep and getting compounded and...when they ask, we try to help them out."

Hunter knew Amy.

Knew she believed something was going on with Ghent.

The kid was squirrelly.

And for a brief moment, Hunter thought David was going to say something.

Maybe even give in.

But he didn't. He straightened, kept his smile in place and shrugged.

"I'm really getting out of here. But it's good to know the FBI and the FDLE are all warm and cuddly. Good night. And I promise, I'll call if I find myself the least bit afraid."

He waved and took off.

When he was gone, Ryan Anders—in his Navy attire—briefly lifted a glass to Hunter. Then he waved at the bartender, thanked her and was out the door.

"He almost caved," Amy said softly.

"Ryan followed him."

She nodded. "I know."

The bartender came by. Hunter realized they'd been eating through the conversation. They'd probably been hungrier than they had expected.

"Anything else for you two?" the young woman asked them cheerfully.

"That's it, thanks! We'll pay up and get out of here."

"Just like that boy in blue!" she said. "What a cutie and so polite!" She sighed. "That kind never seems to stay around too long. Oh, well."

"Oh, I saw him. Young heartbreaker!" Amy agreed.

Hunter lowered his head to smile.

They followed the bartender to the bar, paid their bill and headed out for their car.

Hunter paused for a minute under the stars, looking around.

"What is it?" Amy asked him.

He shook his head. "I'm wondering where our friend went. We shook him up when we asked about Guillermo. And he wasn't expecting to see us."

"Ryan will stay on him."

Hunter nodded. "The kid needs to come in. To come clean. I don't think he was part of the massacre. But I do think his life is in danger, or he'll put others in danger."

"Hunter, we need to reach John Schultz, too—find out if anyone else opted for protective custody."

"I'll drive, you call," he said.

Amy was already dialing. She spoke to her partner and listened while they got into the car. Hunter turned the ignition on, and pulled out into the road.

"One person took him up on the offer. The Tallahassee attorney, Daisy Driver. The Nevins couple said they had to get back to Illinois, and Audrey Benson in Chicago, she has clients. She is also an officer of the court, and she knows the right people to make sure she stays safe once she gets home."

"Interesting," he said.

"Yep. Well, we didn't make it to interview everyone together, but they've all been offered help."

"There's one more person we haven't considered."

"Jimmy?" she queried.

Hunter nodded. "We'll call him from the room."

"John talked to him and told him what's going on."

"I'd still like to talk to him."

"This late?"

"This late."

They reached their room. He put through the call while Amy disrobed and headed for the shower.

Jimmy answered sounding a little groggy, but he assured Hunter he hadn't really been asleep. He listened to Hunter and weighed his words.

"Here's what strikes me as strange. I think someone knew I brought a tour group that way every day. I think I was supposed to find and report the bodies."

"That's possible."

"I did what I was supposed to do. I don't think I need protective custody."

"My fear," Hunter told him, "is whoever the someone is, they might be afraid Ginny Marks said something that any of you might pick up on, putting you all in danger."

"You think Ginny Marks thinking she saw a skunk ape puts me in danger?" Jimmy asked skeptically.

"No, but the fact she saw someone out there does put everyone in danger."

"You know, I was thinking of heading deep into the Glades for a few days."

"And you think—"

"I think idiots using Plains Indian arrows and tomahawks in the Everglades haven't a prayer of finding my place."

"You may be right," Hunter said.

"Trust me on that."

"It's your choice."

"And my choice is made. But if you need me for anything at any time, Aidan knows where to find me."

"Thanks, Jimmy."

"Good luck with this thing, Hunter. I'm not a man who needs much, and I have plenty of people to keep the tours and the restaurant going. But I'm not a rich man, either, and I'd love to be able to get back out living normally. So if you can get these guys...well, it would be greatly appreciated."

"We'll be doing everything in our power," Hunter assured him.

When he ended the call and turned around, Amy had already emerged from the shower and lay on the bed.

"That was fast," he told her.

"FDLE agent," she said sweetly. "We learn to move quickly."

"Ah."

"I wonder if the FBI is half as good."

He removed his holster and Glock, setting them by the side of the bed.

"The FBI can work quickly," he assured her, stripping off his jacket and shirt next. "But we can also be slow and thorough."

"Hmm," she murmured, reaching for him as he cast aside his clothing. Her fingers teased his bare flesh, a touch that aroused him right away.

"We're considered to be excellent at what we do," he assured her, meeting her eyes and brushing aside a sweep of her rich, dark hair.

"Really? I would need evidence of that."

"Oh, I do intend to prove my case."

"And make this world go away for a bit," she whispered.

He smiled and nodded, and his mouth found hers.

And for a while they both made the world, other than that which existed entirely between them, go away.

There was no doubt about it—traveling via one of the bureau's private jets was a nice way to go.

"It's a small aircraft—not tiny, but small—and you can hit some bumps," Hunter warned her.

"I don't know, I like it! A coffee machine that brews anything your heart desires, a copilot who does double-duty making sure you have anything you could want...not bad. No wonder you're so spoiled," she teased Hunter.

He made a face back at her. "I rarely travel this way. It's

just that recent events are considered top priority. So we get some special treatment. Nice for me, too."

Amy laughed. "The best thing is the plane can pretty much go when you want it to go! Doesn't work that way on commercial airlines." She grinned at him. "When I was a kid, one of the girls I went to school with was überrich. We were all together in New York for a theater event—"

"You were into theater? Thought you always wanted to be a cop?" he asked.

"I did, yes, but that didn't mean I didn't have other interests," she said. "But you're missing my story! She came to say goodbye to me when it was over. She was the nicest kid, really, but I'd be going on into high school, and she was leaving for a boarding school in France. We were hugging and crying and all, and I finally told her our plane was going to leave. She was truly baffled. She told me to have my parents tell the pilot he needed to wait. I tried to explain things like that just didn't work in my world. Hunter, she'd never been on a commercial plane, just her parents' private jet! Anyway, now I get how easily one could get into enjoying this!"

"Yes, the best thing is it can wait when you need it to—and pretty much go when you want it to, as well," Hunter said.

"I know," Amy said. "And it'll be useful to get back quickly. We have a lot to pursue in Florida."

"Obviously, this thing is going to reach across the country. We may learn something in New York we can't learn in Florida. So..."

"I get it. John and Aidan and Ryan and a whole task force are all on it."

Hunter had his tablet out and was studying it. "All right,

first thing, we're to meet with a Detective Gil Logan. He's been working the case. Local FBI has been working with him, but they've left it in his hands. Other than the red horse element and the call you received, it is a local matter. But Garza and the powers that be have said we're welcome to any information and assistance available should the cases prove to be related."

"The answers lie in Florida. Maybe there's a clue in New York, but I believe we'll find the real answers in Florida."

Amy leaned back in the big, plush seat. It could hold a team of six very comfortably, she thought.

"What is it? You're almost smiling," Hunter said.

"I'm enjoying the jet. And I guess I was thinking about Adriana."

"Adriana?"

"My überrich friend. She was such a nice kid, and her parents were great, too. I was always glad I'd met her, because I knew you could be poor and be nice, middle-class and be nice—and überrich and be nice and caring, too."

"People come in all kinds," Hunter said. "And their backgrounds, their colors and their sexual preference don't matter. We get humanity or we don't. Are you falling asleep while I'm talking?"

She laughed. "Maybe!"

He let out a soft sound.

She didn't sleep, but she enjoyed the comfort.

They were met at the airport by Detective Logan and his partner, Detective Richard Chan. They were friendly and serious.

Logan was a lean man who appeared to have been around the block several times—his face was as haggard as a bulldog's, but his manner was energetic. Chan was younger, taller and fit, with close-cropped black hair and serious dark brown eyes.

"Word on the street is gang warfare," Chan told them as they walked to their car. "I'm afraid this could bring us back to the warring days of the old, organized-crime groups. The gang members might be going for one another, but they don't usually care a lot about collateral damage."

"Has anything happened since the event?" Hunter asked.

"No, it's almost as if there's a strange stillness in the air. The city's waiting for the other shoe to drop."

"In the Big Apple," Amy muttered.

She watched the traffic as they moved from the airport and through the Bronx and Brooklyn to Manhattan. Endless cemeteries stretched on either side of the car for a while, interspersed with areas of family homes, business developments and bits and pieces of what could still be considered suburban life. Then they reached the city, with horns honking, cars everywhere, pedestrians weaving through them, all in a hurry to get somewhere.

Detective Chan apparently noticed her watching. He smiled. "When you live here, you get used to it all. And you can spot a tourist easily from a resident."

Amy laughed. "How?"

"Tourists look up a lot. Which is cool. It's nice when a lot of the architectural detail in a tall building is noticed. New York architecture itself is an amazing homage to time and life and the feats created by engineers and architects through the years."

"So," Hunter said, "someone looking up is usually a tourist. But not all tourists look up."

"Well, they actually wait most of the time at crosswalks—a good thing," Chan said.

"They move a little slower, as we all do when we're not sure about where we're going," Gil Logan offered.

"Oh, and in winter! Poor things. They step off a curb—not realizing they might be stepping into six inches of ice water beneath the icy crust," Chan said.

"And they look at their smartphones a lot," Logan added. "Used to be maps—these days, it's smartphones. Of course, it's true that tourists and locals alike might be headed down the street wearing earphones and carrying on business or personal calls as they move about. It's a busy, busy place!"

"I love this city," Amy assured them. "All of it!"

"The good, the bad and the ugly," Logan said, shaking his head. "You're going to have it all. Millions living here, millions more flooding in for work every day." He looked at her. "Born and bred here. I wouldn't live anywhere else in the world."

"He really loves New York," Chan said.

"And you don't?" his partner asked him.

"You know I do! But there is a lot to admire and appreciate in other places, too."

Chan glanced back at them and rolled his eyes. Hunter looked at Amy and shrugged with amusement.

"Anyway, we're taking you straight to the site of the massacre. Twelve men with bullets in them. The bullets have been analyzed. Two guns were used—semiautomatic pistols—and we know there were two guns because of the markings on the bullets. The weapons are typical of those we've taken off several different gang members. The men killed belonged to something called the Saints of the City. They're supposed to be an offshoot of one of the big cartels, but that's street rumor, as we don't have any facts. We mainly know about them through vice. They pick up kids with drugs, and the kids tell us about the 'saints' who run around making sure they're supplied. I interviewed one of the kids about the group, and I asked him if he wasn't afraid of saying who they were. He told me that no, they wanted the world to know they were out there. The cops would never find them. Well, we found some of them," Logan said. He pointed down the street. "We'll park here. See the major walk-through pedestrian-type area between the buildings? The alley from the bar leads out from there."

Chan was driving and drew over against the sidewalk. He found a space easily enough. There were no parking signs anywhere around it.

The walk-through was typical of several in the city. Stone paving, no roof, a few trees and even a few benches outside a coffee shop.

Amy noted the giant office buildings, and many with retail stores on the ground floors. She saw the coffee shop Logan had mentioned and the benches. They walked beyond that several feet where a narrow alley—somewhat dark and dingy even by day—met up with the walk-through.

"I don't know what you'll get from this. Forensics is still going through a mountain of debris because it's an alley where the bar and coffee shop dump their trash. The coffee shop had been closed for hours before the attack took place, the bar a few hours. Both had dumped their trash at closing, so…" His voice trailed.

"But there is only one way into this alley," Amy said. "And one way out. It's still just about inconceivable these men walked into this alley—and were killed without firing a shot back!"

"They were cornered," Hunter commented. "Once they were here, they were cornered."

"But they were all shot execution-style?" Amy said.

She pulled her sketchbook out. She knew there were crime scene photos. But she wanted more than the bodies and where they lay. She was puzzled by the way the men had been lured to their deaths just as they had been in the Everglades.

Hunter was observing it all, as well.

"A bit different from the Everglades," Chan said.

"Yes, and no. The men who came were blitzed—taken by surprise. Someone had to be offering something to bring them in like this. They were expecting a business arrangement of some kind and, whatever happened, they had no concept that they were about to be murdered. There had to have been an arrangement made before they got here...but what? If we can discover what lure and bait are being used, we may put a stop to it."

Logan nodded. "There are those in the city who think it's not such a bad thing gangs are murdering each other, you know. The woman who owns the coffee shop was horrified about the blood in her alley, naturally. But she has a teenage son, and she said he had a friend who died from a heroin overdose—supplied by a gang member, she believes. Some people don't mind this."

"But it's turning into war," Amy said softly. "And war takes the innocent, as well. And as we remind ourselves, we are not judge and jury."

"Right," Chan said. "Don't worry—we believe that."

Amy smiled. "I wasn't doubting that. I know how many people feel. Especially many with children. I understand. It's just not our position to judge. Murder is—"

"Murder," Chan said. "The woman who owns the coffee shop—or the franchise—is usually working now. She leaves a crew to close at nine at night, but she should be here now, if you wanted to speak with her. We interviewed her, and we interviewed Kenneth Lemming, who manages the bar for a business conglomerate. They didn't see or hear anything or notice anything at all unusual during the day. The bar is the last thing to close in the area. These are all office buildings—nine-to-five kind of offices—and there are no residential apartments or condos in the immediate area where someone might have been looking out a window. Naturally, we put out a bulletin asking for help, but we've gotten nothing that's substantial in any way." He shrugged. "One lady said she saw people in the alley all day—and then asked me if I could make her neighbor get rid of her poodle, said the dog barked too much."

"Whoever planned this knew there wouldn't be witnesses around in the buildings," Hunter said. "Again, the same. No witnesses in a city of millions. No witnesses in the Everglades."

"You're welcome to prowl the alley for as long as you like. Our forensic team went through it for hours on end, and two of the city's top medical examiners were on the bodies."

Amy believed they should start with the woman who owned the coffee shop franchise and the manager of the bar.

She glanced at Hunter. "I'll take the coffee shop."

"I'll bring you in and introduce you to Mrs. Breyer," Logan said. "Chan—"

"I'll bring Special Agent Forrest in to meet Kenneth Lemming."

They walked back through the little alley to the pedestrian path with Hunter and Chan slipping into the bar while she and Logan continued to the coffee shop.

A clerk went to the back office to find Mrs. Breyer. Amy wasn't sure why, but she was expecting a sturdy matron.

Mrs. Breyer was in her midforties, Amy thought, and exceptionally attractive with stylishly cut blond hair, bright blue eyes and a figure that was a testament to a gym somewhere.

Logan did the introductions.

"Mrs. Breyer, this is Special Agent Amy Larson—"

"The FBI! Good!" the woman said.

"I'm not FBI. I'm Florida Department of Law Enforcement," Amy explained.

"Florida?" Mrs. Breyer seemed appalled.

"My partner is Special Agent Hunter Forrest with the FBI. We're here together because—"

"Then why isn't your partner here—what does Florida have to do with a New York crime?"

"I'm on loan to the FBI, Mrs. Breyer, because we've had a similar situation down in South Florida. I would seriously appreciate it if—"

"I'd appreciate it if you'd send in the real FBI!" the woman said.

Amy could have—and would have—put her politely in her place.

Except she had noticed a young woman sitting near the window. She was a pretty girl with soft eyes, an oval face, dark blond hair—and a look of infinite sadness. She'd paid attention to Amy and Logan when they'd entered. And Amy believed there was something about her that seemed to suggest she had something to say.

Why, she wasn't sure.

Gut instinct kicking in?

"I shall be happy to send Special Agent Forrest—real

FBI—in to see you as soon has he's finished his current interview."

Amy gave Mrs. Breyer a nod and turned around and walked out. Logan followed her.

"Detective, do me a favor, please? Walk away from me. And please, tell Hunter how well this interview went."

"She's lucky you didn't slug her."

Amy hid a smile. "You know we can't do that."

"No, I know we can't. But I was tempted to slug her myself. And no, I wouldn't have, either. But do you want to be alone?"

"I think someone may speak to me because I'm not 'real' FBI," Amy said softly.

Logan understood. He nodded and turned toward the entry to the bar.

Amy leaned against the building, out of sight from the front of the coffee shop.

A minute later, the pretty young woman walked out of the coffee shop, still looking sad, and anxious.

She started when she saw Amy.

"Hi," Amy said. "I just want to help. Why don't we take a walk—there's a clothing store just ahead. We can window-shop."

For a moment, she thought the girl would bolt.

But she had been right. The young woman had wanted to speak with someone. But not in public.

She swiftly handed Amy a bit of ripped napkin with the coffee shop's logo.

And she whispered, "Please!"

She turned and walked quickly away.

Amy looked at the scrap of paper. The girl had scratched a note on it.

The park, please, you'll see the back of my head from the road.

Amy hurriedly walked the few steps to the entry to the bar. Detective Logan was just coming out.

"Please tell Hunter I'll be back," she told him. "I'm heading to the park, but I think I'm best alone. I'll be back shortly."

"I... Okay," he said.

She didn't wait; she turned and hurried in the direction of the park, careful to watch her surroundings.

Careful to watch the people around her, as well, careful she wasn't followed.

She didn't want to put the girl in danger.

To that end, she walked a jagged path—adding a few New York blocks to her journey.

But as the young woman had said, Amy saw the back of her head when she reached the park. She was seated on a bench by a large oak tree.

Amy walked around and sat by her. "You know who I am," she said softly.

"I'm Nell. Nell Blackstone," the girl said. She didn't look at Amy. "I was... I was in love with a guy... Byron Malone. He—he was one of the men who was killed. He kept saying we couldn't be official. We kept our relationship secret. He didn't even want to be seen in public together. I guess I thought I was the other woman or something. I knew I should call it off, but... I loved him. We—we met in the coffee shop. I never thought he'd die so near it."

"I'm so sorry. How long were you seeing each other?" Amy asked.

"A couple of months. I mean, I almost thought I was a one-night stand as he could be so secretive. But he was passionate and wonderful and told me he had to get out of something he'd gotten into. And again, I kept thinking he had a wife, or another woman, but he swore to me he loved me, and as soon as possible, he'd proclaim it to the world."

"You didn't know he was in a gang."

She shrugged. "A gang is one thing...frightening. Maybe even deadly. But he'd be so...frustrated and afraid. And I tried to get him to talk...and he'd say once you got in, you couldn't just get out. But he was talking to someone who understood and..."

She suddenly turned to Amy, sliding her hand into her pocket. "I found this after I learned that...that he'd been killed."

She handed Amy a crumpled paper. Amy looked at it, straightening it out.

Hand-written in block letters were the words *WE WILL NOT TOLERATE.*

"Do you know what this means? Did Byron write this—or did he receive it?"

Nell shook her head. "I don't think he wrote it. I believe it was something given to him by...by whoever ruled whatever it was he was doing. I couldn't get him to say too much. He just told me people were trying to make deals so they could get along, but even if deals were to be made, they had to make a show of strength." She looked as if she was going to burst into tears, and Amy placed a hand gently over hers where it lay on the bench.

"I wasn't really anything to him—not even a known girlfriend. He was a foster kid and said he never ended up anywhere that a person cared for anything more than collecting money for keeping a kid. They're going to dump him in a potter's field—they'll bury him out on Hart Island. And it may be stupid, but I have a good job and I want to have a funeral for him. He deserved that… I was the best thing in his life, he told me, and I can pray that at least in death he's at peace. And remembered."

"I believe I can help you," Amy said. "I'll speak with the right people."

"But…you really are from Florida—investigating a crime here in New York."

Amy gave her a grimace and tried to smile. "But I have friends in the right places," she assured her. "The state always hopes someone will claim the dead, so I don't think that will be much of a problem. But for the time being, I'd rather you keep laying low. I'll see to it that Byron's body does not go to a potter's field, and you take care not to talk about him to anyone." Amy reached in her pocket for a card. "You can reach me anytime. If you think of anything else you might know, please call me."

Nell closed her eyes for a minute. "He told me he thought he was supposed to be selling pot. Just grass, marijuana. Then he found out the Saints of the City sold a lot more than pot. Even before he met me, he didn't want to sell hard stuff to kids—or to sell guns."

"Did he ever talk about anyone else, any other gangs?"

She was thoughtful. "I don't know… He would talk about 'the people.' I don't know if he just meant other people, or if there is something that is called 'the People.' I just don't know."

"Nell, what do you do for a living?" Amy asked her.

She realized she was growing nervous for the young woman. Obviously, Byron had kept her identity a secret from everyone because he was determined she wasn't going to be used against him—or harmed in any way.

But what if someone had known about her?

Was she in danger?

Nell's face lit up. "I'm an illustrator. Children's books. And I work from home."

"Good. Because I'm not sure you're safe at home," Amy said.

Nell's eyes widened. "You don't mean that—"

"Yes. I don't know. We're investigating the murders here because they resemble a massacre in the Everglades in Florida."

"Oh!" Nell gasped. "I heard about that—I mean, it was all over the news! They said someone was trying to cause real trouble, and the dead men were gang members and they suspected a rival gang and...of course. The same as here."

"Right. And what worries me is a woman was targeted by someone who thought she might know something."

"Oh!" Nell was stricken, turning white as a sheet. She laughed dryly, a sob catching in her throat at the same time. "I was so heartbroken about Byron... It never occurred to me I could be in danger!"

"I'm afraid you might be—" Amy began.

And just as the words left her mouth, she heard an explosive crack and then a whizzing sound.

One she knew too well.

It was a bullet speeding through the air.

Imbedding in the old oak near them.

"Down!" she commanded, thrusting Nell to the ground and falling low herself. She quickly figured the trajectory in her mind and rolled for cover behind the tree.

The bullet had come from the street.

She heard someone on the street start to scream, and she saw a man standing on the sidewalk, searching for Nell Blackstone.

189

People were screaming; horns were honking.

"Drop it!" Amy shouted. "FBI!" She could legally make the claim, she reckoned. She was on loan.

The man waved the gun in the air, aiming it at her.

"Drop it!"

The command was shouted again; this time, not by her.

Logan, Chan and Hunter were on the street, all aiming at the man.

He looked furious at first, and then he started to laugh. And he took aim and almost fired a shot.

He never did.

The three men fired as one, all three faster than Nell Blackstone's would-be executioner.

10

Paperwork and psychological evaluations could be the bane of law enforcement everywhere.

But Hunter knew that it was necessary.

Most of those who went into law enforcement did so with a true desire to hold up the laws of the country, to protect the innocent and to bring the guilty to justice. There were bad eggs that could pop up anywhere, and of course, it was the responsibility of law enforcement to remove the bad eggs as soon as possible.

That made it necessary for any shooting—no matter how obvious—to be investigated.

He knew he would be in New York for another few days.

The good thing was the young woman Amy had discovered—or who had discovered Amy—was safe.

And she, too, would now go into protective custody.

The negative was it seemed that dozens of people might well need to be in protective custody; and even with various task forces and agencies involved, the numbers were creeping up.

But Garza himself made an appearance in New York, speeding up the processes that needed to be followed.

Autopsy showed that any of the three men's weapons might have made the kill shot. And while different states and different cities had different laws governing the use of deadly force, he, Logan and Chan would be involved in evaluations before returning to work.

There would be little difficulty. Dozens of people had been on the busy street, terrified of the man wielding a gun and firing at a park where adults relaxed and children played.

But even while the paperwork was ongoing, Hunter was able to work with Amy. The New York field office offered conference rooms and the tech that allowed them to work together on developments in both New York and Florida.

Charles Garza was an impressive man. In his midfifties, he was tall, lean and fit, with steel-blue eyes and short-cut iron-gray hair. He had pulled everything he could regarding the street gangs in the city, especially revolving around the Saints of the City and, with Amy's information, a budding group called the People.

"The People claim to be nothing but a political group seeking freedoms as laid out in the Constitution," Garza told him. "They lobby for gun rights and the right to assemble, freedom of speech without censorship from private concerns. It seems they have been suspended from various media platforms for incendiary comments. They claim they want the government out of their lives. But if Nell Blackstone was right about what Byron had been saying to her, they are involved in a great deal more than just talk. Our offices have been watching them. A lot of the speeches you can find on social media are fanatical, and of course, any kind of fanatic is frightening."

"Do we know of any local members who might be involved in this?" Hunter asked him.

Just as Garza had come to New York, Amy's supervisor, Mickey Hampton, had joined the task force in Florida. Mickey, John Schultz, Aidan and others involved in the investigation in Florida were with them via teleconference, displayed on a large computer monitor.

"No," Garza told them. "The activity we know about occurs in the northwestern states."

"We've nothing down here regarding a group called the People," Mickey Hampton said. "But I'm wondering if this group is starting to travel. It doesn't sound as if they're interested in promoting any legitimate agenda, but rather that they're a group of anarchists."

"My thought, as well," Garza said.

"What about the man who was killed while trying to assassinate Nell Blackstone?" Mickey asked.

"Ronald Rubio, Idaho native, joined several groups out west and left them, dropped out of high school, went from job to job—last legal address is a house he hasn't lived in for about a decade. He's been drifting here and there. No known address in the city of New York," Garza told them. "We found him through his prints. He was arrested once in DC for assault and battery."

"But we can't connect him to anyone else," Mickey said.

Hunter spoke up. "From Amy's conversation with Nell, it appears Byron had gotten himself involved with the Saints of the City. And it sounded like an old Mafia deal—once you're in, there's no way out."

Amy picked up the thread. "But he was also mentioning 'the people,' and Nell was never sure about the way he was saying the words, which suggests he was referring to the group 'the People.' With what we've learned here, I believe they may be the group responsible for the murder in the Everglades. We know the victims were gang members, as they were here. The People may be trying to deal with these various criminal groups—luring them to certain locations where ambushes are awaiting. And there's something cultlike about the way the group demands loyalty."

"I'd like to interview Ethan Morrison's sons," Hunter said. He hesitated. "And Morrison wants to see Amy. I suggest we let him do so."

"Garza?" Mickey said, looking for the lead's sign-off on that strategy.

"Hunter, if you think it will get us somewhere with this, see what you can get from the Morrison clan. I hope we're not just entertaining Ethan Morrison, obliging him by sending Amy in."

"It's good if he thinks we're falling for his games," Amy said. "That's how people slip up."

"All right, then. Our forensic teams will stay on the physical evidence we've collected, and we'll have our people across the country watching for these various groups," Garza said. "Detectives Logan and Chan, thank you, and we'll keep you and the agents on the task force here in New York. All information should come to me, and I'll see it gets out to everyone. Let's stop this. Quickly."

The meeting broke.

Garza looked at Hunter. "I take it you want the jet to bring you straight to Morrison and his sons?"

Hunter nodded.

"Then do it."

Garza stood, smiled grimly at Amy and left the room.

"Well, we'll get you to the airport," Logan told Hunter.

"We're sorry to see you go," Chan said. "Nothing moved here...until..."

"The frightening thing is the number of innocents who seem to be in danger," Amy said. "Things have happened so quickly we haven't been able to follow through on a few interviews I've really wanted to happen. But...we'll keep in touch."

Chan nodded. "Hey, Hunter, by the way, did you get to talk to Mrs. Breyer at the coffee shop? The one who wanted a 'real' agent?"

"The virago?" Hunter asked. He'd had a chance to talk to her, all right. She had done nothing but complain about the police. And whine that she'd been inconvenienced when the forensic crews had been in "her" alley.

"Yeah, briefly. She has a mean streak in her, but I do believe it's just that. A mean streak."

"And the bar manager?" she asked.

"I believe his place was simply used," Hunter said.

The man had been upset; he had been horrified. He'd told Hunter he was trying not to drink up all the profits.

"But don't worry, we'll still be watching them. If anything transpired in either location that had to do with the massacre in any way, we will discover the truth."

Hunter gave him a smile and a nod. "I know you will."

Ninety minutes later he and Amy were on the jet and headed back to Florida.

Amy was studying her sketches of the crime scene. Hunter found himself going over his notes and the sheets of information he'd received again and again.

"Hunter, there is no way into that alley except through the alley—or the coffee shop or the bar. From the coffee shop, there's a little hook. It would make more sense for people to come out of the bar, but single file. The men—and their killers—had to have just traveled through the pedestrian alleyway or through one of those businesses."

He nodded.

"That woman at the coffee shop…"

"Yes, she's a monster. But we discover constantly that being a total jerk doesn't always make you a criminal. Sometimes, the more charming a person, the more able they are to sway others."

"Right. The Ted Bundy effect," she murmured. She frowned. "But Nell Blackstone was in the coffee shop when she heard that woman going off on me. That's how she managed to get to me. Do you think the man who attempted to kill her might have been sent out?"

"It's possible. But we can't be everywhere, Amy. We're going to have to trust Logan and the local bureau office people to follow through. They will. The chief of police and Garza are all over this. They don't want New York looking like a playland for those who want to indulge in a shooting spree."

She sighed softly. "You're right. I'm anxious to get back—"

"We'll be in Florida soon enough."

"North Florida. Hunter, we need to find a way to pick up David Ghent."

"Ryan is following him. They're watching the bar. Team, Amy, task force. This thing involves tons of people and, luckily, we have tons of good working officers and agents."

"I know. But there's something…"

"Squirrelly. No insult to the little rodents intended," he said.

She grinned.

"Sorry, I like squirrels."

"That's okay." She sighed. "I rather like them, too." She was quiet for a bit. "I think he's involved. And I think he knows he's in trouble."

"Why the hell doesn't he come in and tell us what he knows?"

She shook her head. "I just don't see how he can be more afraid of us than…whoever. He knows people wind up dead if it's even suspected they could say anything that would give us a real lead."

"Maybe he thinks he's high enough on the chain."

"Then he's a fool," she murmured. "Whoever the ultimate 'god' is, they appear to get rid of people right and left. I don't think anyone is high up enough in the chain other than the person who is really calling the shots."

"We'll figure something out. You're getting the same reports I'm getting. Ryan is working with another agent—they're tag-teaming—and they haven't lost him once, and I don't believe Ghent has any idea he's being followed."

Amy nodded.

"So, any suggestions on dealing with Ethan Morrison?" she asked.

He smiled. "Just be your charming self."

"He probably asked for me just to rattle you."

"He'd never know he rattled me." Hunter smiled again. "Trust me, if I didn't really know what our roles were in law enforcement—and as human beings—I'd have jumped over the table to strangle him already for attempting to create a sacrifice out of you."

She grinned at that.

"I do consider myself able, but I'm glad the man will be chained to a table. Though he's not so tough himself. He likes to instruct others to kill."

That was true.

"He knows something," Hunter said. "I don't know what, but something."

"Tonight…" she murmured.

He frowned. "Home? Your place is in the center of the state—a short flight since we get to keep the jet tonight."

She shook her head and laughed. "No, home as in our cheap hotel near the massacre site. I want to talk to Celia and Geoff Nevins tomorrow, and to Audrey Benson."

"Audrey, via the phone. Geoff and Celia Nevins, maybe we can still see. They're still here, but I think they're planning on heading back to Illinois soon," Hunter said. "If they make it."

"And since they don't seem to be worried…"

"Yeah?"

"Maybe they're involved, and David Ghent…just happens to like the same bar where Guillermo was recruited." She leaned forward. "Hunter, they're going to make a mistake. One of them is going to make a mistake. We're going to find the right person to talk, and we'll stop a murder before it happens."

He nodded. "We will," he told her softly. "Methodically, we will solve this with the help of others."

She nodded. "Of course. But…"

"But?"

"Someone sent a red horse to us."

"Right."

These were the times when he remembered the years in which he'd lived in a cult.

His parents were educated people. But he knew his mother had been offended by the times her father had valued money over kindness to others. She had been ripe for believing in a society where members helped one another, and where she believed decency, kindness and integrity were valued above the dollar.

His parents had soon learned that, even in a cult, there was a world order. And it took a few years, but then they realized those in charge were willing to commit many crimes, including murder, to stay in charge and to continue with their agenda—including stockpiling arms and perhaps preparing for a next step in their world order.

His parents had been lucky.

They'd escaped.

And while this didn't appear to be a cult in the same manner—or in the manner of the cult killings that had brought him and Amy first working together—there were shades of cultism in what was happening. The unwary were seduced with promises of a better life. They swore loyalty. They believed...

But there was someone at the top. Someone calling the shots. And the grip was so powerful that none dared disobey.

"Hunter?"

He arched a brow to Amy. She was watching him worriedly.

"Are you all right?" she asked him.

He nodded gravely. "We're going to get these false 'gods,'" he told her.

She was sitting across from him. They were the only people in the passenger section of the small but comfortable plane—one that had been set up for the few passengers to work while they were aboard. The seats were wide and comfortable.

Not all that wide…

But she wedged in next to him, half on his lap, half in the chair, and she curled her arms around him.

"You're a remarkable human being," she told him.

"Just a lucky one," he said softly.

She stayed with him there in a comfortable silence until the pilot warned them that they would be landing in another twenty minutes or so.

He knew why he had become an FBI agent. Still, sometimes he wondered why anyone—including himself—chose a life where they constantly saw so much of the ugliness a human being could cause.

But he was lucky. Lucky in the life he had. Lucky his parents were alive and well and living under assumed names. And lucky because he'd been a child when it had all occurred, and they'd gone into WITSEC, so he was still able to see them, and they were leading fairly normal lives. They'd found new lives and careers, writing and illustrating children's books.

And he was lucky he had found Amy, or they'd found one another.

Their commitment to their work was accepted.

Their commitment to one another was beautiful.

Lucky, yes.

Extraordinary, no. Luckier than many people? Beyond a shadow of a doubt.

Hunter had opted for another rental car when they reached the airport. They had just picked it up when Amy's phone rang.

It was Aidan.

"Hey, has anything else—"

"No bodies, thankfully," Aidan told her. "But something. You know Jimmy went out to his place deep in the Everglades. He's the kind of guy who makes use of his time, so he set to cleaning and doing little repairs on his boat."

"Okay. And?"

"He found a cell phone, and he got it to me right away. I've already checked it."

"Burner phone?" she asked.

"Yep. But I was able to trace numbers on it. Guess who called it?"

"Well, no one else on the boat," she said. "So—"

"One of the calls on it came from the exact place you're going. Obviously, it doesn't trace to a particular person, but…"

"Morrison!" she said.

"I'd be willing to bet. Jimmy thinks whoever had the phone intended to drop it into the water, missed, and it fell into a wedge in the boat and then deep into the structure under one of the seats."

"Most probably. Thanks, Aidan."

"I've reported it to both Mickey Hampton and Garza, but you're my second call. I knew where you guys were heading."

"And we'll be back there by tonight, Aidan."

"Can't stay away from cheap hotels, huh? See you soon, then. Who is going in—you or Hunter?"

"I'm taking a stab at him."

"Well, now you're armed."

"I am. Thank you!"

She ended the call and told Hunter what Aidan had told

her. He nodded to her. "The info is already coming through on our messages."

"You still want me to tackle him?"

"I'm going for the boys. Morrison wanted to see you. Head in there as if you're going just because he said you should, and we're hoping to do anything that will get him to talk. Then hit him with what we've just learned."

She nodded.

They soon reached the Florida state facility, turned in their weapons and split up.

Morrison and his sons were being kept in separate wings of the facility.

Warden Carver walked with Amy to the room where she would meet with Ethan Morrison.

"He's chained—his crimes warrant that his cuffs be chained to the table. He wasn't much of a physical danger to other people. He lets others do his dirty work. He's the kind who likes to rule the masses. He has some of the prisoners here believing he is a messiah. He's polite to others and he preaches in the yard sometimes. He steers clear of Harvey Harrison, though. You can tell Harrison thinks he's a laughable fraud."

"Harvey Harrison?"

"Killed three men in a bar brawl. Someone insulted his mother. He's six-six and built of pure steel. Morrison is smart to steer clear. Anyway, as I said, Morrison has been a model prisoner. It's as if he's trying to prove—even in here—that he is innocent of others misinterpreting his words."

"Others? Like his own sons?"

"Of course! They were good boys. They were just fighting for God!"

Amy shook her head. "Why would anyone think one

man had really been touched by God—and knew what He wanted?"

"Beats me. And…well, whose God, to begin with? We have everyone in here, you know—Christians, Jews, Muslims, Buddhists…you name it. Mostly, we really do practice freedom of religion."

"One of the greatest and most important freedoms," Amy said.

The warden shrugged. "One of our most important freedoms, right." He shook his head. "Sometimes people can think it's freedom for their religion—and not everyone else's! But we keep an eye out—especially with Morrison in here. But as I said, so far…all our groups just do their own thing. Even the atheists who just shake their heads at everyone else. Anyway, I don't think Morrison will give you any trouble, but there will be a guard right outside the door—though I hear you're pretty tough."

Amy smiled. "Everyone needs someone at their back. I'll bet even Harvey Harrison."

"He has his friends, and yes, they do have little cliques that look out for one another. Here's your door—good luck."

The warden ushered her past the guard standing at the door and into a small room with two chairs and a table.

Ethan Morrison was shackled to the table. He looked at her and offered her a broad—creepy—smile, one she thought that was to put her in her place. She was a woman, tempting and young, and worthless for anything other than a man's brief enjoyment.

"Looking fine, Special Agent Larson," he said.

"Well, looking alive, I believe, despite the fact you came close to killing me."

"I did nothing to you—"

"No, you just ordered that I be strung out as a sacrifice. I'm still amazed people could fall for your lines. I guess you convinced them I was part of a disease since I meant to save the lives of those you'd labeled as a disease on humanity. How did you explain it when you were simply mad at a follower? Wait, never mind, I've got it. Anyone who gave you any trouble whatsoever was part of the disease!"

He shrugged. "Ah, seriously, what a waste to sacrifice you," he said. "Such a truly fine specimen of female."

"No more than any other," she said sweetly. "So, what is going on now?"

He lifted his hands. The chains dragged on the table. "I'm in here. Guilty of nothing. And my lawyers are going to make you wish that...well, that you weren't around to see what's going to happen! But you will be, won't you?"

"You didn't think of the horses," she said.

"What?"

"You were an effective cult leader. You made people believe you had God's own whispers in your ear. You didn't believe a single thing that you preached. You hoodwinked people. Good show, though! You did a bang-up job of it. But you didn't think of the horses—the little toy horses—or the Four Horsemen of the Apocalypse."

She leaned closer to him, still out of reach. "I'm not even sure you thought of the power of your cult. Because whoever is really running this show is using a lot of the same basic principles. I don't think many drug pushers are doing it in the name of God, but the same concepts of absolute loyalty with dire consequences for disobedience are being maintained. And wow, can they twist anything the way they want. They managed to take the concept of disease as in the Revelation to be seen as people. Now war! Yes, send law enforcement running all over the country, investigating mass murders. You knew that more would follow. And you still believe you will get out of this. Someone is promising you that."

"I run my own world, missy. You'll see. I am an important man. I will not lose."

"You've already lost. And here's another thing. You should help us in any way you can. Because we have seen what goes on. You're alive. So far. But...well, there are always ways. Ways to communicate from in prison. And ways to die in prison, too. Unless you really do believe it doesn't matter if you die or not. That you'll sit in heaven surrounded by...what? Fun and mischievous angels?" She was quiet for a minute. He just stared at her. "We've seen them, Morrison. The victims slaughtered in this 'war.' And we've seen a man blow himself to bits, a shot straight into his face, rather than reap the repercussions for failure. These people can get to anyone."

He smiled. "You can't get to all of them. People will keep dying. It's a powerful force. War—the red horse!"

"Live by the sword, die by the sword."

"I never lifted a sword."

She smiled in return. "No, and it's likely whoever is ordering all this hasn't lifted a sword, either. They just command others to kill."

He shrugged, but for a minute, he looked downward.

He was uncomfortable.

She might have managed to scare him. And she thought she knew how to go further.

"Ethan," she said softly, using his given name, "that man who blew off his face—he did it to protect his wife and child. Guess what? Killers went after them, anyway. I don't know… I always thought a man like you believed in his progeny. I mean, your sons are murderers, but they could live to see the light of day outside these prison walls. Get a second chance. If they live."

He shook his head and leaned toward her, and this time he wasn't playing games or trying to flirt or put her in her place. He was suddenly earnest.

"The final horse is supposed to ride, and ride he will," he said. "That I know. But you must have figured that out by now." He hesitated. "Four Horsemen."

"But we stopped your horse, didn't we?" she asked sweetly. "And…well, in my book that was a failure on your part."

"I didn't fail. I created havoc!"

"Ah, but you were supposed to create so much more. You were supposed to kill me. But you failed. You really should be throwing yourself on our mercy." She leaned closer again. "You know, when we want to, we keep people alive."

"I don't know names. I don't know people."

"Someone must have communicated with you," she said.

He smirked. "God whispered in my ear."

She had heard about the gods of money already.

"A different kind of god?" she asked.

He shrugged.

She nodded. "Of course you know all about the massacre in the Everglades and the dead men in the alley in New York. But I believe you knew more about the situation in the Everglades. One of the killers talked to you right before the event."

"What?"

"Oh, please!"

He frowned. "What do you mean?"

"Someone talked to you. Seriously, the law respects your rights. That's far more than you ever allowed to anyone. You get to make phone calls. And you called someone who was involved with the murder in the Everglades."

He sat back, staring at her. "The idiot lost the phone?"

"The idiot lost the phone. And we found it. We're assuming it was supposed to be four feet deep in muck, but…yeah, the idiot lost the phone. Probably doesn't know it. But you know what that means?"

"That some people are idiots."

"Way more than you'd imagine."

"Maybe that's why so many have to die," he said.

"Maybe you don't have to be one of them."

He sighed, and for once she thought he might be about to tell the truth.

"I don't know names or people."

"Someone was communicating with you."

"All I know is I was given a number to call because I know the area. I needed to give them some coordinates of a place that was truly isolated but reachable off the highway."

"And you didn't know that people were going to be murdered."

He sighed. "They know me because I'm here. Because the 'white horse' already rode out to create the beginning of the end."

"How did you know to call?"

"A piece of mail from one of my flock."

"What member of your flock?"

"I have no idea. And the info was encrypted so that only I could find the number to call and the information that was needed."

"How can you not know who sent it?"

"Well, it was signed Mary Jones. If there is a Mary Jones in my flock, I don't know about it."

"But it was given to you."

"I'm allowed to receive mail. It's read first, of course."

"And it looked like a sweet note for you as a spiritual adviser?" Amy asked.

He nodded. "People do love me." He gave her a strange grimace. "You might say some of them worship me."

She leaned back. "Some might worship you. But we found that phone, and we know you're involved. Some could see that as you really screwing up."

"I didn't lose the phone."

"Do you think it's going to matter?" Amy asked pointedly. Again, she leaned closer to him, staying just out of his reach with the chains. "A man killed himself, shooting himself in the face, to make the sacrifice for his wife and child. Another man went after them to kill them, anyway. Just because he might have mentioned the place where he met his recruiter."

He was silent a minute and then he said, "I'm still the 'white horse'!"

"So, the 'horses' are the second tier. Some second tier if you don't know the god controlling it all. I'm curious— what did you get? What was your reward? I mean, without killing people, you had a heck of a thing going. Your flock! People willing to do anything for you. People who believed you were the next thing to God, the man with whom He shared His thoughts and goals!"

"Give unto Caesar," he said.

"Oh? They were going to pay all your taxes for you?" she asked dryly.

"The world runs on money."

"You were a rich man."

"I *am* a rich man. But…there's a lot that would stand in my way. Stupid Everglades."

"The ecosystem is your enemy?"

"You should listen to all the namby-pamby people out there. Sugar manufacturing causes runoff. Lake Okeechobee could wind up in trouble. Lands could become tainted. Drinking water could be affected. Do-gooders have all kinds of protests going on, and fighting their crap takes a lot of money and…" He broke off, shrugging. "I like money."

"And you like power."

"Money brings you power."

"And yet here you are, living in a cell, wearing cheap inmate attire. And talking to me for amusement because there isn't much else."

"I don't have any names to give you," he said.

She wasn't sure why, but she believed him.

"Okay, you had a number to call. It was a burner phone. You were supposed to provide coordinates for the perfect massacre, off the beaten track for the murders to take place. Did you arrange for the little toy horse to be sent to me—or was it for Hunter?"

"I didn't send you a horse," he said. "I really didn't. I'm not surprised you got one, but I didn't send it."

"So, you made a call to suggest a lovely place for a massacre. I hope you're not the one who suggested tomahawks and arrows."

He made a face that expressed his disgust. "Stupid. Trust me, I had nothing to do with that. I was just asked for a place."

"And who did you speak to? A man or a woman?"

"I doubt it was a woman."

"You don't know?"

"No, I don't know. The voice was…distorted. Purposely, I'm sure. As I said before, I'm the 'white horse.' Others… well, they're down the chain."

"And yet you just never know," Amy said. "These people…they really like to tie up loose ends. If you had to guess, was it a man or a woman?"

He smiled pleasantly. "If I had to guess? It was a man. But that's nothing to do with a voice. Everyone knows the male is…well, God made Adam first."

"And yet a woman helped take you down," Amy said sweetly.

That angered him. He could never admit to being bested by a woman.

"The game isn't over."

"It isn't a game, Mr. Morrison. You're not going to get out of here. Now, we could give you better odds on living, but…well, I'm bored. Imagine. A woman—bored with you. And I can walk out of here and you can't. What a world!"

She rose and walked to the door, turning back to wave.

His expression was strange.

"Come back," he said.

"I have people to see, places to go," she told him.

"No, I mean…"

"That you'd like to tell us what you know for protection?" she asked.

"I have nothing else to tell you," he said. "I don't know names." He hesitated. "We're only drawn in if we're needed. I…gave the caller the information that was needed."

"I'll see they keep an extra special eye on you," she said softly. "And if you do think of anything, let one of the guards know. The warden can reach me."

"I could call you if—"

"Just let the warden know."

She tapped on the door. The guard let her out. She didn't look back again. He would have liked her doing so too much.

She was surprised to discover the warden was waiting for her.

"We need his mail," she told him.

The warden frowned. "We go through everything—"

"Yes, of course, and thank you. But we need someone on it who can see cyphers in the most innocuous words, an expert in that field. If you don't mind, we'll get someone out of the offices here to be on call to see anything Morrison receives."

"Of course."

"Where's Special Agent Forrest?"

"Still in with one of the boys. But he did tell me that when you finished with Ethan Morrison you should join him. He is in a room with the eldest now."

"Can you take me to him?" Amy said.

Later, when they were driving south, she would tell Hunter everything Ethan Morrison had said.

She believed there was little more they could get from him.

Unless Morrison was contacted again.

She wondered if giving advice on the landscape had been his only involvement in what had happened.

One thing was sure, she thought.

There were four separate pieces in what was happening.

Ethan knew more than he was saying...

And his sons may have figured out something. Whatever it was, there would be dozens of small pieces to unravel.

Someone had a true endgame in mind.

11

"The boys" were eventually going to cave, Hunter thought.

He'd spent some time with Ethan's son Aaron, who told him his father had been anointed by God, and everything they had done had been to cleanse the land.

Aaron had not been hostile toward Hunter, and he'd quickly discovered Aaron believed what wasn't true—that he was going to get off on the murder charges that could result in the death penalty. "My father can hire the best lawyers in the world," he'd told Hunter.

"But I'm afraid the evidence is against you. But I suppose that's all right—if you believe you died doing God's work, then...well, death will be nothing."

"Death?"

"By lethal injection. Surely, you've been warned about the possible consequences?"

"I— No. My father's lawyers will get us off. What we did...we have freedom of religion in this country!"

He meant it. Hunter had almost laughed.

"I'm sorry. You must realize freedom of religion must still lie within the laws of the country. And murder is against the law."

"But...no, no. We won't get the death penalty!"

Hunter shrugged, leaving Aaron worried.

"What do you know about the 'red horse'?" he'd asked next.

The look of total bafflement on the young man's face had not been feigned.

"The 'red horse'? Well, I suppose he's out there. I mean, everyone's heard about the gang warfare, the massacres, so..."

"Okay. Well, if you think of anything that might help you, let me know."

"Help me? Or help you?"

"Oh, no, Aaron. Help you."

With a smile, he'd left him.

And now Hunter sat with Zeke, who tried to tell him about the lawyers, too, and who Hunter had told about the deaths of those now involved with the "red horse."

"But... I'm not involved with any of this," Zeke was telling him as Amy entered the room.

He had the grace to look uncomfortable.

Zeke had almost killed Amy. Only her own talents and resilience, and the arrival of a host of officers and agents, had kept her alive and brought down the "white horse."

Zeke stopped speaking and looked away.

"It's okay," Amy said, sliding into a chair next to Hunter. "I forgive you."

"I really thought you were part of the disease," Zeke said, still looking away. "I mean…"

"You know that's not true," Amy said. "People aren't a disease. I'm so sorry you were caught up. I know your father loves you, but he's been mistaken in many ways. We can all be mistaken. We're human. We're here today because we're afraid for you and your family and… Well, I imagine Special Agent Forrest has told you what has happened to the people involved. How their families were attacked when they performed the ultimate sacrifice. You're young. You can't want to die," she said.

"But I'm not involved."

"But your father is. He helped plan the massacre."

Zeke was startled by that.

Amy leaned in. "Families are attacked, not just the guilty party. We believe your guards are honest and law-abiding, but these people get to anyone they want, and you are in the general population here."

"I can't tell you anything!" Zeke said. "I—I didn't even know my father had been involved. Talk to him. Tell him we're in danger!"

"He knows," Amy said softly.

Zeke inhaled deeply. He exhaled and started to talk.

"All I know is the apocalypse is coming. The Four Horsemen are coming, and we were all supposed to do our part. Doing our part assures us a place at the end. My father…my father is a holy man. He told us doing the work right often involved doing things that seemed wrong but were part of the greater good."

"You grew up rich," Hunter reminded him. "In the best

214

schools, golfing, riding, joining the hottest fraternities. How did all that fit in with believing in some greater good?"

"My father told us," he said quietly, "that I was born white and therefore I was meant to have the good things that were offered in this world. Fun, parties..." He looked away again. "Women."

"While doing God's work," Hunter said.

"We were chosen."

"Ah. And now?" Amy asked softly.

Zeke shook his head. "I don't know what I believe. They don't let us see our father."

"Your father is going to get you killed. See where you are as it is. The parties are over. But it could be a lot worse," Amy reminded him.

A look of loss and desperation fell over Zeke's face. He had learned some hard realities. The parties were over. He was no longer the rich kid, laughing, playing, enjoying all that money could buy.

"I've told you what I know. Honestly." He sighed. "The first horseman carries a bow and wears a crown. Some saw him as Christ. But I know my father symbolized the first, as whispered to him by God. He brought with him pestilence and disease. The next horseman carries a sword—and he is war. The black horseman will bring famine, and finally the fourth horseman will ride a pale horse and he will bring death. Don't you understand? It was all right for us to enjoy the things of this earth. Because in the end, death will come to the many."

"Wait—to the many?" Hunter said.

Zeke sighed. "Death comes to all eventually. But when the fourth horseman arrives, he will control life and death."

"Other than what's happening now," Amy said.

Zeke shook his head.

"Come on, Zeke," Hunter said. "You're far from stupid. You don't believe God is really ordaining any of this. Your father is a master at manipulation, and you wanted to believe you could do all the things you did—and it was all right."

"I don't know what I believe anymore," Zeke admitted. "All right, all right, when it was all over and the rider on the pale horse came, we would be...well, like the hands of God. Left with time to enjoy the good things on this earth, and then yes, sitting in a high position for having helped bring it all about."

"So, who is the 'red horse'?" Amy asked softly.

He shook his head. "I don't know. I swear, I don't know." He winced. "All I know is...war. The 'red horse' is supposed to get people killing each other." He hesitated again. "Starting here and moving across the world."

This could all become so much worse! Hunter thought.

He refrained from looking at Amy, and he knew she was thinking the same thing.

They had to stop this.

Before the 'red horse' really managed to start a war.

"I don't want to die!" Zeke said. "Please, I'd tell you anything...help me. Don't let one of these other guys come at me. Please."

Hunter stood and Amy did the same.

"We'll see you're protected awaiting trial."

"And talk to the right people? Please?" Zeke begged. "If I know anything, if I figure out anything, I swear I'll tell you."

Hunter nodded gravely.

They left him sitting reflectively at the table, waiting for a guard to return him to his cell.

Thanking the warden, Hunter and Amy left before discussing what they had learned.

"So, Ethan Morrison admitted to suggesting the location for the massacre," Hunter said, looking at Amy.

She nodded. "But he doesn't know who called him. He doesn't even know if it was a man or a woman. But according to him, it had to be a man."

"Why?" Hunter asked, puzzled.

"Because he can't believe whoever is orchestrating all four horses would put a woman in charge of anything."

Hunter was silent a minute, then he grinned at her.

"It will be great if the judge who determines the punishment for his crime is a woman."

"I don't think that even occurs to him."

"Guess he never heard about Ruth Bader Ginsburg."

She smiled and nodded. "A beacon to all little girls," she said. "But, Hunter, I don't like what we learned. It sounded as if...as if the 'red horse' is supposed to start causing all kinds of trouble here. We don't have any real communication with the gangs involved in these killings, but I don't think it's rivals or a territory thing. But it's supposed to look as if rival gangs are killing one another's members so that they seek revenge."

"That certainly appears to be true."

"It's all just a dress rehearsal for something far worse."

"I agree."

She turned to him. "We know someone on that boat was in communication with Ethan Morrison before the event. Not Ginny and Ben. And probably not Daisy Driver since she was quick to go into protective custody. That leaves David Ghent, Celia and Geoff Nevins and Audrey Benson."

"And we will get to all of them—whether they're in Chicago or not." He glanced at her. "Call Mickey Hampton and make sure he talks to Garza immediately. Other agencies are going to have to be warned. Even if the 'red horse' hasn't gotten that far yet, I'm willing to bet his 'war' is supposed to eventually involve the whole country."

"Right."

Amy put through the call. They had several hours to drive, and she made other calls as they passed through miles and miles of the peninsula, checking in with John Schultz, Aidan and the New York City police.

Nothing had changed since they'd landed.

It was just after six when he pulled into the parking lot of their chain hotel. Hunter looked at Amy. "I'll call the Nevinses, tell them we're just checking on their welfare."

"I'll see if I can pin down Audrey Benson. And check in with Ryan."

He nodded. "I just have one call to make first," he told her.

"Oh?"

"Pizza."

They headed to their room, both on their cell phones. Hunter did order a pizza for them first, then called the number Geoff Nevins had given him. He thought he was going to get voice mail, but the man answered after several rings.

"Mr. Nevins, it's Special Agent Forrest," he told the man.

"Yes, sir, of course—I have you on my caller ID. Is everything all right with you?" Nevins asked him.

"Yes, fine, thank you. We're checking on you. You may have heard we're concerned—"

"Yes," Nevins said softly. "Ginny was attacked. But we left Florida and we're home in Chicago. I have work—too old to be cool and not old enough to retire," he said lightly.

"Well, we do want you to get to retirement age," Hunter said. "You're sure you don't want protection until we can get this thing unraveled?"

"I hope I'm not being a fool," Nevins said. "But Celia wanted to get home—far away from all that—and back to our normal lives. Look, I have no clue what was going on."

"Mr. Nevins, we know someone on your boat was involved with whoever planned the operation."

"What? I never heard that!"

"It's recently come to light."

"Oh, come on. We all talked before we left the dock. Those were all nice people. A kid, some retirees and two attorneys!"

"Mr. Nevins, I can't make you accept protective custody. I do still recommend it."

"I'll talk to my wife. But, Special Agent Forrest, we are miles and miles away."

"Yes, and you might have seen there was another massacre in New York."

"And you don't know that was related."

"We have every reason to believe the two events are related," he told the man.

"I'll speak with Celia again. I can reach you at this number, right?"

"You can reach me at this number or dial 911 at any time. Law enforcement across the country is aware of what is happening."

"Thank you. We'll talk again."

They ended the call and he looked at Amy.

She shook her head. "Audrey Benson is starting a campaign for the next House race. She can't hide, and she's convinced she has the majority of a very fine police force looking after her, not to mention guards and everyone else involved with the courts."

"She's a defense attorney. I'm sure there are a few prosecutors who might step aside if she was falling into a puddle."

"You had no luck?"

"Nope. Nevins believes he's far, far away, and I'm making things up when we don't give out details. But—"

"One of them had that phone! And was in contact with Ethan Morrison."

"Were you able to reach Anders?" he asked her.

She nodded. "David Ghent has been a model citizen. He's gone to lectures and hung out with his friends. Yes, he's hung out at the Wing House, but with groups of friends all talking sports or the latest movie."

"Maybe he does know he's being watched."

"Hey! I hardly recognized Ryan."

Hunter shook his head. "Not because he'd make Ryan or Ryan's partner on this as someone watching him, but just because he probably knows we suspect him of…something."

"I called his cell phone—David Ghent's cell phone—and left a message because he didn't answer. Ryan texted me that David looked at his phone and put it back in his pocket, so he apparently doesn't want to talk to me."

"Lots of people don't answer their phones when they're hanging out with their friends."

"Ryan said he looked at the caller ID. Hunter, he's at the bar now."

"So…"

A ding on Hunter's phone alerted him to the fact the pizza had arrived.

"Pizza," he said. She was staring at him. "Pizza is here, but you want wings. At a place called the Wing House."

She grimaced. "We're so close, Hunter. I just want to set up a meeting for tomorrow."

"Wings. And besides, what college kid hasn't learned to appreciate a cold pizza? I'll just grab it and throw it in the room, then we'll head to the Wing House."

She smiled.

Hunter shook his head, smiling back. "Morrison really is a fool."

"Oh?"

"No one is as persistent as a woman."

She shrugged. "Well, this woman, anyway!"

The parking lot was crowded. The bar was busy.

Tonight, Ryan Anders was clean-shaven and wearing a sandy-colored wig that was long; he was sporting a heavy-metal-band T-shirt. He was at the bar, animated as he talked to the man next to him who was wearing a uniform for a local construction agency.

David Ghent was at one of the high-top tables again with a group of friends. He looked at the two of them as they entered and rolled his eyes.

But he quickly excused himself to his group of friends to join Hunter and Amy near the door.

"Oh, my God, you people!" he said. "I have a life I'd like to live!"

"We'd like you to get to live it, too," Amy told him sweetly. "We'll get out of your hair right away, but it is imperative that we speak to you. There have been…developments. Someone on the tour group was involved. We know it."

"But—"

"We recovered a cell phone," Hunter told him. "We're

not giving that information to the media, but we are worried about you."

"A cell phone?" David Ghent said, frowning.

"A cell phone was found on the boat. What we call a burner phone. Anybody could have bought it at many, many places, paying cash for the use and not associating the number with a name. But a call on it traced to someone involved with other murders."

David was dead still for several seconds.

"Please, I'd like to speak with you again. See if I can't—" Amy began.

"Tomorrow! Please. I promise I'll call you in the morning. And…did you really find a phone? And you traced it to…?"

"Yes, someone who orchestrated several murders," Hunter said.

David nodded. "I'll call you in the morning. I swear," he told Amy. "Right now…well, there's someone here. And if I'm going into hiding, well, hell—I'm going to get lucky tonight."

He turned and left them, shaking his head as he rejoined his friends.

"Think he will really call me?"

"I think if he doesn't, we'll know where to find him. And we'll know where to get him through Ryan. And we *will* get him."

She nodded. "Well, then. Let's not cramp his style. He wants to get lucky tonight. And if he does take us up on protective custody—"

"Then he's not as squirrelly as we thought."

"Right. That will leave those folks up in Chicago."

"Or it will be a ploy."

"Did you want some wings?" she asked him.

"No, I'm into cold pizza. And maybe I can get lucky to-night, too," he teased.

"I don't know...hmm. Shouldn't seduction be practiced with something a little...more appetizing than cold pizza," she said, grinning as she shook her head. "But I'd give my eyeteeth for a shower. So you can enjoy cold pizza, and I'll enjoy some hot water."

"Did you want wings?"

"No, I want hot water." She shrugged and turned to head back to the car.

"You mind driving?" Hunter asked her. "I want to text Ryan."

"Sure."

He texted the agent to let him know it was imperative they not lose David Ghent overnight. Ryan texted him back.

No way.

Amy hadn't lied. She didn't even glance at the pizza but went straight for the shower.

Hunter was hungry.

He looked at the pizza.

But the pull of the hot shower was stronger, and a different kind of hunger much greater.

Amy seemed to expect him. She leaned back against him, and he wrapped his arms around her. For a few minutes they just stood there, allowing the sweet sensation of the hot steaming water to slip over them, cleansing their flesh, and cleansing the trials of the day and all that had been ugly from their minds and souls, as well.

She turned into him.

They kissed and teased, stroked and caressed...

And he nearly slid against the porcelain of the tub, which left them both laughing, emerging, reaching for towels and falling sweetly damp into one another's arms again.

They tangled in the towels and tripped and laughed more as they fell upon the bed. Then sensation took over, and they made love with a fierce energy that was passionate and urgent and beautiful.

And when they had climaxed, they lay in one another's arms. He thought that the time they shared before and after, sleeping together, waking together...all were beautiful, too.

He was about to say something sweet and sentimental when Amy suddenly jumped up, walking naked to the desk, comfortable with him and herself, fit and sleek and curvaceous.

"What?" he asked her, worried.

She turned around with a grin. "Pizza. Delicious cold pizza. Hey, I went to college, too!"

"Mmm, that would be good now!"

It had been a while since he'd been in college. It wasn't good, but it wasn't all that bad.

They ate in bed, then cleared it of crumbs and laid down again, checking their cell phones and messages for anything they might have missed. But it had been a long day and a long night. Finally they were curling up together, sleeping with that touch, something that made their private world right.

Hunter woke easily; he'd done so since he'd been a boy. Any slight sound could awaken him.

But the sound seemed loud and blaring.

It was Amy's cell phone. She answered it quickly, frowning as she saw the caller ID, and put her phone on speaker.

"Special Agent Amy Larson," she said.

"It's David. David Ghent."

"David! Great. You did call. It's…uh…early. Six to be exact. That's fine, I'm happy to hear from you."

"I think I need to be in your protective custody," he told her.

"Okay, that's excellent. Are you home? May we pick you up at your place?"

"No, no, I'm not home. I'm… I'm afraid to be home. People were following me last night."

"Agents have been watching you, David."

"No, no…not agents. People I've seen before. People… who I think are part of it. I can't explain now. I'm on the move. There's a place in the Everglades. It's an old hunter's lodge, the kind people can't have anymore, but it's abandoned and falling apart and deep in, and…that Seminole man knows how to find it. Jimmy knows where it is… I'll be there."

"David, agents have been watching you. I'll call them, and you can just go straight to the man who has been following you. I'll get the police—"

"Amy, I got scared last night. No one is watching me because there's a way out the back at the apartments, through the bathroom window. I'm gone. Find me at that old lodge. Please. I don't—I don't trust anyone but you."

The line went dead.

Hunter was already up, donning his clothes. Amy quickly did the same, her phone in her hand.

She woke Ryan up. His partner from the local bureau, Sean Masters, was on duty.

Ryan gave her Sean Masters's phone number and she dialed it.

"Special Agent Larson! I'm here, right in front of his place—"

"Not your fault, Masters, but I don't believe he's there.

Go up to the apartment and see if he's gone—through a window out back."

"Right away. But—"

"Just do it. We'll worry about the consequences later," Amy said.

"Let's go," Hunter told her. He had his phone out, too. He was calling Jimmy Osceola.

Hunter swore as the phone rang.

"If Jimmy went into deep hiding, we'll never reach him. Do you know where this cabin or lodge or whatever might be?"

"Probably not too far from the place where the massacre occurred."

Hunter's phone rang. He didn't recognize the number of the caller, but he answered it quickly.

"Forrest."

"Hunter, Jimmy here. I didn't bring my cell phone out with me, but my manager has it there at the restaurant and he saw that you called. Hey, I'm in hiding. I bought a burner phone myself."

Hunter put his phone on speaker, letting Amy hear the conversation.

"That was good thinking, Jimmy. We need to find one of the old, abandoned hunting lodges in the Everglades. The kid, David Ghent, is in hiding. He's running scared. We had an agent watching him, but he slipped out through his bathroom window. Do you know the cabin? Can you send me coordinates?"

"Right now," Jimmy told him. "Coming through in your messages. It's along the same waterway where the massacre occurred. Other side, deeper in. Watch out for the gators and the moccasins. Oh, yeah, and these days the pythons."

"Thanks, Jimmy."

"Are you on the way?"

"We are."

"I'll meet you. There's a turnoff a mile south of where the massacre took place. Take it and come and park on the embankment. I'll get you across the water."

"That'll work."

Hunter and Amy were already at the car. It was the bureau's, though it didn't have any flashing lights or a siren. He sped his way through traffic, anyway, neither he nor Amy speaking much.

Jimmy was coming along in his boat just as they parked. Both ran to him and hopped on and he ferried them across.

"Jimmy, if you can point us in the right direction, you might then want to wait here—" Hunter began.

"Hell, no. I'll be with you two—the people with guns. Don't you two ever watch horror movies? You never leave someone behind and alone!"

"Right, then lead the way."

Jimmy could move. And it wasn't easy. The terrain was muck interspersed with tall grass and trees, some growing so close it didn't appear there was a way through them.

Then Hunter saw the cabin ahead, dilapidated, the roof caving in, boards that had been on glassless windows caving in, too.

They ran the best they could, stopped at the door, looking through a broken window, weapons ready.

She nodded to Hunter; he easily kicked the door off its hinges.

And they found him.

12

Amy had seen a lot in her days as a cop and then with FDLE.

But she had seldom felt quite so ill.

Because she had known. She had known David Ghent was in-volved with what was going on, and she hadn't forced him in.

"He made his choices," Hunter said quietly.

"But—"

"Amy, it's not anyone's fault but his own. He knew what they did to people. He had his chance. I'm sorry. I hate to see this, too. I hated to see a woman and child who weren't involved almost murdered. There's one thing we can do— find the head and cut it off." He winced. "Figuratively," he added.

Because David Ghent's throat had been so savagely slashed his head was almost severed from his body.

They had stepped outside.

So had Jimmy—luckily, before he had vomited on the crime scene. He'd followed too quickly in their wake, seeing what he shouldn't have seen before they could usher him out of the place.

The ME and the crime scene techs were on the way.

"Hunter!" Amy said suddenly.

"What?"

"He hasn't been dead long. The killer is probably still near here!" She had her phone out quickly, calling the local county police and the Seminole police. David Ghent's killer was probably hiding out in the trees, perhaps even going across waterways and through different hardwood hammocks.

Jimmy had overheard. "Maybe we can hope, for once, the denizens of this place get ahold of whoever it was," he commented.

Hunter started around the back of the old cabin.

"Hey!" Jimmy said. "Don't leave me here!"

"Jimmy, he—or she—is not coming back. They're fleeing now."

"Great. I'll get behind you. I'm not carrying a gun—you are."

"True," Amy told him.

But walking around what was left of the rotting structure, she saw Hunter had already moved on, and quickly.

She wondered if the killer had planned on the terrain here.

Because there were prints easily seen in the muck just beyond the house. They then disappeared as the muck turned into water.

Hunter headed that way.

"I hope he knows this area is a haven for moccasins," Jimmy muttered.

Amy opted not to follow Hunter.

The two men were wearing boots. She wished she'd chosen boots, too, instead of her sneakers.

And they weren't going to get whoever had done this. The Everglades might get him, yes. But they wouldn't. With luck, maybe one of the law enforcement agencies would find him.

"We'll wait for Hunter. He'll hopefully get a direction to give all the cops and the FDLE people who are heading out."

Jimmy smiled as they heard sirens.

"And here they are! Well, someone is here."

The first to arrive were officers from the Seminole police, and Hunter appeared again just as they were pulling in. Hunter and Amy described what they'd found—and their certainty the killer was still around.

"We'll find what we can of the trail and then keep our eyes open," one of the officers promised. "We've got an airboat coming around. We'll leave the forensics to FDLE and get out and see what we can find." He was a handsome man, tall and bronzed with his dark hair worn to his neck. "We'll have everyone we can on it," he promised.

He and his partner quickly moved toward the water where an airboat was already arriving.

John Schultz—still with Aidan—arrived next, and then the ME.

And Hunter and Amy explained why they had come, and just what they had found.

"He was hiding out, seeking protection," Amy said.

"Well, evidently," John said, "someone knew he was hiding out."

"And knew about this place," Aidan added.

Jimmy cleared his throat. He still looked peaked. "You know, the kid found out about this place because I was talking about the way lots of people—lots of guys who claimed to be fishing or hunting alligators—used to keep these cabins until they were outlawed. Most guys who had them just came out to drink and maybe shoot up their beer cans. But I talked about them on that tour. And I remember the kid asking me more about them, and how I pointed out the fact there was one ahead."

Amy looked at Hunter. "We'd thought David might have been the one who had been talking to Morrison. But someone else on Jimmy's boat is probably involved, too. And I'd say we're looking at Audrey Benson and/or Celia and Geoff Nevins."

"Who have all gone back up north."

"Thankfully, I can still question people in Chicago," Hunter said. "And so can Amy. She's 'on loan.'" He looked at Amy. "Some answers are in New York," Hunter said. "But I think we're looking at small fry there, too. But the same plane that flies to New York can go to Chicago, too. I just have to give Garza a call."

She smiled sweetly. "And I do love the Windy City," she said.

"You know it's 'windy' because of the politicians not the weather?" John asked.

"You know what they say, don't you?" Amy asked John. "They have to have some lousy weather or else everyone would want to live there. Hey, seriously, Chicago is a great city. Sounds like a…"

Her voice trailed. An image of David Ghent's nearly severed head, lying at an improbable angle in a pool of blood, flashed across her mind.

The lightness in her tone dropped.

"Sounds like we need to stop this. As soon as possible."

"You know we'll be working it here," Aidan told her sincerely.

She nodded and looked at Hunter.

"Call Garza and find out what airport he wants us to be at."

Hunter already had his phone out.

The upholstery was nice.

Everything about the small plane was nice.

Hunter had been given use of it before, but only when time was of the essence and a situation was dire.

A situation in which it was believed his experience might be useful.

"You know," Amy told Hunter, sitting across from him again. "This is really nice. I could get use to traveling this way."

"Well, don't get too used to it. Even though I'm considered an 'expert' on certain types of killers, I don't travel in it all that often."

She smiled. "We don't fly often, though we do sometimes. I mean, we are one state. But from Key West to the Georgia border, it's over four hundred miles. And almost nine hundred miles from Key West to the Alabama border."

"And have you driven that distance often?" he asked her.

She shook her head. "No. But I do enjoy it when I have to go down to the Keys."

He laughed. "I enjoy it more when I don't *have* to go down to the Keys, but just have the free time to go down to the Keys."

"Okay, that's true, too. So when this is over, we could take a few days in the Keys," Amy said. Her smile faded. "Think we'll get another little toy horse if we go to the Keys?"

"We can make sure we eat out, and that way we won't get one with room service," he told her, turning to look out the window. "I don't know, Amy. I don't know what is really going on with this. I think about it a lot—Morrison was easy prey."

"Prey?"

Hunter nodded. "You had an extremely rich man who was also an expert at manipulation, who had a family who loved being rich, and more—they loved their father's power over people. Morrison easily convinced people he had a direct line to God. But his greed and ego made him easy to control, too. Now this…gang warfare, starting with the lower echelon of international drug cartels. Get law enforcement running all around trying to stop the violence. These people rule with even more fear—kill or be killed, and watch your loved ones die, as well. That's potent. But what I'm afraid of now is that it's all a rehearsal or a setup for something far worse."

"Yeah, I know. What are you thinking?"

He sighed softly. "We know most people are decent, whatever their feeling on many issues. But we've also learned it's easy to stir up hate. I'm afraid of race wars, religious wars, you name it. And then even taking it out of the country."

"We really do have to stop this."

He smiled. "All of us, Amy. And you can't keep feeling guilty about David Ghent's death. You tried to talk him in. We hadn't figured out just what his role might have been, if he'd had one, and we had nothing to arrest him on."

She nodded, looking out the window.

"So, uh, where are we staying?"

"We're heading straight to an apartment downtown that's kept and maintained by the Chicago office—just for occasions like this. And we're going to surprise Audrey Benson at her work, and we'll meet up with Geoff and Celia, too, without letting them know we're coming."

"You're sure we're going to find them?"

He nodded. "I'm extremely patient. I've spent hours upon hours sitting in a car, watching and waiting. I'm sure you have, too."

"Yes, I have. And tonight—"

"We're going to engage in this thing called sleep."

She smirked. "I was thinking something else."

The world could be going to hell, and Amy could still make him smile.

"It is cool to have a woman with such a seductive mind," Hunter said lightly.

"Wow, it would be. I was actually thinking about dinner," she told him.

"Oh, yeah, well, that, too. You know, Chicago has some of the best steakhouses in the world—if we make it in time."

On landing, Hunter talked to the local director in charge, his FBI liaison, Mario Cutter, who assured him that the large restaurant at the corner of the block where they'd be housing was wonderful. "It might be one of the reasons we specifically keep that condo," he told Hunter.

The place was decorated in Western fashion. Two life-size cow mannequins flanked the large double doorways. Saddles were displayed on beams and pictures of cowboys lined the walls.

Hunter was starving by that point and quickly ordered their "cowboy rib eye," certain he would eat every ounce.

He was surprised when Amy ordered the salmon.

"If they want you to order beef, they shouldn't make the cows at the entry so cute and lifelike."

"You know they can be quite stinky—"

"They're mammals. They have huge brown eyes and soft noses."

"So, I brought you to a steakhouse and turned you into a vegetarian?" he asked.

"Pescatarian. I just ordered fish."

"I'm sure the mother salmon thought her baby was cute, too," Hunter said.

"Maybe I should have gotten the vegetarian lasagna."

"I can catch the waitress—"

She stopped him. "I'm not making any lifestyle choices at the moment—just opting for the salmon."

He grinned at her. Leave it to Amy.

His steak was delicious. It was odd how good a meal could be when you spent so much time running—and trying to stop a roller coaster with twists and turns that were almost impossible to fathom.

"Hunter?"

Amy was staring at him, concerned.

"Yeah, I know. I'm not supposed to obsess."

She smiled and shook her head. "No, I'm obsessing, too. This is...almost a cult, isn't it?"

"In the aspect that gangs can be like cults."

"What about satanic cults?"

"We know they exist."

"Do you think that...?"

"No, not really. The gangs that are involved are being goaded into this somehow. I think David Ghent was sent out to spur trouble—maybe to cause the massacre. If you get one faction believing another gang is in—in effect, determined to bring it down—you create warfare. But I do believe this just a beginning. These massacres have been trial runs. First, to really start a problem with the country, and then maybe across the world."

"How do most wars start?" Amy murmured. "Power, land, assets…"

"And often in the name of religion," Hunter said.

"Yes, but do you think you're jaded?"

He shook his head. "Even my dad will tell you—there's nothing wrong with most religions, especially the traditional religions across the world. Christianity, Judaism, Islam, Hindu, Buddhism…you name it. Most teach us to look out for the aged and respect our fellow man. It's what man can do in the name of religion that is horrendous, that any god would find despicable. Well, except for those practicing satanism, and in truth in this matter, I don't think we'd be seeing what we're seeing. More people would be out just for themselves—screw a higher-up on the chain. And once you're fearing the hellfires of eternal damnation, what more is there?"

He paused, studying her.

"What have been some of the horrible events here?" she asked softly.

"Church and temple attacks," he said.

"We need to speak with your liaison," she said.

"Yep!" He pulled out his phone, noting it was nearly ten o'clock and apologizing when he got the man on the phone.

"Hey, if you need something, call me. Even if it's 2:00 a.m.," Cutter told him.

"Well, we're worried this thing might be coming to Chicago."

Cutter sighed. "They started in the South, they hit New York. Chicago is a nice big city in the Midwest."

"Right. But I'd like to know if you'd had any religious extremists in the area."

"Uh, no. Not lately. The country has gone through a lot of turmoil in the past years. We have a largely mixed demographic—mostly good people, all just wanting fairness and to get along. But nothing bad happening—nothing that has been brought to my attention. Most folks leave other folks alone. Sometimes there's a group that likes to stir things up, but you think we're going to have a religious problem here?"

"No. But I think someone might make it appear you have a problem. Would you speak with the local police and other agencies? I'd like to have extra vigilance at temples and such for the next week or so."

"Yes, of course. It's always better to prevent a crisis than try to repair whatever may come of it. I'll get started right away."

"Thank you."

He ended the call and looked at Amy. "I guess people have faith in us. He didn't ask me to second-guess myself."

"That's good. And the salmon was good."

"And I did say we should sleep."

She grinned. "I said we should eat. That's done, so…"

They left the restaurant.

Amy went straight to the shower; she tended to do so after a long day. He had been serious that they needed sleep, but he found himself on the computer looking up everything he could on the religious scene in Chicago. It was a big city. Besides traditional churches, there was a group called "the Science of God," as well as more predictable off-the-main practices such as voodoo and Wicca.

But he didn't think someone would try making war with

a small group of people. The horsemen killers wanted more. They would be attacking the city's big three, trying to cause problems between the Christians, Jews and Muslims.

Amy came out of the bathroom in a towel, and he looked up and blinked. "Oh, I was going to join you!"

She laughed softly. "Too late. But did you find anything?"

He shook his head. "You know, Cutter didn't think I was off the mark, but... It's true, I believe in God, and I believe in man's goodness to man. But also the fact I have no right to tell anyone else how to believe. I truly thank God for our Founding Fathers and the separation of church and state, because we can be a unified country with different religions. The things people have done in the name of faith... But I'm ranting. Sorry. I'm going to the shower."

She stopped him before he could go in. Smiling, she stroked his face and pressed against him. "You are an amazing person, Hunter. A crack agent—and simply a good man."

He kissed her lips. They were moist and warm from the shower. She tasted sweetly of mint toothpaste.

"I'll shower quickly," he promised.

It was the fastest shower he'd ever taken.

When he emerged, drying himself as energetically as he washed, she rose to meet him; then they crashed down on the bed together.

She whispered that he was hot, then teased she was only referring to his body temperature lest he get a big head. They laughed and teased, caressed and seduced, kissed and teased more with their lips and fingertips; they came together and let the night take them away, as a fiery wind, where there were moments when the world did abate, and they were just two.

Then they curled together.

And he whispered they did have to sleep.

They didn't talk anymore.

But Hunter knew Amy would be thinking, just as he was thinking, until sleep claimed them both at last.

"Cops are watching every church, temple, mosque and house of worship they know of," Hunter assured Amy, buttoning his jacket. "I thought we'd start by visiting Audrey Benson at her law offices. Right downtown. Geoff and Celia Nevins are a bit out in the suburbs. We'll see what we get from Audrey, and we're going to meet up with Director in Charge Cutter for lunch. He'll fill us in on any reports of unusual activity from the CPD and the captains from surrounding areas."

"Audrey is..."

"Pretentious."

"A shark," Amy assured him. "I have a feeling that—"

"Hey, I know some great attorneys and they're not all sharks," Hunter protested.

Amy grinned. "Calm down. I know a lot of great attorneys, too. Defense attorneys and prosecutors. Okay, so I deal with the prosecutors more often, but I believe in defense attorneys and I do know a lot of good ones. I wasn't even referring to attorneys. I just think the woman is a shark."

"But a shark—"

"Hard-core. A go-getter."

"That could mean she's just strong and determined."

"Absolutely."

He grinned. "Okay. Let's head on out to see the shark."

Amy hadn't been lying when she'd said she loved Chicago. She'd first come with her parents and brother when she'd been about ten. They'd gone to a jazz festival at Grant Park where they'd listened to great music and stared with pleasure and fascination at Buckingham Fountain. They'd been to the Museum of Science and Industry where her brother had gone crazy over the train exhibit and then on to the Field Museum of Natural History where he'd tried to scare her with stories about mummies coming back to life when the lights went off. Then on to the Shedd Aquarium where their dad had gotten them tickets to put on waders and step into the water with beluga whales.

They'd shopped the Magnificent Mile downtown where she'd stared in wonder at the massive buildings and loved the fact they'd been there for Saint Patrick's Day, when the river had been green.

"The office is just down there a bit past the Sears Tower," Amy said, looking at her phone app.

"A lovely walk," Hunter said.

"What if she's in court? Or with a client? Or wriggles out of seeing us?" she asked him.

Hunter shrugged. "We wait or we find her. That's not so hard."

Amy laughed softly. "Yep. You're a fed. You can figure anything out."

"Hey! What's wrong with feds?"

"Not a thing. Well, you know—"

"Forget I asked."

They walked down the busy street. Somehow, just the few blocks made Amy think about people in general. It was true. Most were decent. Some were kinder than others. But in all, most people just wanted the same things: to love and be loved, have a job that provided for their family, a certain amount of security and some fun with family and friends when a workweek was done. Or just some rest. Most people...

Of course, some were ambitious and aggressive. Those were traits that were okay, so long as ambition and aggression were to move forward and not knock off others along the way.

Some wanted money, more and more of it, badly.

Some wanted power. She'd heard power was like an aphrodisiac to many people.

And this, it seemed, was someone seeking a truly despicable power, killing people as if they were no more than insects in the way.

"There," Hunter said. Then he added, "Wow! Will you look at that!"

"Look at what?" she murmured.

He indicated the sidewalk. She looked down. There was a poster beneath her feet—slightly trampled and dirtied but still legible. There was a picture of Audrey Benson on the paper, along with the words *Audrey Benson for the Senate! Vote for honesty and integrity in government!*

"Senate, huh?" Hunter asked.

"I grant you, our senators have power. But, Hunter, there are two senators from every state. Now, if she were running for president—"

"Maybe she's starting with the Senate," Hunter said. "Then she would be thinking long-range. And this must just be a test flyer. I think she's gearing up for her campaign. Strange, though. Someone who has defended some serious offenders is running on honesty and integrity."

"Maybe she honestly believes all her clients are innocent."

Hunter gave her a skeptical look. "Everyone is entitled to the best defense. Even if they are guilty."

"Devil's advocate?"

"Always have to look at everything from two sides," Hunter told her.

"No, actually, you have to as far as the law goes. Inside, not so much."

He frowned.

"I always act within the law!" she said.

"Ah, but then you're from Florida."

"Hey!"

He laughed. "Just kidding! I wanted to get a rise out of you. I can't wait for that trip to the Florida Keys. We need to play devil's advocate with each other. It's good for reason—and discovery."

"I'm glad you look down as well as up," she told him.

He frowned.

"Down—as in at the pavement. We can ask her about her run for the Senate."

"Ah, yes. Let's move slowly into it, shall we?"

The law offices had a handsome waiting room with several chesterfield sofas, a pod coffee and tea maker and a large-screen TV playing the news. The receptionist sat behind a large mahogany desk with her computer, intercom and matching file cabinets.

Amy displayed her credentials and asked the young woman at the desk if they could please see Audrey Benson.

The young woman, smart and sleek in a high-necked black dress, swept-up hair and artful makeup, looked at her quizzically.

"What is that?" she asked Amy.

"My badge. I'm sorry. I'm with the FDLE—"

"And what's that?"

Amy forced a smile. "Florida Department of Law Enforcement. And—"

"Honey, you're a long way from home. This is Chicago. Illinois."

Hunter stepped forward before Amy could say anything else, producing his badge. "FBI. Stands for Federal Bureau of Investigation. Good all over the country—even in Chicago." He gave it a beat, just as the young woman had done. "Illinois."

"Oh." She suddenly looked flustered. "Well, she said that...well, she isn't in."

Luck, however, was with Amy and Hunter. Audrey Benson, in a white shirt, navy pencil skirt and spike heels, came out into the reception area escorting a middle-aged woman and a teenage boy while speaking evenly but reassuringly.

"I'll be doing my research and getting back to you. It's possible we'll be able to get probation and community service. Now—"

Audrey stopped when she saw Amy and Hunter.

"Yes, what?" the middle-aged woman asked.

"Luke needs to think about life when he's doing that community service," Audrey said sternly. "I'll be in touch soon."

The woman nodded and prodded the teenager toward the door.

"How nice," Hunter told the receptionist. "Audrey does seem to be here."

"Hello, yes, I was with a client as you saw." She glanced at the receptionist. "I guess Rhonda didn't see me slip in after coffee with a client, right, Rhonda?"

"Uh, no. I mean, right!" the receptionist said.

"Come on in, my office is down the hall," Audrey told them.

They followed her down a carpeted hallway and passed

closed wooden doors and expanses of glass-encased conference rooms.

They reached her office where two wooden chairs sat
conveniently in front of her desk, handsomely appointed.
Her law degree was framed and hung on the wall along with
pictures of her meeting with various dignitaries.

"Have a seat, please. I heard about the latest, of course, and
I'm sure you've come to offer me protection again," Audrey
said, swinging around to take her swivel chair and indicate
the wooden chairs before her desk. "I think that...well, no.
I have to admit. My radar wasn't out on David Ghent. He
seemed like any other young man his age. He was serious
about law school, but he also wanted to be a...well, be a kid.
He asked Daisy and me all kinds of questions, and they were
good ones. But every now and then, one of those questions
seemed a bit underhanded. Almost as if...as if he were asking
about ways to cheat the system. And looking back, he was
more interested in me than he was in Daisy, or I should say,
more interested in defense tactics than in prosecuting criminals. But he was a nice kid, basically. I'm so sorry to hear he
must have been wrapped up in all that in some way—and
that he was killed. He didn't deserve that."

"Audrey, he had called me, wanting to come in. Wanting
protective custody," Amy told her.

"How sad! He was killed before he could get to you."

"Audrey," Hunter said. "This is getting worse by the minute. Are you sure you don't want to come and be in protective custody yourself?"

"He was killed in Florida. I'm up here. I'm a defense attorney. And supposedly, I'm the enemy to good prosecutors
everywhere. But we need each other, and I'm loyal to my
clients, but I know how to work with the prosecution, too.

I know when there's a deal to be made that will help law enforcement catch bigger fish. I… I'm sorry. But I do assume you're here because of what happened to David? Oh, and I didn't say anything about the investigation to anyone, I promise. I just…well, the news reports everything within seconds these days. When I heard about David… I don't know what he was into, but I'm sorry. So young to have become involved in such a mess."

"Yes. But we are afraid for you, Audrey," Hunter said.

"We were the ones who discovered David's body," Amy told her quietly.

Audrey nodded thoughtfully.

"We understand you might be on a political trail and realize you want to stay in the public eye, but is it worth it if you're not here to enjoy it?" Hunter asked.

Audrey frowned. "I'm not sure. I've thought about a run. I may be a defense attorney, but there are certain cases I will not touch, and there are many things I believe in—passionately. But I haven't even decided what I want to do. I have thought I would be good. I know the law, and I know many things that need to be done. I know people and causes and…" Her voice trailed and she frowned.

"How did you know I was thinking about a candidacy?"

"We saw a flyer outside," Amy said.

"Outside? Oh, those were done up as a possible promotion. I still have to run!"

"Well, the point is, it's all moot if you're not here, right?"

Audrey sighed, looked down and shook her head. "I'm not in Florida. I didn't see a skunk ape. I don't know anything about anything. I'm serious when I say I'm respected by both sides. Police watch out for me, and I'm either here in my office—and trust me, we have some fine security here—or in a courtroom. One of the guards escorts me out every night. I live in a high-rise just down the street. I know you're thinking of me, but... I will do everything to make sure I'm safe. I promise you. I will not be alone anywhere. I've spoken with the local police. And with officers at the courthouse. I do have people who care about me and are looking after me," she said. "I have your cards, of course." She smiled. "I'm honored, too, that you came up here for me. Well, Celia and Geoff Nevins are local, too. Maybe they'll want to come in and be protected, but I know Geoff feels the same. It was a Florida incident. Ginny Marks talked and put herself out there. Now we know David Ghent was involved, so he probably warned someone she might be dangerous. So...well, thank you. But again, no thank you."

Hunter stood and Amy did the same.

"There is nothing else you remember, right?" Hunter asked her.

Audrey grimaced. "Please! If I knew anything at all, I would have told you by now. You must know that. I'm an officer of the court!"

"Of course," Amy said. "And thank you for your time."

"I would love to be able to give you more," Audrey assured them.

"We know the way out," Hunter said.

They left the office. Amy made sure to thank Rhonda, the receptionist.

When they were out on the street, Hunter said, "How timely for her to walk out just when we heard she wasn't in."

"She couldn't have known we'd be in Chicago," Amy said. "So, it was strange. I told you—shark."

"Attorney, politician!" he said.

She elbowed him in the ribs. "Some people really want to serve their country."

"And you think she does?"

"Okay, I think at best she is a glory hound. But you don't need to play devil's advocate. Liking the limelight does not make a person evil."

"No. Evil deeds make a person evil," Hunter said.

His phone rang.

He answered it quickly, glancing at her with a frown as he listened.

He ended the call, still staring at her strangely.

"What is it?" Amy demanded.

"Cutter."

"Right. We're supposed to meet him for lunch—"

"No. We're supposed to meet him right now, along with Imam Ali and Rabbi Schwartzman of a local mosque and temple."

"Oh, no! Did something happen?"

He shook his head.

"Something didn't happen. We put them on alert. They both reported strange vans parked in their lots and, having been put on alert, they called them in. Separately, of course. When police went for the vans, one was empty, and the driver of the other escaped before backup could arrive to help the two officers chasing him."

"And the vans?"

"Were filled with explosives," Hunter said. "Somehow, together, we were right. The 'red horse' is ready to take this up a notch and kill dozens at worship and start a real war right here in Chicago. Illinois. USA."

13

"Believe it or not, Rabbi Schwartzman and I are good friends," Imam Ali Jabal told them, shaking his head as he leaned back in his chair in his office at the mosque. He was a man in his midforties, with a full, rich beard, dark brown hair and eyes and a lean physique.

He was sincere and earnest as he spoke with them.

"The police gave out the warning, and we'd already spoken to one another." He gave them an odd smile. "Some people can speak about their beliefs and respect another's beliefs, as well. We have lunch once a month—with Father O'Brien—Catholic priest, his church is barely a mile from here—and Father Liffey. He's an Anglican. Liffey is a popular guy—always warns the congregation the sermon will be quick when his teams are going to have a game on a Sunday afternoon. Sure, there are haters. There are haters everywhere. But we don't teach hate here—nor do they. And trust me, hate is something that is taught. What toddler have you ever seen playing at a day-care center where one child even knows there are differences in their color or ethnicity?"

"None," Amy agreed.

"Sir, we believe you," Hunter told him earnestly. He paused. "Is it all right to address you as sir?"

The imam nodded. "We have many titles. We are teachers in my faith, those who bring others to understand the ways of Allah. Call me Imam Ali or sir...and I answer to almost anything."

Hunter glanced at Amy, who was smiling.

"Imam Ali, Amy and I get to see all kinds of things, and certainly, blind hatred is taught. But one day...well, we can hope. And while we're certain you and your fellow religious leaders are friends, we greatly fear—which appears to have been proven—someone is going to try to start a war between you. Not between you, but between those who don't know they're being played. We'll be asking all of you to think hard—to think about your people. Is there anyone you know about who may be angry for a slight—real or perceived—who might have been willing to meet with someone and plant the explosives in the truck?"

The imam was quiet, thoughtful. He suddenly brightened and smiled when there was a tap at the door.

"That will be my friend Rabbi Schwartzman now," Imam Ali said.

Mario Cutter quickly nodded and rose to answer the knock.

There was little to fear from it as the hall was guarded by several of Cutter's people.

The person arriving was indeed Rabbi Schwartzman. He greeted Ali with obvious affection, but he looked worried as he took a chair to join them.

Like Imam Ali, he was in his midforties or maybe fifty, a taller, sturdier man. He had a warm smile; and when he greeted them, he seemed deeply concerned and confused.

"We're stunned. I'll admit, when we heard to be on the lookout for anyone attempting trouble or carrying arms, we thought the government was simply being overly vigilant. I know that attacks have taken place at synagogues and mosques across the country, and that we could be a target. But we've been so fortunate here. Many of us have worked together to promote tolerance and understanding. And... The police told me that while the bombs were homemade— nice to know anyone can build a bomb off the internet— they could have caused tremendous injury and death. But... how can we watch every second, every minute?"

"We'll be watching for you," Mario Cutter promised quietly.

"And still...we don't even know what the one man looked like. The other escaped when the police came, and I don't believe they got a good look at him," the rabbi said. "I hear he was wearing a dark hoodie. They should have stores for crooks that sell dark hoodies! Seems to be what they all wear."

"I'm afraid we'll know soon enough," Amy said.

"How?" Imam Ali asked.

Hunter glanced at the two men and at Cutter briefly; they had to know what they were dealing with.

"Whoever is at the top of this organization, they don't tolerate failure. I believe we'll find a few bodies in the next day or so."

"You mean the would-be killers will be killed?" Imam Ali asked, glancing at the rabbi with a sinking expression. "So…if they had gotten in and been caught, they'd know they'd die, anyway, and there wouldn't be much negotiation with them?"

"We had a man shoot himself rather allow himself to be taken, yes."

"Dear God," Rabbi Schwartzman murmured.

"For the love of Allah!" Imam Ali murmured. "Then we should be afraid. Very afraid."

"Only to the point where fear is useful and creates vigilance," Amy said softly. "I believe you both know we can never let fear rule us, but we do have to be extremely wary, alert to any little oddity and cautious and smart in every way."

"The FBI will be protecting your houses of worship," Hunter said. "What we need from you is help with people. Rabbi, we were just telling Imam Ali we need you to think about those you know among your congregations. Is anyone angry with the country, angry with life? What we're looking for is a person who is feeling put-upon, hurt, betrayed or dissatisfied. A person who may feel they need to strike out. And someone who can be convinced that someone of a different faith intends to persecute them for their own faith."

"Is this…a strange form of a holy war?" Imam Ali asked. "I'm confused. I thought you were here because of gang killings in different states."

"There's nothing holy about this war at all," Hunter assured him. "This is being manipulated by someone who hasn't a faith of their own—other than power and money. They're hoping to escalate the bloodshed."

"This is…terrorism," Imam Ali said.

"To what end?" Rabbi Schwartzman asked.

"We don't really know. The world in chaos, and perhaps someone rising to rule the world. We don't have the full picture yet," Hunter said.

Amy leaned forward. "Do either of you know of such a person? Someone struggling, but anxious to prove their love for their religion?"

"I have to think," Imam Ali said.

"And me," the rabbi murmured. He looked at Hunter. "And we need to speak to our friends in the Christian communities, as well."

"Indeed. Of course, the warning has gone out—" Cutter said.

"They'll understand the seriousness when they hear from us," Imam Ali said. "We will be vigilant, smart and wary." He smiled at Amy. "Everything you said. We will use our fear and put it toward our strength. And I think we'll have a well-publicized supper this evening, and show we are a united front. Putting forth the truth in an American promise that all men—and women—have freedom of religion. Their own religion. Not one religion. We are all free to practice whatever our faith might be."

Hunter couldn't help thinking about his parents then. Now they were clearheaded, smart, savvy and happy to live freely. But he understood how his mother had felt. She hadn't been seeking any specific religion. She had just wanted people to care about other people.

But she had been vulnerable, in rebellion against a world where it had seemed to her material goods meant more than people.

Many things could cause that kind of vulnerability. He didn't believe either of his parents could have been talked into killing another human being for any reason other than self-defense. Of course, this was different, because the puppet master was trying to make it appear houses of worship were after one another for their differences.

But finding the vulnerable was just the same.

He liked these men. Really liked them. They knew they were different from one another, but they wanted to understand and to celebrate those differences.

"A dinner would be great," Hunter said. "A united front. That's a great idea."

He glanced at Cutter.

"A well-protected dinner," Cutter said.

"That will work for me," Rabbi Schwartzman said.

Hunter nodded, looking at Amy. She smiled and rose. "Thank you so much. And please do think about your people. We've been able to stop one man and keep him alive. If we can find others before they fall prey as either killers or instigators and then victims, we can learn more and more. Thank you again."

Everyone in the room stood. The imam and rabbi agreeing they would go through their physical and mental files and come up with the names of anyone who might be feeling disenfranchised—prime for a puppet master.

Heading out they spoke with Cutter, who was a lean, hard and unassuming man, level in his tone, and yet when he spoke it was with authority.

"I can't tell you how relieved we are that you brought a timely warning. This whole thing is absolutely insane. How do you get people to kill for you, set bombs for you…and start with gangs and move on to religions?"

"I wish we had all the answers. Getting someone to talk is a hell of a game," Hunter told him. "I'm hoping these men will be able to help us. I can see someone who is very religious being convinced they're fighting in the name of God—their god as they see him. People have done it for centuries. This is probably easier than getting a gang member to infiltrate another gang and convince them someone is coming after them. We still haven't figured out what happened in the Everglades. We know two of the men who were killed had checked out the area a few days ahead of the event. They'd been promised something. I have a feeling David Ghent, another victim, convinced the other dead men they'd be partners with the killers on a major money-making deal. And the goods to be sold would be delivered in the Everglades in the middle of nowhere. Instead of an equitable partnership, they were murdered."

Cutter nodded. "Garza told me they're still looking for the murderers down there. But he didn't think they'd know anything, other than they'd been told 'the Shoes' were after them, and they had a chance to take them down first. As you are both well aware we have people on it, working national and international levels, plus your team at FDLE, Amy. We know some of the cartels better, but you know the terrain and the people in the state."

"Thank you, sir," Amy told him.

"I'll let you go. I know you want to see the couple that were on that boat. Beats me why anyone would refuse protective custody when this thing is so deadly."

"We saw Audrey Benson already. She's still refusing protection. But she wants to go into politics and also believes she has enough protection what with court officers and local police," Hunter told him.

"Well, try with the couple. I don't know if we'll be able to stop this or not, but..."

"It can't be an 'if,' sir," Hunter told him. "It has to be a 'when'—and the 'when' has to be soon. We don't know how far this can go."

"Call if you need anything, we'll be there. And keep me in the loop."

"We will," Hunter said.

Cutter nodded. "Don't worry about the mosque and the synagogue. Trust me, we've got them covered."

They left him and went out to the car Cutter had provided for them.

"Next stop, Des Plaines, Illinois," Amy said.

"Think they're home from work?" Hunter asked her.

"Do you really think they're back at work already? I'm willing to bet they decided to get out of Florida—"

"And away from us?" he asked her.

She shrugged. "Or away from a bloody massacre."

He was quiet for a minute. "This devil's advocate thing isn't bad. Amy, if we hadn't thought of the religious angle, it could have been bad."

She was thoughtful. "The explosives were homemade. I'm willing to bet that means the 'red horse' dragged young, impressionable men into it. Made them believe they were martyrs for God. And made them believe the other was responsible for their repression."

"Maybe they'll come up with names for us," Hunter said.

Amy sighed softly. "Or bodies," she said.

"Or bodies."

They arrived at the Nevinses' house in Des Plaines. It was a ranch-style home, with flowers bordering a chest-high brick wall. But there was a wooden gate with an intercom to electronically allow entry.

Hunter noted the security cameras at the house.

He could clearly see the one that watched the gate and the front door.

But he wondered if there were cameras to cover the distance of the brick wall. An agile man or woman could hop it easily enough.

Amy pressed the intercom button. A voice came over a call box.

"May I help you?"

"Mrs. Nevins?" Amy said.

There was silence for a minute, and they realized they were being seen from inside via the camera.

"Special Agents Amy Larson and Hunter Forrest?" the voice said quizzically.

"Yes, Mrs. Nevins, we need to speak with you. Please."

"What are you doing out of Florida?" Celia Nevins asked.

"Trying to speak with you."

"Um. Sure."

The gate opened and they walked up a tile path to a brick porch. The door to the house opened as they reached it. Celia Nevins was there. Her husband was right behind her.

"I guess you didn't have to be back to work yet!" Amy said cheerfully.

"Uh—no. We just wanted to come home. After what happened and all," Celia said.

She backed up awkwardly.

"Um…come in."

The front door opened right to a large living room complete with a handsome brick fireplace, soft sofas and chairs and a fifty-two-inch television screen. A pile of knitting lay in a basket on an occasional table by one of the sofas.

"We figured we'd just kick back and watch TV with the rest of our time," Geoff Nevins said.

"Please, we're being so rude, sit," Celia said. She was staring at Amy. "We just didn't expect to see you in Chicago."

"You are a Florida law official, right?" Geoff asked.

"I am. I'm on loan to the FBI," Amy told them.

They sat on the sofa.

"Uh, coffee, tea? Goodness! I sound like a stewardess!" Celia said.

"Flight attendant, dear," her husband said.

"Well, whatever! May I get you anything?" Celia asked.

"No, no, we're fine," Amy said. "We've come because—"

"We heard about it! That the young man on our boat was found in the Everglades, murdered! And his killer hasn't been found. Well, you still don't know who killed those other men, right?"

"Yes, but that's the thing. He's dead. Ginny Marks was attacked, and when her attacker failed, he killed himself, and people still went after his wife and child. We wanted to ask if you remembered anything else at all. And we want to encourage you to accept protective custody."

Geoff Nevins sat in one of the sofas across from Amy and Hunter, hands folded before him. "It's tempting because, of course, we do want to be safe. But you might have noticed, I have a fair amount of security around here—"

"You have a wall that can be easily leaped. Do your cameras cover the entire wall?" Hunter asked.

"Well, no. But my windows and doors have alarms."

"And no matter how good your security is, police can only get here so fast," Amy said.

"But—but we have never had a speck of trouble!" Celia said.

"You were never on a boat before with someone who was

probably the instigator in the attack that left twenty men dead," Amy said.

"Twenty bad men!" Geoff said. He waved a hand in the air. "Yes, the New York thing. More bad men killed in an alley. I can't cry over gang members who kill one another," Geoff said irritably.

"Ginny Marks never hurt anyone. And she was marked for death," Hunter said.

"But she was so ridiculous! Skunk ape," Geoff said. "Maybe someone wanted to kill her just for her stupidity."

"You really feel that way, Mr. Nevins?" Amy asked.

"I just…" He winced and broke off. "I like my life! What if you don't find out what's going on? I don't want to give up my house or people or—"

"Your house will remain your house. If you love people, don't you want to make sure you'll see them again?" Amy asked him.

He looked at his wife and then shook his head.

"You do know," he said, "the world is going to hell. They found vans with bombs in them. Someone is always trying to do something horrible to someone else."

"All the more reason to make sure nothing bad is done to you," Amy said.

Geoff looked at his wife, then looked at Amy and Hunter again.

"What about Audrey Benson?" Geoff asked.

Hunter answered honestly. "No. She feels she's friends with most of the police force, and she's an officer of the court, and therefore she has protection."

"Well, there you go." He tried to joke next. "I mean, seriously, if you were going after someone, would you want it to be Celia and me—or a powerful lawyer like Audrey?"

"I've heard she wants to run for the Senate," Celia said. "She was talking about her political ambitions when we were on the tour."

"See there—even worse! I wouldn't want anything bad to happen to anyone, but don't you sometimes think all of Congress should be scooped up and put out on an island, and we should all start over?"

"Geoff!" Celia said.

"I'm just being honest!" he protested.

"They're federal employees," Celia reminded him.

Amy gave her a tight smile. "Not me. I work for the state of Florida."

Celia frowned. "Then what are you doing here?"

"As I told you, I'm on loan," Amy said.

"You can loan people out?" Celia asked, confused.

"We're actually all part of a task force," Hunter said. "Look, we can't force you to do anything. We can only warn you your lives could seriously be in danger, and we strongly suggest you accept our offer of protection."

They looked at each other again.

Celia murmured, "Geoff, maybe..."

"We've been home, and nothing has happened. Up here, we just suddenly need to worry about whackos now and then, but that's not a personal thing."

Hunter looked at Amy.

"Mr. Nevins, we believe the plot to blow up the mosque and synagogue is related to what has happened elsewhere," he said.

Geoff Nevins gave him a look that insinuated he had to be as unhinged as whoever was dealing with bombs.

"Oh, please!" he said. He shook his head. "I don't have anything else to tell you about what happened in the Everglades, and I don't think bomb-making idiots have anything to do with us! We're agnostic, so we won't be going up in any church bomb. And you know what? I have a shotgun in a case in my closet, and I'm damned good with the thing. Celia can even shoot. Look, I know you mean well. But if Audrey Benson thinks she's going to be okay, then Celia and I aren't giving up our lives over what you *think* may happen. But if we change our minds, we'll call you. And please... Special Agent Larson! I'm sure they need you in Florida. You don't need to fly up here on our account again."

Hunter and Amy rose as one.

"As you wish," he said.

"Um, goodbye, and thank you!" Celia said.

They were already out the door.

Hunter tried to take a deep breath. There was no way in hell he would do it, but it was one of those times when he wanted to deck someone.

"Breathe!" Amy told him.

He stopped at the car. "They're either idiots—or involved," he said.

"Cutter and the cops can keep an eye on them," she said.

"Right. I know."

"Let's get back. We haven't eaten. Dinner and then... hopefully either Imam Ali or Rabbi Schwartzman will have thought of someone."

He nodded. "Right. We haven't eaten. Food would be good."

As they left, he looked back at the Nevinses' house. Cameras, yes. The guy had a shotgun. But could he really believe he could protect himself from a hardened killer—one with everything to lose?

"Steak?" Amy asked.

"You're going to eat meat?"

"Maybe. We'll just pick another steakhouse. One without cute cows at the entry."

He grinned and got into the car.

His phone started to ring. He pulled it out and put it on speaker.

"Special Agent Forrest." It was Mario Cutter. "Your suggestion saved a life. We have a serious situation. Father O'Brien stopped to speak with one of our agents who was arriving to guard the church, and the timing kept him from being in his office...when it exploded. Someone bombed the church."

Father O'Brien seemed like a nice man, a fellow who had walked straight out of Ireland to come tend to a congregation in Chicago.

He looked the part, with snow-white hair, ruddy cheeks and bright green eyes.

And he was polite and courteous, and charming with his accent. He was grateful to Amy and Hunter.

He'd been ordered out of his church so that the explosion could be investigated by the experts. He was standing on the sidewalk outside when Amy and Hunter arrived, shaken, still trembling, but he'd been given the all-clear by the paramedics and was determined to help in any way that he could. And he remembered his manners—and his calling.

"I do believe the Lord is my Shepherd," he told them. "But like as not, I'm grateful my meeting with the Lord will come later. I feel I've a wee bit more to be doing here in this world before I'm joining loved ones in the next!"

"Everything is a team effort, Father," Amy assured him.

He dropped his voice to a whisper, "Aye, lass, but I heard

you and Special Agent Forrest are the part of the team worried for my friends in faith and me, and we are grateful!"

"We're grateful, as well," she assured him.

"God bless you!" he said, reaching out to touch the top of her head. "I don't mean to offend if you don't... I mean—"

"Father, I am always grateful for a blessing. In my line, one might go a long way," she said.

Hunter nodded. "Amen. Father, we have to leave you here. Officers will see to anything that you might need. We need to take a look at what happened."

"Of course!" he said. "I'm due for dinner with my colleagues now, at any rate. We're still having it. I need the support of other communities of faith now more than ever."

Hunter and Amy made their way inside to where Father O'Brien's office had been. The effects of the bomb were shattering. Bits and pieces of wood from what had been sculptures and a cross, Amy believed, were stuck here and there in the remnants of the inferno. Everything was blackened and charred.

She could only imagine the effects on the human body that had most probably been intended.

The smell, too, was staggering. Cloying and tearing at her gag reflexes.

They didn't stay long; members of the bomb squad were there. Amy and Hunter knew to keep their distance and observe. Hunter lifted a hand to one of the investigators who nodded in return.

This was his expertise, and he and his team would discover what they could.

Amy and Hunter were due at the police station where a press conference had been called.

The mayor arrived just as they did. She was a slim and

serious-looking gray-haired woman, smartly dressed in black pumps and a skirt suit with a white shirt beneath.

She exchanged pleasantries with the agents.

"We considered this carefully, of course," she assured Amy. "We were worried about details and left the final decision up to Assistant Director Garza and Director in Charge Cutter. But we need to warn people, they finally decided. And we need to get the word out that Chicago is a city where we believe in unity while embracing our differences, and acts of hatred will not be tolerated."

The mayor went to take her place at the podium in front of the news cameras. She briefly described what had happened, and that a terror attack had been averted. She reminded the citizens of Chicago that they were safe, but that they should stay vigilant for anything out of the ordinary, and look out for one another. Someone was purposely trying to create havoc and cause unrest in the city.

Amy assumed Garza or Cutter would speak. She was stunned when the mayor turned to her, indicating she should explain the case.

Cutter and Garza were both looking at her and Hunter.

"Take it," he said softly. "We'd say the same thing. You're just prettier."

"Depends on who's looking," she told him. But without it turning into an awkward situation, she needed to move. She stepped in front of the cameras.

She tried to be concise, starting with the event in the Everglades, giving no details but stating several people who had barely touched upon the situation had been attacked or killed. She went on to talk about New York and how that led them to believe with a fair amount of certainty there was a criminal working just to sow discord and cause whatever death and mayhem was possible.

"We're lucky this person tried to play a game of hate in a place where it just wouldn't work. And we have task forces in several states working night and day to put an end to what is happening. If you've been involved in any way, if you've been approached, if you even know of anyone who has been approached, every little bit of information helps us. There is a hotline number for information, and I believe...yes—" she saw the mayor indicating it would flash across the screen at the news stations "—the number is dedicated to this situation. Please call. Please ask for help. Your life may be at risk. Thank you. Thank you for being smart and vigilant, and for any help you may be able to provide."

She left the podium. Hunter nodded his approval. She just hoped that anything she'd said hit the right ears, and someone would come forward with new information.

Amy noted on the bedside clock it was just seven when her phone rang. She swung to sitting to reach for the bedside table and answer.

No caller ID.

A distorted voice came to her.

"Special Agent Amy Larson! Far from home and interfering!"

Hunter was awake, staring at her. She hit the speaker button.

"This is Special Agent Larson, yes. What do you want?"

"I want you to know the 'red horse' will ride. You just don't understand how far and how fast! Neither does that fed you sleep with. He's a real...well, just a gem. You think you're so clever, between you. You don't know how hard and fast that 'red horse' can go. But you will. You'll see soon enough!"

The line went silent.

14

"A lawyer who wants to be a politician or a middle-aged couple who just go about suburban life? On a boat in the Everglades. So, which one is it?" Hunter asked Amy.

Amy managed a smile.

"I guess most people would say politician. Some believe the word *politician* is synonymous with liar. But maybe this goes against type. I don't know. Hunter, if David Ghent was the person on the boat who had the phone, and Ginny probably did hear him call his accomplice an 'ass...'" She hesitated. "We still don't have anything to lead us to the person who was there making sure the job was done."

"Well, we have a problem in general. We don't know who killed the men in the Everglades, and we don't know who killed the men in New York, and worse—we don't know who is trying to create war here in Chicago."

They were heading to the local offices where they'd meet up with Cutter and video-link with Garza and Hampton. The distance wasn't far; they could have walked it. But Hunter wanted the car, since he was afraid they'd have to move at a moment's notice.

"Their tech people will check the call," Amy said.

"Yep. But it will be a burner."

"But maybe they can trace the location of the call," Amy said.

"Here's hoping."

They had just parked when Amy's phone rang.

She glanced at the phone and at Hunter.

"Just a number, no ID," she told him. She answered it and hit the speaker button almost instantly. "Special Agent Larson, FDLE," she said.

A whispery voice came through her phone.

"Um, Miss Larson. I mean, Special Agent Larson. I... I'm scared. Is there a way to talk to you where no one else is around? I mean, where no one can see me talk to you or hear me talk to you. I don't know. I need to hang up. I'm scared. All this is bad, so bad."

"Please don't hang up," Amy said quickly. "If you can help in any way..."

"I don't know. I just think that maybe... I think I know someone who may have been involved with those bombs. But I'm afraid to talk. I'm at school. I go to the institute. I have a friend and his major is in chemistry and..."

The voice trailed. Obviously, it was that of a young person, a boy, Hunter believed.

"This friend of yours—"

"I mean, we aren't close friends. I see him at the institute.

I want to be nice because no one else hangs out with him. I'm not popular, but I have a few friends."

"You think he might build bombs?" Amy asked softly.

The caller didn't answer the question. He kept talking, but he seemed to be speaking to himself. "He talks about building bombs, and about how simple it is to build a bomb. He's such a strange dude, a loner, kind of creepy looking. I always try to be nice to him. But I'm a nerd and an introvert myself, and loners can get lonely, and…"

Hunter motioned to her he had an idea. He pretended to be writing, then reached out his hand; she understood and passed him her sketch pad. He wrote on it quickly.

Tell him we'll come to his school. A young agent will get him into a car while we visit the dean. He didn't take the time to write why it would appear to be a simple visit with an escort, but Hunter knew that the dean at the science institute was a military vet—a man who had been a demolitions expert in the field.

But Amy nodded, whether she knew his reasoning or not.

"Hey, we're grateful for your help. What's your name?" Amy asked quietly.

The boy didn't answer the question, but just started talking again.

"I'm scared. I'm so scared. I mean, if I'm right, and he knew I was talking to you…"

"Okay, slow down," she said softly. "First, I'm going to be honest. I'm here with my partner—"

"The tall guy who was waiting for you when you finished speaking?"

"Yes, that's Hunter. And I think it is important for you to tell us what you know. This person might be responsible for people dying, and we don't want more people to die."

"I know, I know, I don't want people to get killed! But I don't want to die. I shouldn't have called."

"No, no, you did the right thing. What is your name? Tell me, please."

"Mike."

"Mike—what?" Amy asked softly.

"Mike Norcross," he breathed.

"Thank you," Amy said.

Mike started to laugh nervously.

"You're welcome. But you could have gotten my name through my phone. I'm not...well, I wouldn't even know how to get a 'burner' phone. My mom still pays my phone bill."

"My mom and dad paid my phone bill when I was in college," Amy told him. "We can guarantee your safety—"

"Doesn't sound like anyone can guarantee anyone's safety. There's a whole lot of dead people!"

Hunter mouthed the word, "School."

Amy nodded.

"Mike, you say you're at the institute. You're there now?"

"Yeah, I'm hiding out in the back of the library. I can see anybody coming in from here. But I don't know what I'd do if he did come in. I mean, unless he was right here, he wouldn't know who I was talking to. If I hang up quickly—"

"Mike, this is Hunter Forrest. The tall guy. Okay, so listen," Hunter said. "We'll arrange to come to your school as though we're just there to speak with the dean. If I remember right, he's a genius, especially when it comes to fireworks and explosions, chemical reactions."

"Yeah, Dean Braxton is supposed to be a genius. He's a good guy."

"Okay, we'll have another agent with us. He'll pretend

to be an out-of-town relative, and he'll come and get you out of one of your classes. We'll see you're clear of the place and meet up at one of the local offices where no one will see you enter or leave—straight through a garage entry."

"Right. I don't want to die. But...he's talked to me about building bombs. About how easy it would be and how a single bomb could cause all kinds of crazy confusion. It's not always the politicians who will rule the world—it's the bomb-makers."

"Go about your normal day," Amy said. "Special Agent Forrest and I will head there straightaway. Mike, how will we know you? And please, what is the name of the friend you're talking about?"

"What if I'm wrong?"

"He'll never know you were involved in any way."

There was a beat of silence and then Mike said, "Owen. Owen Thompson."

"Thank you. Now how will Director in Charge Cutter know who you are?"

"I'm wearing a plaid shirt in blues and greens, blue jeans. Um, I've got longish hair—brown. Okay, that's me, easy. How will I know who to go with? How will I know it isn't someone who wants to kill me?"

"Mike, I'm going to get the big man in charge up here to be your pretend uncle. His name is Mario Cutter. He's tall, gray-haired, wears a suit, and I'll see that he has a bandage on his cheek. He'll find you, though. When you see him, make sure to act like he's your long-lost uncle Mario, and you can't wait to spend time with him. Where are you supposed to be now?"

"Advanced Calculus."

"He'll find you there."

"Okay. And you're coming now. Straightaway? You promise?"

"We promise."

Amy cast her head to the side, giving Hunter a quizzical look as she asked Mike, "How did you get my number? This isn't the hotline that was shown at the press conference."

"I watched you talk. I believe you mean to...save people, I guess. So, I looked you up. Your contact info is on the FDLE website. Hundreds of people will call that hotline. If I was going to call, I needed help fast."

"Smart kid."

"I hope so. I guess that's why I'm at the institute."

Amy smiled. "All right. See you soon."

Hunter was already dialing Cutter. He'd spoken to him earlier, to report the phone call Amy had received when they were just waking up.

Now, he asked him to meet the boy who had called Amy. And to start the team researching background on Owen Thompson.

"We've received hundreds of calls, you know. Fielding them is a nightmare. One lady said she knows her neighbor is crazy because he talks to his dog. You're sure this kid is the real deal?"

"What he's saying about his friend fits the profile of someone easily deluded into believing blowing up a place of worship would be a good thing." Hunter gave Amy a grimace Cutter couldn't see. "You weren't on camera. And you're careful to stay out of the news, from what I understand. It's unlikely the kids who see you will connect you with law enforcement of any kind."

"I'll get ahold of the dean, tell him you'll be coming to

his office," Cutter said. "And I'm taking the kid to the satellite office, garage entrance."

"Yes, sir. And thanks for paving the way to the dean's office. We'll distract anyone from wondering about a random student and his uncle Mario. There's no surprise in us consulting with an expert in the field."

"Good thing the kid wasn't an art major. But you'd have figured something."

"Sir, you need a bandage on your face."

"What?"

"A bandage. That's how he'll recognize beyond a doubt it is you."

Cutter muttered softly.

They ended the call.

"Let's go get our kid," he said to her.

As they approached the institute, Amy thought about Chicago: the impressive buildings downtown, the river and the pier—and then how one passed Grant Park, the beautiful fountain and miles of space that wasn't so crowded and allowed for the museums and the aquarium. She had friends who lived in the city or were from there, and they liked to joke about the weather. It could be bitterly cold in winter and scorching hot in the summer. According to them, they had to have bad weather; because if they didn't, everyone would want to live there.

Amy had to admit that since she'd been born in a state where snow never fell, she wasn't sure she could get used to such extreme, changeable weather. She glanced at Hunter as they drove. She had been "loaned" to the FBI. She was still an employee of the state of Florida, but it made her wonder.

Where did they go when this was over? Assuming there was a time when it would be over.

"Do you think Mike Norcross knows the real would-be bomber?" Hunter asked, and she wasn't sure if he was asking her or himself.

"More than one person had to be involved."

He nodded. "There's a text from Cutter. Want to read it?"

She pulled out her own phone; they were all receiving the same information at the same time when anyone had anything relevant to report.

The text had come via Garza.

Amy read, "'Vans stolen separately a few days apart last week. Disappeared, making the police believe they were stolen and kept in a garage until they were to be used transporting bombs.'" She paused and looked over at Hunter. "There had to have been several people involved."

"One person or two people to steal the vans. Two driving. Whether they were just to deliver the materials or set them up is another question. We need to talk to Mike and make sure he is safe, and then see what we can discover about Owen Thompson."

"I wonder if they're getting anywhere in Florida," Amy said.

"Something will break," Hunter assured her. "There is so much they need to sort through. But there was something really important about the call you received this morning."

"That we weren't able to have the last number traced?"

"It's going to be a burner phone, we know that. No, I think the call was made out of frustration this time. We stopped something from happening. The 'red horse' had to swerve."

"And the 'red horse' is probably pretty angry."

"I would assume."

Amy realized Hunter had parked the car. She looked up at the facade of the institute and wondered which of the architects known to create in the area had imagined the great white buildings, the columns and the spaces of green in between.

"Let's go."

"There's such amazing architecture in Chicago," she said.

He'd been walking and he turned back with a smile. "Maybe we'll find time for a Frank Lloyd Wright tour," he told her.

She made a face at him. "Seriously?"

"Yes, seriously."

Hunter had long strides, but she could and did keep up with him. As they headed for the administration building, she saw Director in Charge Mario Cutter had also arrived. He was looking at his phone. He'd drawn up an internet map of the institute, she thought, and was looking for where to go.

He didn't glance toward them.

There was, however, a bandage on his cheek.

"Too bad we don't have Ryan Anders up here," Hunter said quietly.

"Why don't we get him? I mean, your local people are great, but it would be good to have Ryan, especially since he seems to have an entire Broadway basket of identities to don. And he's familiar with the case."

They found the office of Dean Vince Braxton. The man was expecting them and came out to meet them when his secretary announced their arrival.

"Welcome, and I'm hoping I can be of some assistance.

Now, I haven't seen the mechanisms, but I can tell you what I surmise from my experience."

Braxton looked like a dean should look: tall, lean, a little world-weary, both serious and empathetic. Amy knew from Hunter that he'd been in the service, called upon to defuse many an enemy creation. She could imagine his military years had been tough, but they had also forged him into a man who could run such a school and be admired and respected by his students.

He led them into his office. "I can't tell you anything the police and FBI experts couldn't tell you about the bomb. And you probably know that. I'm assuming you've come to talk about my students."

Hunter nodded. "The explosives experts have said that there were remnants of cardboard, and they believe that the bomb was in a box on the Father's desk, a pipe bomb with a timer set to explode. One that could have been created by an enterprising student—or by someone who took a simple course online. It's amazing what one can learn on the internet. Though I bet there aren't that many people who sit around idly thinking they want to take an internet course in bomb-making."

"Well, I think we'd all be surprised by what some folks do. I have several dozen students here who could create the kind of explosives that were confiscated. But I understand a priest is alive because he was summoned from his office right before a bomb exploded." He walked around his desk and took his chair and indicated the seats before the desk. "Please."

They sat.

"Thankfully, an officer stopped Father O'Brien to speak with him before he entered," Amy said. "We don't know who might have been in his office. No one noticed anyone in the parking lot and no one noticed anyone heading in. There are no cameras. And with what happened, it was just a matter of lucky timing."

"I've been thinking about it, and I've pulled up a list of students who seem to like to play with fire—more or less. I believe two, however, are genuinely looking to join law enforcement in the field. And two are intending military careers, and one has a dad with fire rescue. I've noted all that. Anyway, I don't know that any one of these kids is the culprit you're looking for, but I did my best."

He handed them both sheets of paper. There was a printer right in the office; Amy didn't think he'd wanted to share any of this with anyone—not even his secretary. He'd done the collecting and printing himself.

She scanned through his list.

The name Owen Thompson was on it.

She looked at Dean Braxton.

"What can you tell me about Owen Thompson? He's here on scholarship?"

"Brilliant kid—just brilliant. But he's got a chip on his shoulder a mile wide. Sad life. My heart kind of bleeds for the kid. His mother was an alcoholic who died in a house fire when he was four—luckily, he was already in foster care, taken away due to neglect. Thompson was the mother's name—there is no father listed on his birth certificate. Unknown. He was tossed around from house to house, but graduated at the head of his class, already having university credits. He lives in a tiny apartment in a snowbird's basement rent free—all he needs to do is check the pipes and keep the house going through the winter. If he has friends, I don't know who they are."

A snowbird's basement. A perfect place to construct bombs without being bothered.

"Thank you. We'll be studying these. And please don't worry. If anyone knows we were here, it was strictly to learn what you could tell us about the bombs."

"I appreciate that," Braxton said, nodding. "That's it?"

"That's it. We have to meet up with our task force," Hunter said. He carefully folded his paper, seeing Amy did the same. They thanked him and left.

"We'll talk to Mike Norcross, and I'll see what Cutter can do about getting us into Owen Thompson's basement apartment."

"If the owners of the house give us permission—"

"Yes. If they give us permission, we're home free," Hunter said.

"You know where you're going?" she asked. "You've been here before?"

"Briefly, a couple of years ago." He glanced her way and made a face. "What appeared to be a ritualistic killing. It turned out the husband had taken out a huge insurance policy on the wife, who was in the way of his new relationship. He figured if he killed her in a bizarre manner, they'd suspect Wiccans, satanists or someone else. He thought he had a great plan—he just didn't realize he'd be leaving his DNA all over."

"Ah," Amy said. "You've had some gruesome cases."

He glanced her way. "A few. Other than those we've dealt with together. And so have you. Dismembered bodies in oil drums in the muck in the Everglades."

"Right. Yeah, well, that one wasn't pleasant."

They hit a call button to enter the gated garage. Cutter and Mike Norcross were waiting at the elevators.

Mike was, Hunter thought, a good-looking young man despite his lack of confidence in himself. His hair was long and curling around his neck. He was tall and almost skinny but had a nicely crafted face and large brown eyes that registered his nervousness. He clutched his computer case to his chest.

"I have a conference room ready for us," Cutter told them. "Let's get settled."

Amy grinned and glanced at Hunter. The bandage was still on Cutter's cheek.

"Ah, sir, you've got something there," Amy said.

Cutter scowled and reached for his face. "A bandage, right on my face? Seriously, you couldn't think of something else?"

"There wasn't time to have you shave your head," Hunter told him seriously.

Cutter looked as if he was about to growl, but Hunter was glad he had joked.

Mike smiled at last.

"Let's go," Cutter muttered.

In a matter of minutes, they were together in a small conference room.

When Amy glanced at Hunter, he nodded. She should take the lead now. Mike Norcross had called Amy based on seeing her speak on TV. He believed in her.

Cutter sat down to watch and listen.

"Mike," Amy told him. "We understand your friend Owen had a horrible childhood. Did he ever talk to you about that?"

Mike nodded. "Yeah, but...well, he said it just all sucked. He always said people treated him as if he was a creep— but a new world order was coming. Guys like him, they'd rise above."

"Did he have anything in particular against the Jewish faith, Catholicism or Islam?"

"No, he mocked them all equally. The real gods were not in any kind of heaven. They were aliens. He had theories about all the different structures around the globe that show a greater power came in the past. And when they come back, they will want allegiance. But… I just thought that…well, I mean, I watch shows about 'ancient' aliens, too. I mean…" His voice trailed.

"Do you have any evidence he might have created the bombs we discovered?" Amy asked him.

"No, but I actually went by his place the other day. I don't live that far from him. We're both just a bit north of the airport. Suburbia, except I'm in an apartment with two other guys. He's in a basement. Anyway, I was going out for a snack. I thought I'd see if he wanted to come with. Except he didn't invite me in. He came out of the main house. Most of the time people invite you in if you know them, and you stop by. But he was really weird about it. But, I mean, that's not evidence."

"Did you ever see a van at his place?" Hunter asked quietly.

"At his place? No. But once, a couple of days ago, I did see a florist's van across the street from the house where he lives." Mike looked at them and let out a long shaky breath. "Should I be afraid?"

"Would you like to stay here tonight?" Cutter asked him. "We have a room. Dull, plain, but it has a television and cable."

Mike nodded, frowning. "Are you going to go see Owen?"

"We'll be paying him a visit. But we'll say we're checking up on several students," Amy assured him. "Still, this place is filled with good people and if you need anything they'll get it for you."

"Maybe I will stay here. Tonight. Until I can quit acting so nervous," Mike said.

"Well, that's true," Amy said. "Don't give yourself away. Do you play poker?"

"Hell, no. Everyone would know what I had!"

"Stay here tonight. We're going to see Owen from here," Amy assured him.

"But what will you find? He'll come out the main house. And you can't just—"

Cutter leaned forward. "We have permission from Mr. and Mrs. Englewood to check out and safeguard their property. Owen will be inviting us in whether he likes it or not."

Hunter glanced at Cutter, giving him a nod of admiration. Cutter had moved quickly.

They left Mike with one of the satellite's young cyber agents who was quickly setting Mike at ease.

"Wonder if we've just created a future cyber agent," Amy murmured.

"Maybe," Hunter said.

"SWAT will be joining us," Cutter told them. "Because we are going in."

"Did you want to let me try to reach him first?" Amy began.

"Yep. I'll give you all of three minutes," Cutter told her.

They took one car with Hunter driving. They had barely arrived when police cars rolled in behind them and officers poured out taking up positions.

Hunter almost stopped Amy from getting out of the car to walk to the door.

"I can take this one—"

"Hunter, Mike trusted me. Maybe Owen will trust me, too."

"Right."

They walked to the front door together. They rang the bell, and there was nothing. They rang again. Nothing.

"We'll have to break it—"

"It's open," Hunter said, frowning as he realized the door had not been fully shut.

There had been rain recently. The wooden door and frame were swollen.

He shoved against the door with his shoulder, turning to wave at Cutter.

Several officers scampered after them. They all entered the house, moving in different directions, calling softly to one another when each room had been searched.

"Clear!"

"The basement," Amy whispered. "The entrance is usually through the kitchen."

She hurried back around to the kitchen. Hunter followed.

Like the front door, someone maybe had thought they had fully closed the basement door.

But it wasn't locked.

Hunter completely opened the door so they could enter.

Carpeted stairs led the way down.

There was light.

The basement had been finished and made into a pleasant apartment, carpeted, with a futon bed, a desk, coffee table, TV and several dressers.

Books lay about, a few open.

The area appeared small, but Hunter realized there was another room behind it; there was an opening past a kitchenette that featured just a small refrigerator and countertop and microwave.

Their weapons drawn, he looked at Amy and indicated he was going first to the left; she fell back and to the right.

When he walked around the wall, he came upon a workshop.

Maybe the owner of the house used it sometimes to store firewood and to whittle pieces from wood; there were carved horses and dogs and other little creatures on the shelf.

There were rows of tables there, as well, with beakers and burners and other paraphernalia.

There was also a large barrel that appeared to hold gunpowder.

"Hunter!" Amy cried.

He turned to look.

Owen Thompson had suffered the same fate as others who had failed the "red horse." He lay on the floor, a stream of blood pooling from his sliced neck.

Amy had already moved; she was down by his side.

She looked up at Hunter.

"Hunter, he's still alive! We need medical help and an ambulance—now!"

15

Amy was grateful that Garza, Cutter and Hunter all agreed she should be the one to speak with Mike Norcross after the doctors told them Owen would live. They had found the student in the nick of time to save his life. His assassin just hadn't been that good; he'd missed both major blood vessels in the neck. Owen had lost enough blood and oxygen to pass out, and so he'd been alive but unconscious and unable to dial a phone himself. He would have slowly bled out, but they were able to stop the bleeding before that happened.

They didn't know when they could speak with Owen, but he was going to live.

Mike was sitting at the end of the bed in the room at the satellite office, munching on chips and playing a video game, when Amy and Hunter returned from the hospital. Amy briefly explained it all to Mike.

"Oh, God!" he breathed, and he seemed confused. "But why... I mean, did he make the bombs?"

"Yes."

"Then why would they try to kill him?"

"There is a hierarchy to this, and they rule through fear. You sucker people in, and once they're in, they quickly learn death is the only way out." She paused and shook her head. "All-out war," she explained.

"Um...do you think anyone knows that I talked to you?"

She shook her head.

"There were a lot of people out at the house, but everyone moved quickly. There might have been a neighbor or two who saw something, but we were all out of there before the media showed up. We managed to get Owen out and into an ambulance. As far as the person who was ordered to kill him knows, he is dead. He'll just be a no-show at his classes for a while. He's in the hospital under an assumed name. We've managed to keep everything about it quiet. Since he lived alone in the basement and the family was gone, there would have been no one there to find the body for days, which gives us some time. No media, no one to announce he was found alive or dead."

"But neighbors saw, right?"

Amy nodded. "Yes, and they'll call the family. The family will say they heard about a break-in but the police checked the house out and everything was all right."

"Yeah," Mike said dully. "I guess... I mean, decomposing bodies smell, but it would be a while before it was bad enough for a mail carrier or a garbage man or anyone to notice."

"You saved his life."

"I saved the life of someone who wanted to kill others," Mike said, shaking his head. "Maybe... I don't know. What will happen to him?"

Amy shook her head. "I'm not sure. He was involved in conspiracy to commit murder, but thankfully no one died from his bombs. I believe it will depend on Owen."

"But—"

"He may help us save other lives, Mike, so what you've done is great."

He digested her words for a minute and smiled. "You know what?"

"What?"

"I don't think I have what it takes to run around the way you do—I'm kind of a coward. But I sure like that cyber guy who has been helping me. I think I have skills, too. Owen is a genius, but I'm close. I'm going to look into the FBI!"

"That's great. Anyway, I just wanted to see you myself. I wanted to thank you. You just said you're a coward. You're not. You were afraid, but you called me. We get to learn that courage doesn't mean not being afraid—it means doing the right thing even if you are afraid. I see you as very brave."

He beamed.

From his spot by the door, Hunter added, "Yeah, kid, you did good."

"Thanks. Could I stay here tonight, anyway?"

"You sure can," Hunter said.

"We'll see you later, then," Amy told him.

"Okay," Mike said happily.

Amy joined Hunter in the hallway, knowing he was anxious to talk to her.

"Owen is awake. We've been warned he can't talk long—

his throat is pretty messed up. But he's aware enough to mouth words and write. Garza was with him for a few minutes, but he figured we had the right to be there and I'm still lead on all this, so..."

"Let's get to the hospital!"

As they drove, Hunter told Amy, "According to Garza, we did—thanks to Mike—save someone who might give us solid leads. The kid has been crying. He didn't realize he would be killed. Apparently, he never got word on what happened to those who failed, even if the failure wasn't their fault."

"What will happen to him, Hunter?"

Hunter shook his head. "I don't know. He's not underage, so he'll face charges as an adult. But the justice system is often willing to make deals, and this kid seems to want to come clean. Of course, the higher-ups in this organization have been careful. But since they seem to depend on everyone either following through or committing suicide, they're bound to make a mistake somewhere along the line. And a mistake has been made."

"Let's hope."

"We'll see what he has to say."

It wasn't long before they reached the hospital and found Garza pacing the hallway and probably irritating the nurses. Owen was in an intensive care ward, but other FBI agents were stationed at various vantage points to the room.

They weren't going to lose their witness.

"Thank God you got here," Garza said. "The doctors have to look after the life of the patient. But they say he can talk for five minutes, no more. I was in with him briefly, then spoke with his physician in charge, and decided to wait for the other four and a half minutes." He looked at Amy. "The other kid called you to talk about this kid, and…you have the right combination of authority and empathy, so let's see what you can get."

They walked into the intensive care unit together.

"Owen, these are the two agents who saved your life. Anything you can tell them will help us and help you, too."

The boy was attached to an IV and had an oxygen tube in his nose.

It was difficult to believe he could have engineered bombs to kill numerous people.

He looked like any other twenty-year-old—an adult by many standards, still a kid in so many ways. Like Mike, Owen had long hair, but his was a soft dark blond.

She hadn't really noted his hair color before; his head had been plastered with blood.

His eyes were large and green. His face was thin, as was his body, which seemed especially so beneath the hospital sheets and with all the machinery connected to him.

Amy thought about a way to speak to him, to try to draw him out.

But to her surprise, he spoke in a whisper, exerting himself in his effort to get his words out.

"I don't want to die. I didn't realize… I thought I was a warrior against fools. We needed to clear the way. They were wrong. They were leading people in a…"

His voice faded in a gasp and Amy hurried to his side. She placed a hand on his. "Shhh, please, slow down, we'll get to everything. You're not going to die. You must be careful, but you're not going to die. The doctors say you'll make it."

He motioned for paper, tears in his eyes.

He wrote quickly with surprisingly good cursive hand-writing. Amy read silently as he wrote.

Maybe I don't deserve to live. People could have died. But I did what I was told. And they came to kill me, anyway. They laughed. I failed. But I wasn't one of the drivers.

"Who came to kill you?" she asked softly.

Don't know them, he wrote. *I think I've seen them. I think they live somewhere near. But they weren't the drivers.*

"Did you know either of the drivers?" Amy asked him. "The van drivers who picked up the bombs from you?"

To her surprise, he stared solemnly. And wrote again.

One. Works at convenience store down the street. Only ever saw him once before. I think he's about thirty. Dark hair. Maybe 5'10". Never saw the other guy before.

"Who had you make the bombs?" Amy asked.

She was startled when he wrote, *The red horse.*

She glanced over at Hunter and Garza. Hunter was close enough to have read what was written. He nodded, indicating she needed to show the written answers to Garza.

But first she asked, "Who is the 'red horse'?"

He wrote, *Voice on the phone.*

A nurse poked her head in the door. "Time is up," she said softly.

Amy nodded and squeezed Owen's hand.

"We'll be back. Be a good patient. You need to heal. I need you strong to talk to me."

He grabbed her hand. "They'll try to kill me again," he whispered hoarsely.

She shook her head. "They don't know you're still alive," she told him. "And there will be several FBI agents looking out for you. They'll be here. No one is going to get to you here, Owen. I promise. Just do what your doctors and nurses say."

She offered him a smile.

He grimaced, in pain physically and mentally. Maybe he had never planned to be a terrorist; he'd just been vulnerable.

She squeezed his hand again, then gently pulled her hand away.

Hunter and Garza were already out in the hallway. Garza was arguing with a nurse. And he was winning.

"One of my agents will be here, and in his room, through the night," Garza said firmly. "This young man is our link to the health and welfare of a number of people so large we can't even begin to imagine. The agent will sit out of the way, but he will be here. And he will need to know every time someone walks in here with any kind of medication for that IV—it's to be given with two health care workers in the room. No one is slipping this boy anything he shouldn't be having."

"Sir!" the nurse said. "We know who works here—"

"Two people verify every medication. And my agent will be here. Right here."

"Yes, sir," the nurse said, giving up.

Amy was glad.

In her experience, things had happened to people even when they were in a hospital. A clever person could easily appear to be a nurse or doctor—and slip something deadly into an IV.

"All right, I'll be here, standing right in the hallway, until my agent gets here," Garza said. He offered the nurse a nod. "Thank you. And if the doctor says we can question him again, we'll be back."

"Whatever you say," the nurse mumbled. She gave Hunter and Amy an emotionless smile and moved on to the nursing station.

"Get back to the office—teleconference with John Schultz.

He's got something—not much, but something. I have a young man on his way in. One of my most trusted young agents. He'll make sure nothing happens here. I should be right behind you. And I have agents headed out to the convenience store—luckily, there's only one convenience store near the house where Owen was living."

"If the 'red horse' has already made an attempt on Owen's life just for the bombs being discovered before they could be detonated, I don't see life boding well for the clerk. There's not much to go on, but the agents will need to find this guy fast."

"Right," Garza said. "I sent good people. If there's any way possible, they'll get to that driver before the 'red horse' does."

"Great. What does John have?" Hunter asked, frowning.

"I'm afraid it's not going to help us here. But a man came into the FDLE office. He claimed he had nothing to do with it, but he knew who killed the men in the Everglades. Members of a cartel we have some data on—not much. A group called the Islanders. I'll let John explain." He sighed deeply. "It always comes down to a voice. And that voice, it seems, knows how to manipulate different people in different ways. A voice on the phone. Saying the right thing to the right people—and carrying through with executions for failure. Anyway, John can tell you more."

"All right. Thanks," Hunter told him.

They left Garza in the hallway to head back for the telecom.

Driving back to the office, Hunter glanced at Amy and said, "I'm willing to bet the 'voice' is the same 'voice' who calls you."

She nodded. "You're right. But someone who is such a

puppet master…why send a horse to us, and why call me? The 'voice' has never tried to dissuade me from anything—it even told me the truth about New York. They're taunting me."

"Yes, this 'voice' wants to lord it over law enforcement. Show that he or she or they will do what they intend to do, and we'll be powerless."

"Wait…but they did make a mistake," Amy said. "Hunter, we need to go back to the hospital after the meeting. When they let me, I need to talk to Owen again."

"All he had was a voice," Hunter said softly.

"No. Whoever tried to kill him. He said 'they.' That he thought he'd seen *them* before, that he thought *they* live somewhere near. He meant more than one person. And they live somewhere in the vicinity. Together? Like a husband and wife? We really needed to talk longer."

"Ethically, we have to be glad our doctors protect their patients. We will speak with him again. And it's important now to find out more about the events down in Florida."

Amy nodded. But she had to say, "Celia and Geoff Nevins."

"Anything's possible. We'll follow up. But without more, all we can do is to talk to them again. We have nothing for a warrant—not unless we can get more from Owen. So we're not prejudiced when he's able to talk, why don't you do your sketch artist thing and get him to describe the people who attacked him?"

"Right."

To Amy's surprise, Hunter suddenly swung the car around in a U-turn.

She looked at him with surprise.

"We're going to head back to the hospital. The second we can talk again, you need to make those sketches."

"Hunter, they won't prove—"

"They'll be enough to get us in. And if they realize Owen is alive and he can swear under oath they attempted to kill them, well, it will be something."

"All right. But we're supposed to talk to John."

"We'll do fine from my phone. Secure line. And if we're right on this...the rest of it is going to be tying up loose ends."

In the parking lot, Hunter put the call through to John.

"Hey, guys, things are heating up down here, but I understand they're heating up in the North, too."

"You talked to Mickey and to Garza?" Amy asked.

"Yes, I did. But Garza said things were popping there, and he'd let me give you the whole nine yards. So, I'll bring you up to speed. We have another man for WITSEC. His name is Henri Thayne, and he was involved with a cartel called the Islanders. Like the men killed, he was part of their street gang and a petty pusher. But he was leaving a meeting outside a bar—David Ghent's hangout—when he heard someone telling his boss that Los Zapatos were planning to start picking Islanders off, one by one, because he was supposedly taking over their territory. The headman of the Islanders was told—probably by our dead instigator, David Ghent—that there was a plan to start cleaning out his workforce. I guess he believed the threat. So, in turn, the big boss of the Islanders sent out an offer, claiming that he and his crew needed help to push a big shipment of cocaine—a really big one. It would be lucrative for them all since they didn't dare sit on it, and it needed to move quickly. Everyone would be told where to meet to receive shipments of the drug. It was a safe place for a deal to go down, and they'd know that when they saw it. Apparently, Jimmy's 'fishermen' in camouflage went to check it out first, and they saw that it was out of the way. So the Zapatos gang members went to get their drugs and we all know what happened instead. Henri's given us names of people he believes were involved, since he claims he wasn't among them. We'll pick them up and get the questioning going. The good thing is that I think we get our hands on some of the higher-ups in the local drug trade. The bad thing is, with David Ghent dead, I don't think it will bring us any closer to the puppet master on the whole deal," John finished. "So, I hear you saved a would-be bomber's life. Are you getting anything from him?"

"Something, though we don't know what yet," Hunter told him. "We're headed back to the hospital. Our bomb-maker said 'they' regarding the people who tried to kill him. And he believes he's seen them in the neighborhood. Celia and Geoff Nevins don't live in the same neighborhood, but they're not that far. Garza and Cutter have people out looking for the man who was one of the drivers who works at a convenience store. We're going to try to hone in on Owen's would-be killers."

"Who may already be dead," John said. "Failure doesn't pay."

"But no one knows yet that Owen isn't dead. Neighbors saw cops and all kinds of stuff going on, but they were told it was just a break-in," Amy said. "His would-be killers are still in the good graces of the 'red horse.' And maybe they're higher up in the chain than some of those who were so quickly executed. At any rate, it's our strongest lead."

"Okay, then. We'll keep working here and see if there is

anything that can lead back to someone higher up the chain. Keep me posted," John said.

"Will do," Hunter promised.

They left the car and headed back into the hospital. When they reached the unit where Owen was being cared for, they saw Garza was gone—and in his place was a young agent who looked as if he'd be a great linebacker for a pro football team. But he had seen Hunter and Amy at the press conference, and he quickly met with them in the hall.

"He's been resting quietly. They gave him more plasma, and like Garza told me, I had two people signing off on it even though I recognized the doctor and the nurse involved," he told them. "Special Agent Hal Hooper, by the way."

"Nice to meet you," Hunter told him. "We're going to wait until they say he can talk again."

"Apparently, he's doing fairly well. He slept a bit when I first got here. They seem pleased with his progress."

"That's great. I'll find the doctor," Hunter said.

Amy nodded as Hunter walked off.

Hal Hooper smiled at her. "You spoke well, by the way. At that press conference. You have the ability to make people smart rather than panicky."

"Thank you. I'll admit, like anyone, I've been involved with some rough cases. But never anything like this."

"I don't think any of us has ever been involved in something like this," Hooper said. He shrugged. "Garza said I was not to leave my post. If you're able to speak with him, I'll hang in a corner of the room, if that's all right."

"I would not want you to go against Garza in any way," Amy assured him.

Hunter returned with a doctor, who nodded a grim acknowledgment to them and went into the room.

"I should be back in there," Hooper murmured.

"We can see him through the glass," Hunter said.

"Right. I just...when Garza says jump..."

"We all ask, 'How high!'" Hunter finished for him. "He's actually okay. You'll get to see his human side soon, I imagine."

"He's looking at the monitors—and talking to Owen," Amy noted.

She watched as the doctor touched the line to the IV.

She felt a moment's panic.

Was he about to do something to the liquid flowing into Owen's veins?

She almost sped through the door, but then the doctor turned and walked back out to them.

"He's young, strong and lucky. If you had gotten to him just fifteen minutes later... So, I don't like the idea of him talking, but I know it's important. You can have fifteen minutes. Twenty max. Don't excite him or get him going."

"We won't," Hunter assured him. "And we'll be quick."

"Three of you in the room, huh?" the doctor asked, looking at Hooper. He shrugged. "You don't even trust your own people?"

"We just have an exacting boss," Hunter said.

"It's been a rough case. A lot of people have died," Amy said softly.

The doctor gave her rueful look. "I want you people on the case if I'm ever in trouble, that's for sure. Like I said, don't excite him. And don't get him talking long or loudly. And if I or one of nurses tells you that you're done, you're done. I can be pretty exacting, too."

Hunter gave him a grave nod and took Amy's arm, leading her in.

Just as he had promised, Hooper went to stand in the corner at the rear of the room.

Hunter pulled up a chair for Amy to sit next to the bed, close to Owen so that he could speak softly.

Owen offered her a smile.

"I don't know what I was doing," he told her. "I'm really not a terrible person."

She smiled back at him.

"We need your help. Can you describe the 'they' who tried to kill you? Lift a finger to indicate 'yes.' First, was it more than one person?"

Owen raised his index finger.

"A man and a woman?"

Again, he agreed.

"Were they young?"

He did not move.

"But not old. Middle-aged. Maybe late forties?"

Affirmative.

And then she had him describe the pair. The man first. She gave hair colors—balding, a full head of hair, thinning hair, short, long...

And the face... Clean-shaven? Beard? Mustache?

Owen indicated when she was right, and he wrote out a description, too.

Not handsome, but okay. Maybe five-ten. Medium build, but strong.

Amy sketched.

Erased, shaded and winced inwardly as she drew.

Blond, thinning hair. Dark eyes, oblong face.

She was coming out with a fine facsimile of Geoff Nevins.

Then the woman.

Brown hair tied back. Maybe five-five. A little plump. Strong. Lines around the eyes. Not beautiful, average.

Bit by bit...

Just as she created an image of Geoff Nevins, she had now created one of the man's wife.

Hunter stepped out into the hall. She believed he was calling Garza, getting police and/or agents out to the Nevinses' house as quickly as possible.

She showed the images to Owen.

He spoke out loud in a raspy whisper.

"Wow! Yeah. That's them. Yeah. That's them, that's them. She may look like a sweet old schoolteacher, but man can she wield a knife!"

"Thank you. Don't talk anymore. But thank you."

"That's them!" he repeated, barely making sound. He winced. "You'll get them?"

Amy looked out into the hall. Hunter gave her a nod; law enforcement was on the way. Soon they'd be taking off on the chase, as well.

But were the Nevinses the top of the chain, the "voice" she heard on the phone, taunting her and commanding all? Were they the "red horse"?

"We will do everything in our power," she assured Owen, and then nodding to Special Agent Hooper, she hurried out to the hall.

And she wondered if they'd be in time to find Celia and Geoff enjoying a quiet evening at home while they continued plotting and planning. Or if they'd gotten wind of the fact Owen was alive, and were already on the run.

They were on the way down to the car when Amy felt her phone vibrate; she saw Hunter reaching for his phone, too.

They had both received the same text from Garza.

No help from the kid who worked at the convenience store and drove one of the bomb-laden vans. He was fished out of the Chicago River just about thirty minutes ago. Wonder where they might have disposed of the second driver.

They finished reading at the same time.

"This isn't going to stop. It's going to get worse. We have to find the Nevins couple alive, and find out what they know," Hunter said.

Amy couldn't help but wonder if they would find them at all...at least not alive.

16

The local police and agents from the bureau field office were already at the Nivenses' house when Hunter and Amy pulled up.

Hunter knew he and Amy didn't have to be there; Garza had taken lead on the mixed group of FBI and police who were at the house.

Garza was a reasonable man. He knew clues might not lead anywhere; and no matter how diligently people worked, there were those who escaped the law.

He was passionate about justice, a man who didn't bend the law.

He was also angry as hell.

And Hunter was glad. Garza wouldn't let this go.

In Hunter's opinion the scene was bizarre. This area of

the suburbs had a friendly, neighborly feel with big yards and mostly freshly painted houses, and usually there would be kids playing on climbing sets and even playing football in the street.

SWAT had surrounded the Nivenses' house.

Garza, stalwart in his bulletproof vest, was talking to the officer in charge. He was taking this one.

Officers and agents had told the locals to get their children, dogs, cats and any other living creatures indoors.

Garza first tried the intercom at the gate.

There was no reply.

He shouted into a bullhorn.

"Geoff and Celia Nevins! Come out now! We will enter the premises forcibly. This is Assistant Director Garza, FBI! I am here with a host of law officers. Come out, hands up where we can see them clearly. We are asking you to come out and talk!"

There was no reply.

Standing by Amy, with his back against one of the black-and-white police cars on the scene, Hunter shook his head and said quietly, "They're not there."

"Or they're dead," she said softly.

He shook his head again. "They knew. Somehow, they knew they didn't finish the job. Now they're running. They're in hiding. Or...both."

"You think they believe their lives are in danger? Hunter, we didn't let a peep get out about the situation at Owen's house. They must believe they killed him."

"How high on the chain were they? Or are they?" Hunter mused to Amy, watching as events unfolded. He hadn't expected Geoff or Celia to be there. Even though they shouldn't have known they had failed to kill Owen, maybe they just somehow knew.

Or maybe they were already dead. Maybe they couldn't answer Garza because, like Owen, they were lying in pools of their own blood.

He gave a nod toward the house. "Garza is ordering a forcible entry. I don't think they're in there."

"Are *we* going in?" Amy asked.

"There's an amazing force assembled here," Hunter said thoughtfully. "Let them do their thing first, and we'll go in after. I'd say in a matter of minutes the door is going to be rammed."

He was right.

Garza ordered it taken down and it was. Agents and officers, working in tandem, entered the house with every man and woman alert and wary.

They all knew the case. And just how dangerous their targets could be.

"We can start for the house now," Hunter told Amy. "But they're not in there."

"Then they're not dead? You don't believe they're dead? They could be in the Chicago River like another 'failure.'"

Hunter sighed. Amy had a good point.

But he shook his head.

"I really don't think so. I believe they're running, but it's going to be a hard run now because they're running from us *and* from someone who won't give them a chance to turn themselves in."

"We still need to see the house. We need to see what they might have left behind," Amy said.

"Yes. Let the officers do their thing. We'll get in soon enough."

"Hunter," Amy said.

"Yeah?"

"We need to warn Audrey Benson. If she is innocent, she'll need to have protection. And if she is involved, now might be the time *she* decides she needs some protection, too."

Amy stepped back, pulling out her phone. "You want to put a call through?"

"Sure. But I'll see what Garza has to say."

The assistant director was coming toward them.

"The house is clear—they've gone. And it looks like they cleared out in a hurry. I suspect someone in Owen's neighborhood got busy on social media, showed the action at his place, and the Nivenses got worried. Very few people are going to sacrifice themselves. We've sent out an APB."

"Hopefully, that means they'll be picked up soon. But the young agent we're working with in Florida can change his identity in a flash. These two might try something like that."

"Let's be glad the young agent is working for us, and let's hope this pair is not so talented. At any rate, you two can go in and take a look and see if you find anything that resembles a clue as to where they might have gone, or…"

Garza finished by just shaking his head.

Amy rejoined them.

"It's all yours—see what you can find," Garza said for her benefit. And with a nod he moved off.

"Shall we?" Hunter asked Amy.

"Seems strange we were here so recently asking them if they wanted protection," Amy said.

"I guess they thought they didn't need it. It did seem suspicious. And Audrey Benson?" he asked.

"She's scared now at least. She's working with some people on her upcoming campaign. She was telling me about all the paperwork they need to submit, and I was reminding her she couldn't run for anything if she wasn't around. She's going to talk to her people and get back to me. She's at the law offices now, but I guess she already has a campaign headquarters she's setting up."

They reached the house and nodded to a few of the officers standing outside or just inside the house, careful to stay away from the forensic people who were finishing up.

Hunter remembered sitting in the living room.

They hadn't been in the bedrooms or the office.

"Let's split up, though I don't believe they've left anything for us to find."

But there was nothing unusual about either the office or the bedrooms.

The computer had been taken from the office. So had every scrap of mail. There wasn't so much as a scratched-out note left behind.

Hunter looked in an empty file cabinet.

And inside every book on the shelf.

Amy met him, coming from the couple's bedroom.

"Anything?" he asked.

"Clothing—I checked every pocket. But lots has been cleaned out. They packed for an extended trip."

"Any travel brochures?"

"No. Posters on the wall with things like 'Believe!' against a backdrop of fairies, and 'Be the Right Stuff' with a picture of a marathon runner. Nothing that would indicate anything criminal at all. Take a look."

"Okay. You see if I missed anything here."

They changed places, but neither could find any suggestion of where the couple might run.

They were just leaving when Amy had trouble shutting one of the file cabinet drawers. Hunter walked over to help her.

"Something is stuck," she said.

"Yeah, you're right."

Instead of trying to close the drawer, he pulled it out.

Something fell to the floor.

Amy stooped to pick it up. She rose, holding it in her gloved hand.

"What—" he began. But then he saw the object.

"A red horse," he said softly.

"Think they've had it?" Amy asked him. "Or maybe they just received it. Maybe it came to them as a warning not to mess up."

"Yeah. Maybe. And if so, the 'red horse' knows they're on the run. They are probably running because, somehow, the 'red horse' knows they messed up. Anyway…"

Hunter paused for a minute.

Amy looked at him. "What?"

"Basement."

"Basement?"

"We walked through the house. I didn't see an entrance to the basement."

"No," Amy admitted. "I didn't think there was one. In Florida, while there are some basements in houses in the northern hilly areas, anything in the south is because a house was built up on stilts. But…does every house have a basement?"

"I'm willing to bet this one does. We're in the Midwest, where most houses do, and walking around…it feels like there is something beneath. Not only that, but the house is raised—so it's a very high foundation, or there is a basement down there."

"Then we have to find a way in."

Amy started out before him, asking others if they'd seen Garza. Someone directed them to where Garza was standing by his car, speaking on the phone, giving directives to someone. He ended his call, frowning as he looked at the two of them.

"We can't find a door to the basement," Hunter said.

"Yeah, team members have said that. Odd, but—"

"There's a basement. We need the original plans," Hunter said.

"On it. I'll get a team to start inspecting floors."

"And out here," Amy said. "There might be a tunnel that leads to an exit away from the front of the property."

"We'll get on it."

Garza ordered a search; police officers, bureau agents *and* a forensic team started searching, and so it went on.

It took time, but pressure was on from the mayor and the police force. City records were checked. The original plans arrived. The house had been built with a basement.

Recent plans showed it had been filled in.

"I don't believe it for a second," Hunter said.

"We keep looking!" Garza told the search teams.

Hunter and Amy worked near one another, near enough that he heard her phone ringing and knew when she stepped away to answer it.

She walked over to him a minute later.

"I'm going to go over to the law offices and see Audrey Benson. I think she's going to come in, but I want to reassure her one more time."

"All right. We'll go—"

Amy shook her head. "No. I think you're right. And if you find Geoff and Celia, or anything about the 'red horse,' one of us needs to be here. I just don't want to risk Audrey being on her own anymore no matter how many friends she has at court and with the police."

"Let's keep her alive," Hunter agreed. He wanted to protest—and he knew he shouldn't. She was a keen, and far more than just capable, agent.

But the "red horse" didn't care who ended up dead. In fact, the "red horse" seemed to relish every death.

"Amy—"

"I'll take one of these cops with me as backup," she told him, grinning, as she apparently knew what he was thinking.

He smiled ruefully. "Thanks."

"You're going to find them. Text me the minute that you do."

"I will. And keep me up on what is happening, too."

"Will do."

Amy started out. He couldn't stop himself; he followed a second later to see her heading to their vehicle and being met by a young officer on the way.

Relieved—to an extent since somewhere ridiculously in his mind he only trusted himself with her "back"—he returned to the task at hand.

He was right. There was a basement, and the Nevins couple were using it. Whether they were still in it, or had used it for an escape, he didn't know.

But it was there. And it hadn't been filled in.

The search—even with teams swarming the house—was tedious and long. He was sure some of the other officers and agents thought they were on a wild-goose chase.

But that chase finally ended.

It was a member of the forensic team who finally found the entrance, invisible against the grain of the wood in the little closet beneath the staircase.

Hunter was near him, searching lines in the floor, when the young man said, "I think I've got it!"

Hurrying over to him, Hunter used his pocketknife to leverage the tiny crack.

A piece of the floor was the entry.

Stairs led down to the darkness below.

He drew his Glock and his flashlight. He nodded to the officers and agents behind him who were now aware he had, indeed, been right and were awaiting his directive.

He started down the stairs.

Rhonda was sitting at the desk when Amy arrived, the young officer in tow. The receptionist looked at Amy and then sighed softly, shaking her head in dismay.

"Audrey just left maybe five minutes ago. She said she tried to call you and left you a message she'd be at the campaign headquarters. She wanted a final meeting with her campaign manager and some of the workers." Rhonda grimaced apologetically. "She's flustered. So much…and it's her big opportunity. But she's scared. She probably dialed the wrong number and left someone else a message. But it's not that bad—headquarters is just down the street."

"It's okay," Amy told her. "We don't mind. We'll meet up with her there."

Rhonda nodded. "Thanks! And again, I'm sorry. I should have called."

"It's seriously all right. I'm just grateful she's going to take protection. Thank you, Rhonda."

"It's all right? Seriously?" Officer Fletcher asked dryly as they left. "People! You try to help them, and they just kick you in the teeth, huh?"

Fletcher was in his twenties and new at the job, Amy

thought. But he had a helpful manner and assured her he'd keep a keen eye out for her.

"But I'm not expecting too much to happen in a Chicago law office," he had told her, grinning. He had red hair and green eyes, and she imagined he was good with the public. Amy thought he took his job seriously, but still had a good sense of being decent.

But she could see he didn't much care for the way Audrey Benson did things.

Amy shrugged. "She wants to run for public office. That means you need to be out in front of the people. For her, I guess this is a hard decision."

"Let's see—my life or public office. Hmm," Bruce Fletcher said.

She smiled at him. "Yet you chose to be a cop."

"Oh, burn! Yeah, you're right. But you know, I was one of those kids who grew up on reruns—believing in truth, justice and the American way. Honestly, right now, I'm heading up the ladder. One day, I'll make detective."

"I'm sure you will," Amy told him. "Let's get to the campaign headquarters."

Amy wasn't sure what she expected. She had never run for public office, nor had she ever been called in because of trouble at a campaign headquarters.

Audrey Benson had taken the ground floor of a building on the northeast side of the city. Amy imagined it had once held retail space. Now, it was crammed with desks, computers, people, life-size images of Audrey and stacks of campaign posters.

A young woman quickly directed them to Audrey, who was posing again for pictures, looking attractive, put together, serious and capable as she pretended to be speaking to a crowd.

She stopped the photographer as soon as she saw Amy and Officer Fletcher.

"You're here. Already!" she said.

"I hadn't realized you were so into the campaign already," Amy told her. "This is Officer Bruce Fletcher."

"Backup, in case there's trouble," Audrey said, looking at Bruce. "Where's Special Agent Forrest?"

"Occupied," Amy said briefly. "Have you had any trouble?"

"No. No threats. No trouble. But…"

She paused.

Then she shrugged and said, "I found a little red horse. A toy horse, on the steps of my porch when I went home last night. Of course, I know what's going on, and…anyway. I figure that's a threat, maybe? Or a kid left it—maybe. I don't know. But…how long until you catch whoever is doing this? I'm not running away forever. I want to win this race!"

"Hopefully, soon," Amy said. "But Audrey, that little horse is a threat. A very serious threat. You need—"

"Please," Audrey lowered her voice. "I've got my people still working. I've told them I'm just going to be away for a few days. They believe I'll be back and ready to campaign hard when needed. And I believe I'll be back and ready to campaign when needed. Right?"

"Audrey, we're not trying to mess up your life. We're trying to preserve it, We can't ignore that you might be a target," Amy told her.

"I know. It's a serious threat. I just don't want it to be. I need to go by my house. Then I'll go wherever you want. You both shoot well, right?"

"I'm good," Fletcher told her, grinning. "Okay, I'm excellent! Top of my class."

"Well, good for you," Audrey said. "I'm ready. We'll just swing by my house and I'll get some things? Is that okay."

"Of course," Amy said. "I'm glad you're coming in."

Amy drove. Audrey had automatically slid into the passenger seat beside her, and Fletcher slid into the back after making a face behind Audrey's back and grinning at Amy.

Amy just shook her head, smiling. She was going to be glad to get Audrey back to headquarters. She had been so suspicious of the woman.

Lawyers. She smiled to herself as she quickly texted Hunter to tell him she had Audrey Benson, and they were on the way to Audrey's house to pick up some things, and they would then be bringing her in.

She saw a quick text from Hunter in turn.

Found the basement. Looking.

She grinned, sliding her phone away to put the car in gear.

"What is it?" Audrey asked.

"Nothing. I just know people who seem to have a strange sense of what is and isn't real. Anyway, we should be at your house quickly."

Bruce Fletcher leaned forward from the back seat.

"So, Audrey. Sorry, Ms. Benson. What is your platform?"

"Oh, well! I'm not sure you want to get me started on politics! I'm working on all sorts of projects, but mostly things that will make life better for the working American. For all Americans, of course. We don't have a class system—but we do have a class system. We need something for those people who think and feel alike, seeking to obtain higher goals!"

Amy had put Audrey's address into the map system. They weren't far and she was glad.

She found Audrey's platform enthusiastic, caring and all over the place. Her voice droned on as they neared her house.

There was a fence around it, and Amy could see there was a camera and signs that warned the house was protected by a legitimate security system. She slid the car in front of the gate. Lights went on.

"I told you I tend to be safe!" Audrey said proudly.

"Very good," Amy said.

"A smart politician," Fletcher murmured as Audrey opened the gate, and they walked up the path to the house.

"I *am* a smart politician," Audrey said, keying in her code again to open the front door. "I'm all about doing the right stuff!"

They stepped inside.

Her home was perfect. Shiny marble floors with attractive throw rugs here and there. She had a large fireplace with a marble mantel sporting pictures of her with various celebrities and friends. A leather sofa and matching armchairs were placed between the fireplace and a handsome entertainment system.

"I'm going to grab a glass of water—too much talking today, I think—and then just run upstairs for a few things. Please, sit down. I promise I'll only be a few minutes," Audrey said.

She hurried to the far end of the living room where it met with the dining room and the entrance to the kitchen.

Bruce Fletcher wandered over to look at the pictures on the mantel.

Amy thought she heard something odd coming from the kitchen.

A scuffling noise.

"Fletcher," she said softly.

He turned to look at her expectantly. She was already

leaning against the wall, watching for anyone leaving the kitchen, ready to slide along and enter it silently.

But before she could do so, a man in a ski mask forced Audrey Benson ahead of him out into the living room.

He held her tight against him with one arm.

In his free hand he held a gun, and the gun was pointed at Audrey's temple.

Amy's Glock was aimed at the man's head. She wondered if she could hit him cleanly before he could fire off a shot.

Unlikely!

"Let her go," Amy said quietly.

He started to laugh. And he had the right.

Because five other men, all in the same black, wearing ski masks, stepped out of the kitchen behind him.

All with weapons—aimed at her.

"Please!" Audrey whimpered.

And yet Amy had to wonder.

The house was well guarded with all kinds of security. So...

Had Audrey planned all this? Or was she the victim they'd been waiting for?

The basement was a bunker.

It reminded Hunter of all the movies he had seen that dated back to the 1950s and '60s. There were shelves full of food and water bottles and other drinks.

There was a kitchenette, but also a small stove that worked off kerosene capsules readily available on the shelves.

The rest was set up as a tiny house with a bed, a dresser, a wardrobe and a dining table. There were plenty of books and tons of batteries of all varieties.

Garza joined Hunter. "They're prepared for World War III

down here!" he said. "Or a cataclysmic weather event or the damned zombie apocalypse."

"Not the zombie apocalypse—*the* apocalypse," Hunter said. "They're part of this, higher-ups, I believe. Though…"

"Though?"

"Are they the 'red horse'?" Hunter wondered.

"Special Agent Forrest!" one of the officers called.

"Over here!"

"Sir, you were right on all of it! There's a door—leads to a tunnel."

"Be careful. We don't want a cave-in," Hunter warned.

He hurried over to the door—one that again blended in with the paneling that had been put behind the bed and across the back wall. It opened to a dark, dirt-walled tunnel.

The officer waited for Hunter to take the lead.

Glock and flashlight in hand, he stepped into the space.

His light at first gave him nothing, swallowed by more darkness ahead. As he took tentative steps along the floor, he tried to imagine what was above, and he knew they were moving into the small—but richly forested—area behind the Nevinses' house.

The couple had been ready for whatever was coming.

But they had also been ready to escape if their bunker had been discovered.

Then his light hit on something ahead of him in the path.

He knelt when he arrived at the corpse.

It was Celia Nevins. Laid out, hands folded over her chest, a flower placed within them.

She was so peaceful she might have been sleeping.

But she was cold to the touch. The earth below and all around the body was cold, so he wasn't sure how long she had been dead.

Or how she had died.

There were no signs of trauma on her; she hadn't been shot. She hadn't been attacked with a knife.

It was almost as if her death had been carefully and lovingly planned.

Garza was behind him. Hunter heard him shouting back, "Get a medical examiner out here, fast!"

Hunter stood, walked past Celia, shining his light ahead. He hurried onward. Not much farther, he came upon a ladder tossed on the ground. He leaned it against the side of the wall and went up the rungs, seeking the exit.

He found it and pushed. A door swung open to the dying light of the day.

Hefting himself up, he surveyed the area. If he kept heading north, he'd hit a road.

"What do you see?" Garza cried.

"He's gone. Geoff Nevins left her there. He's out now and he's going after Amy or Audrey Benson or both…" His voice trailed.

Or Audrey was in on it and Geoff was trying to get to her. To get rid of Amy. Or he still feared for what had happened and had killed Celia himself rather than see what the "red horse" would do to her.

"Garza, we've got to get to Audrey Benson's house fast, but we can't go with sirens blazing. I'm on my way. Send backup but see they stay quiet and surround the house."

"You're on your way? You're in the middle of trees—"

"And heading out of them! I'm taking your car! Throw me the keys."

"Hunter—"

"Hey, come on! Amy is just on loan to the FBI. We have to give her back in good shape!"

He knew he was trying to still his own fear.

Garza tossed him the keys.

Hunter ran.

17

There was no way out of the fact she was outgunned. In truth, the situation was bleak.

But Hunter knew she was here; if he tried to reach her and she didn't answer...

He was fast, but not faster than a speeding bullet.

Amy's phone was in her pocket. She had one free hand. She tried to keep her stance, leaning against the wall to slide her free hand into her pocket and manipulate her phone, finding the top button for her virtual assistant.

"Hunter!" she murmured as loudly as she dared, shaking her head and hoping that, if they heard her, they imagined that she was wishing that he was there with her or cursing him for not being there. She had to hope that her phone would dial him, and that he would answer it.

That he would hear what was happening.

And she had to talk her way out of this.

"So, here we are," she said. With her right hand, she kept her gun trained on his forehead. She wanted him to know if she went down, he was going down, too.

"You're going to shoot me, Officer Fletcher and Audrey— in her home? All six of you?" she made a point of asking. "For the three of us. There are cameras everywhere."

The man holding Audrey laughed.

"And what will those cameras show? Men in black ski masks. What? Someone is going to see my beautiful baby-blue eyes?"

His speech was odd. Beneath the mask he was wearing, he was using a device to alter his voice.

Much like the caller.

But was this…

The "red horse"?

She smiled, keeping her gun trained on his temple.

"Well, now they know—with or without the cameras— you have baby-blue eyes. I don't agree with beautiful," she said pleasantly.

"Well, you are going to die."

Still by the mantel Fletcher was silent, wide-eyed and watching. He hadn't made a move, but he had guns trained on him before he had been able to do so—no matter how fast he might draw.

"I may well die. But you'll go with me," Amy said flatly.

"Not if I fire first."

"That's debatable. I was the best in my class. I have awards for marksmanship. Oh, and think of it! You'd be killed by a woman. Let Audrey go."

"Let her go? How do you think we got into the house?"

"What?" Audrey said, blinking. "No!"

"Hmm," Amy said. "Well, with one shot I can take you both out."

"Then you die."

"You first!" Amy told him. "I'm law enforcement. I signed an oath. Oh! But you did, too. I used ink, you probably used blood. And I promise you, there are already agents and officers heading here. You'll all die. You know that, though. You sign up, first just thinking you're going to do little things—maybe get yourself out of debt. Then the warnings come, and then the threats, and then you're sent to see the body of someone who failed in their task."

He cocked his head, waving his gun toward Fletcher. "Your friend here hasn't even tried to pull his gun. Maybe he's part of the change that is to come."

"No!" Audrey said. "Amy, don't fire, please. I want to live. Maybe he won't kill us! Maybe—"

But her protest was broken off as he jerked her hard.

"If we're all dying, we can start anytime," the man said. "Your cop can kill you, too, you know."

"Amy, I'm not—" Fletcher began in horror.

A gun went off; Fletcher howled and fell to the floor.

One of the gunmen had shot him in the foot.

"See!" the main man said. "We mean business. And I do have to kill you. But maybe Audrey is a lying sneak at this moment, and I'm just supposed to bring her to the 'red horse.' So, if you're such a noble law officer, die. Then I'll take Ms. Benson with me."

Amy was running out of time. Fletcher was on the ground.

"You shot him in the foot," she said, hoping Hunter was at the other end of the call she had made.

Fletcher was howling, holding his leg, but he still had his weapon.

She didn't believe the young officer was involved, no matter how this man was trying to provoke her.

She frowned.

"Listen!" she said. "They're here."

"Who is here?"

"They're here. You should check. Oh, wait, you have Audrey. But your men should check. I heard something outside. Seriously, what kind of a leader are you?"

That angered him. He replied loudly, and she thought again she knew the voice.

"The right kind. You know, Special Agent Amy Larson, you just don't see the big picture. There is going to be a new world order. Don't you see? It's going to be the mass downfall of the wicked. And the most wicked are those who are proclaiming they're good all the time. The drug lords are going down, the men and women who postulate they know false gods are going down. The apocalypse is on the way, and only those who know true obedience are going to be here when the pieces fall in at the end."

"Nice speech," Amy said dryly.

She knew the voice.

"But come on. The 'red horse' wouldn't be caught like this," Amy said.

Angrily, the man moved, pushing Audrey away and heading toward the door.

With two of the armed men behind him and three keeping their guns trained on Amy, he went to the door and threw it open.

Hunter could hear every word being said. He'd picked up the call while still driving and instantly figured out that Amy was in danger, but smart as always.

He wished he knew the layout of the woman's house, but it sounded as if they were all in one room, probably the living room.

And there was no time.

He parked behind a hedge near the neighbors', listening as Amy drew the speaker out, noting Garza kept an extra bulletproof vest in the car.

No material could make anyone truly bulletproof, but the vest couldn't hurt.

As he donned it, he continued to listen to his phone and the speaker.

The voice was strange, altered. Not a surprise. They even made toys to alter voices. But if he was altering his voice, it was because someone might recognize it, and if that someone wasn't dead...

Geoff Nevins.

The man had sacrificed his wife to prove his loyalty.

He wasn't running; he was proving himself to the "red horse."

Hunter carefully leaped over the fence that encircled the place, making every move behind brick or foliage. Once there he slunk to the ground and inched his way to a window. Now that he could see and hear what was happening in the house, he ended the call with Amy so that he could call Garza and tell him what was happening.

"Team is right behind you. What do you want?"

"I'm in position at the rear windows. There are six armed men. Amy is still armed. Fletcher has been hit in the foot, but he may still have a weapon. Amy put through a call so that I could hear what was going on. We need to surround the place without being seen. And, when the moment is right, surprise them."

"I'll relay. How are you calling it?"

"Have a man where he can see me. I'm heading back to the side of the house. There are two windows here and I can see inside. I'm making a noise at the front and moving back."

As he spoke, Hunter could see a team arriving. The men were doing as he had requested—silently coming over the fence, taking up positions.

He watched inside as one of the masked men—*Geoff Nevins*, he thought—headed to the door and threw it open. He turned back and started to talk to Amy.

"You know, you should have tried modeling or something. Something women are good at. Women shouldn't try to be cops. They hear things, they see things. By nature, as it should be, you're cowards."

Audrey Benson, standing in the middle of the room, was staring at him. Her life was on the line, but she was incensed.

"Women are cowards?" she demanded.

The man sighed through his mask and voice-altering mechanism.

"The 'red horse' wants you alive. Otherwise, I'd shoot you on the spot."

It seemed the right time. Hunter raised a hand to signal. And he shouted through the window.

"Was your wife a coward, Geoff? I'd say you were the coward. She died so you could live!"

The man turned to the window, gun still raised. He fired, shouting, ordering everyone to shoot. Hunter ducked beneath the window, watching shattered glass fly out onto the lawn.

Amy saw Bruce Fletcher draw his gun just as she got off a shot herself at one of the men aiming at her.

She threw herself over Audrey Benson, bringing her down to the floor, out of the hail of bullets.

She saw Hunter crash through one of the windows, taking aim at a man in a ski mask.

Bruce Fletcher fired his gun and brought down another of the masked men.

A team was breaking through a second window.

More men were rushing through the door.

There was a hail of fire.

And then the six men were down, some dead, some wounded. She felt Hunter come to her side, catch her arm and help her to her feet.

Beneath her, Audrey was sobbing. She and Hunter both helped Audrey up.

"Oh, thank God, thank God!" Audrey breathed.

Hunter was looking at Amy. "Thank God," he murmured.

She smiled.

Audrey wasn't letting them go. Hunter nodded toward one of the team members who came over and gently offered to help her, find her a chair, get her a glass of water, anything.

He was good. Audrey hung on him as he walked her away.

Others were sorting through the living and the dead.

"Hey, Amy!" Fletcher cried, trying to stand. "I got one!"

"Yes, you did," she said.

"You're pretty tough, pretty darn tough!" Fletcher told her.

"Thanks," Amy said. "And for a man with a bullet in his foot, you held up."

"I did, didn't I? Guess I'm lucky it wasn't in my head. Couldn't have held up too well if that had been the case," he said ruefully.

"Get that taken care of," Hunter told him.

"Yes, sir!"

Hunter turned to Amy.

"You are pretty cool. You're not even shaking. That was... an experience," he said.

"Yeah, but..." She paused and smiled at him. "I knew you had my back." Her smile faded. "Geoff Nevins killed his wife?"

"I believe so. We found her dead in a tunnel that led out of the basement. I don't know how she died—Garza was calling the shots when I left. He got the team out here, and he's getting the medical examiner out there. But it looks like Geoff Nevins sacrificed her and came out on this job, I imagine, to prove he was worthy. But...he's down. A few of these men might make it, but not Geoff Nevins."

"You're sure?" she murmured.

She looked toward Nevins.

Yes, he was dead.

Pulling off his ski mask confirmed his identity. The baby blues he had boasted about were open and glazed, staring sightlessly at the ceiling.

"Let's get out of here," Hunter said. "The local agents can wrap up. And there will be paperwork coming out the wazoo. And we'll need psychological evaluations. And..." His voice trailed and he shook his head.

"And we still don't have the 'red horse,'" Amy said.

"Yeah." Hunter sighed softly, looking perplexed. "I keep thinking Ethan Morrison knows something more, and then I don't. And I go over Revelation, and try to figure it out that way, but as often as not, whoever is doing this is interpreting words however he or she wants—disease, famine, swords—all taken however they fit their needs. But Ethan..."

"You think he was just the first. The 'white horse.' And we don't have the 'red horse.'"

"Well, it wasn't Geoff Nevins. Or Celia. They're both dead. And while we had to get into that fight since six guns were aimed at the innocent, it could have helped if Nevins were still alive."

"Let's get out of this house."

They walked out to the front. Darkness had fallen, but the night air was sweet. Amy thought that just breathing the fresh air felt good.

She hadn't realized just how bad the tinny smell of blood in the living room of Audrey Benson's house had been, along with the harsh and burning smell of so many shots having been fired.

They were standing by the gate entry when Garza arrived.

He looked at the gate, but it was standing open now—one of the team had broken through so others could enter quickly.

"Strange," Amy murmured. "When we were questioning them, whether I thought they were guilty or not, Geoff and Celia seemed...like a loving married couple. And you think he killed her?"

"She wasn't left a mess. No marks on her whatsoever. I'm assuming poison of some kind. She was laid out like she might have been at a funeral parlor, prepared for mourners to come and say their final goodbyes."

"It hurt him, but I guess he was more into self-preservation," Amy said. She shook her head. "I'm trying to fathom it. It was easy enough for David Ghent to get gangs to kill one another, believing rivals were after them. Then they started trying to create religious havoc, but thankfully we were able to stop them. But what was it all about?"

"It seemed the Everglades was just a prelude—a practice, really. Then New York City and...the attacks here."

"With Geoff and Celia here," Hunter said. And he added thoughtfully, "And our would-be victim in there—Audrey Benson."

"A politician. Doing the 'right stuff,'" Amy murmured.

She looked at Hunter, frowning. "Hunter, there was a poster in the Nevinses' bedroom. The astronauts were pictured along with the words *the right stuff.*"

"That's...everywhere," Hunter said. "But..."

"Audrey said a few times that her house was protected. But the men were already in the house. Whoever ordered Geoff Nevins to gather troops and to be here had to have started this hours ago at least. Geoff was told to get here and to take out Audrey and me in one sweep. Geoff probably killed Celia when he was given a chance by the 'red horse.' He hightailed it out and met the other men and got into the house. Probably just minutes before we arrived. How did they get in?" Amy wondered.

"How, indeed. And...poor Audrey was terrified. Not to mention he had been ordered to deliver her somewhere."

"Geoff Nevins, with his altered voice, suggested Audrey might be involved and also tried to cast doubt on Officer Fletcher." Amy sighed. "At least I read him right. His poor foot will never be the same again, but he was ready to move when it became necessary."

"Fletcher is young and a good man. I hope they fix his foot for him. He's lucky they only shot him in the foot."

"Nevins didn't want to die. He was trying to get me to drop my weapon."

"Audrey is still in there. She'll have to come to our offices," Hunter said. "Even traumatized, she'll have to make statements. She is still supposedly coming in for protective custody. But she is feisty. Terrified for her life, she still went into a fury when Nevins suggested women were cowards."

"Didn't make me terribly happy, either," Amy said.

Hunter grinned. "Ah, well, he was a fool. Women are far more ferocious than men."

"Also, Hunter, this may not be anything—when we got here, Audrey made a point of saying she wanted a glass of water. Maybe she really was thirsty. Or maybe she knew one of her crew was in the kitchen, waiting."

"And Geoff Nevins suggested she might be in on it."

"Well, I doubt he knew. But he was ordered to bring her in—not to kill her. The 'red horse' usually kills, leaving no witnesses or failures behind."

"So, why take Audrey and not kill her?"

"I don't think Geoff Nevins thought she was the 'red horse.' He was just obeying orders. In his mind, it couldn't have been her. She's a woman."

"All right. What say we get back in there and talk to her a bit? Be sympathetic."

"You think we can trip her up?"

"I don't know. But we can try and maybe learn something."

"Well, we might as well. Nothing else to do except tons of paperwork," Amy said.

They turned and went back into the house. Forensics, EMTs and two medical examiners were on the scene along with their assistants, working their way around the bodies, sorting the living from the dead.

Audrey was nowhere to be seen.

But Officer Bruce Fletcher was there, having his foot bandaged up by one of the EMTs.

"They brought Audrey into the office, off to the left!" he said.

They walked into the office. There was a sofa facing a desk, several chairs, file cabinets and more pictures of Audrey with various politicians and celebrities.

And there was a poster on the wall—Audrey's main campaign poster probably.

It was Audrey dressed in business attire looking approachable and yet serious.

And the words *Vote Audrey Benson! Vote for the right stuff!*

Amy glanced at Hunter.

He had noted it immediately, too.

Garza was seated behind Audrey's desk talking on his phone. Audrey was on the sofa between two of the officers, clinging to one man's arm.

There was a lot for Garza to be doing; events had moved quickly. He was answering questions on the Nevinses' house and dealing with all the people involved now at Audrey's house.

He covered his phone, nodded to Hunter and Amy and told Audrey, "We'll move down to the local offices soon. Maybe you'll feel better there," he said, assuring her.

"Audrey, you showed a lot of courage," Hunter said.

Amy walked over to the campaign poster.

"That's a great poster," she said.

"Thank you," Audrey said. "We try."

"The right stuff!" Hunter said. "Well, good. We want all our politicians to be about the right stuff. No big words or lengthy explanations, just the way to go. I like it." He turned to Amy after studying the poster from afar. "I saw those words somewhere else recently."

Audrey shrugged. "They're good words."

"They are. Really good words. You know, I think I saw them somewhere else today, too," Amy told her. "Where was I?" She paused, shrugged and shook her head. "Oh, well. And I agree with Hunter. You showed some amazing courage today, and I have to say I loved it! You were so frightened, but when Geoff Nevins took a swipe at women, you came after him like a bear!"

Audrey shrugged, but her voice was a little tighter when she spoke.

"I'm a politician. And a huge believer in the fact both sexes are equal."

"So commendable," Hunter said.

Amy noted Garza and the other officers were silent but focused.

The officers were confused.

Garza was frowning, probably wondering what they were up to.

And he wasn't about to interfere.

Amy turned and stared at Audrey.

"Audrey, how did the men get into the house? How did they get past your great security system—the alarms, bells, cameras and buzzers?"

Audrey was visibly irritated. "I'm not a technician! I don't know," she said.

Amy shrugged. "And it is curious you wanted a drink of water—when the men were waiting right in the kitchen."

Audrey lost it then.

No tears fell from her eyes. Amy could almost hear her teeth clench.

"What? Is it a crime to need a drink of water? What the hell are you getting at?" Audrey said.

Amy just smiled at her. "We saw 'the right stuff' at the

home of Celia and Geoff Nevins. Celia was discovered dead, but then you know that—you let Geoff live just long enough to pull off this charade. But when the police search your house, office and campaign headquarters, they're going to find a mechanism to alter your voice. And I'm betting they'll also find a stack of burner phones and files on all kinds of people—people you can lure in. You'll have criminal records on some and interesting bits of blackmail to use against them—to start. You have a knack for first finding those who will kill without blinking, and then having them find people you need to start your 'war' who are terrified once they're sucked in."

"Obey or die. Die horribly," Hunter said. "And Geoff Nevins wasn't just out for himself. He killed his wife rather than let her die at your hands." He shrugged. "Well, he was willing to sacrifice her, but he did care about her and wanted an easy out for her."

"You're insane!" Audrey said. "And you have nothing on me! And no right to search—"

"Oh, but we do have enough for a search warrant," Hunter said.

"And we'll have you in custody until it's executed. I mean, of course we do want to keep you in protective custody, and now, well…"

Amy didn't expect what happened next.

None of them did.

And no one, not even the far-seeing Garza, was prepared.

Audrey Benson pushed away from the officers and leaped to her feet.

In an instant, she pulled a compact gun from her pocket and took aim directly at Amy.

Amy reached for her Glock, but in a split second, she knew she'd be too late.

Audrey Benson fired.

But the bullet never touched Amy.

Hunter did a magnificent flying leap in front of her.

The bullet pounded into him and he crashed to the floor.

Experienced, cool, collected FDLE agent Amy let out a scream and fell by Hunter as the officers wrested the gun from Audrey and brought her to the floor.

Garza was up and next to Amy.

"Hunter!"

Tears filled Amy's eyes, and the pain hit her with worse than any physical damage that could have been done to her.

Hunter. There on the ground. He'd thrown himself in front of a bullet for her!

To her amazement, he opened his eyes.

And he smiled at her.

"Told you I had your back. And your front," he said.

She smiled in return, and then realized the bullet had imbedded itself in the bulletproof vest he was wearing.

Tears were still falling from her eyes. Hunter reached up and brushed them away. He looked at Garza. "I am awfully grateful, sir, that while you are an assistant director, you're also a man ready to be in any field action. Thanks for the vest."

"Glad it was there," Garza said. "Damned glad it was there!"

"So am I!" Hunter said. He winced at last. "I think... I think I might have a few broken ribs."

Garza was up instantly calling for EMTs.

Audrey, from her spot held to the floor under two agents,

was spewing out hatred. She kept promising Amy she would die, and Hunter would die, and they would all die.

As the EMTs moved in, Amy rose and stepped away to give them room. Cuffed, Audrey was back between the two officers, glaring at Amy with hatred.

"You will die! War is coming!" she spat out. "I will be among the chosen, no matter how you try to stop me."

"I really can't just shoot her, can I?" one of the young officers said.

"No, sorry," Garza told him. "But you can get her the hell out of my sight!"

They had to drag her out. She screamed all the while.

"I am the 'red horse'! I, a woman. I am the 'red horse.' I have commanded life and death, and it is in my hands!" She tried to wrench away from the officers, still lashing out at Amy. "I am the 'red horse'! I command life and death. I am war!"

"Looks like you're going to have to be at peace now," Amy told her.

She turned away. Hunter was accepting help but insisting on getting up.

"The 'red horse,'" he said softly. Then he shrugged. "A sad day and a good day. So, uh. I'm going to let them wrap me up."

"And you're going to get X-rays and take downtime!" Garza barked. "You're going in an ambulance!"

"I can ride with him?" Amy asked.

"You can. Don't get him riled up. Both of you—behave." He paused. "There will be a search warrant, and we will tear apart her offices and her house. Amy, we will find all those things you mentioned?"

"I believe so."

"The 'red horse.' Go figure. You found the 'red horse,'" Garza said. He turned to the EMTs. "Get him out of here, please. And chain him down if you have to."

"Hey!" Hunter protested. "I'm going to be a lamb. And yes to time off. We'll take it."

Hunter rode to the hospital in an ambulance with Amy at his side.

X-rays showed two broken ribs, and he was duly wrapped up and told the best way for them to heal.

Garza insisted he stay in the hospital overnight. That was fine. Amy stayed with him through the night, glad of the comfortable chair that turned into a not-so-comfortable bed, and when he woke he spent some time just watching her sleep.

It was still very early when she woke, maybe feeling his eyes on her.

"Hey," he said.

"Hey."

She rose and came to his side, frowning. "Is anything wrong?"

"I was just wondering if you were homesick for Florida."

She grinned. "I was thinking that, really, home is now wherever you are."

"Ooh, I like that. But say that you're homesick for Florida."

"Okay. I'm homesick for Florida."

He let out a sigh. "Good! So, I get convalescence, and I get better, stronger and tanner! When they let me out—and those thousands of pages of paperwork are done—I say it's time to head for the Keys!"

She kissed his lips gently.

"I wouldn't mind a tan myself," she assured him. Then

she said softly, "Hunter, you threw yourself in front of a bullet for me."

"I was wearing a vest."

"You would have done it, anyway," she said softly.

"We'll never know. I don't even know," he told her. "But I know two things."

"Oh?"

"I know I love you."

She smiled.

"I love you, too. And you may begin to imagine how much!"

He didn't smile. He was still serious.

"And the second thing?" she asked.

"We're only halfway through. The 'white horse' and the 'red horse.' Two more horses, Amy. And something else I'm afraid of."

"What's that?"

"A grand puppet master. Someone commanding all four horses. But..."

"But?"

He gave her a smile again.

"For now, the Florida Keys. Diving, sand, sun, boating, fresh fish, romantic sunsets, wild nights! Hot days, hotter nights!"

"That will work for me," she assured him.

And she would cherish the time.

Because he was right.

The black horse would soon be riding out with purpose and vengeance.

And they were going to need to be ready.

★ ★ ★ ★ ★